"I TELL YOU SHE HAS GONE!"

the squire cried.

Lord Mallory came to him at once. "I will get my horse."

While Mallory went out, the squire explained to the company that his daughter Mary had run away, leaving behind most of her belongings and a note.

"It is nothing," Lady Babik apologized to the throng, which gaped in astonishment. "She is only a very eccentric young lady who runs off and does just as she pleases. But it does not signify."

"Why should she run away?" someone asked.

"She does not wish to marry his lordship," cried the squire.

At that, Mallory entered and made a hasty excuse to his hostess. To the squire he said, "Where do you think she has gone?"

He was handed Mary's note, and after perusing it a moment, he said, "I will bring her back, Squire Ashe, I promise you."

"Bring her back a bride or do not bring her at all!"

☆   ☆

MARY ASHE

MARY ASHE

Barbara Sherrod

WARNER BOOKS

A Warner Communications Company

"Without contraries is no progression."

—William Blake

CHAPTER ONE

"This is the difficulty with Miss Ashe," declared Mrs. Chattaburty. "She is eccentric."

Her listeners, who had gathered in that august lady's sitting room for a morning's netting and gossip, did not dispute this assessment of the young woman in question. Harriet Chattaburty's pronouncements, emanating as they did from a booming voice and a granite face, carried the weight of law in Burwash. Indeed, even Lady Babik, whose rank and beauty entitled her to the first position in county society, deferred to her friend in all matters that required exertion of intellect and the formulation of an original opinion.

"Eccentric!" repeated Lady Babik. "I should say she is eccentric. I have never approved of her having such black eyes. And how do you suppose she contrives to make them so large? They are nothing if not outsized."

Sensing that it was safe to find fault with Miss Ashe's appearance, the parson's wife, Mrs. Venable, ventured to say, "I think her hair objectionable on that account as well, for it is as black as her eyes."

"And wild as a gorse!" added Mrs. Turnbull, the widow of a magistrate.

Miss Mary Ashe, who had formed the subject of the ladies' conversation for half an hour, had claimed their entire attention by the simple expedient of her absence.

"Her begging off today is a case in point," Mrs. Chattaburty pointed out. "Theo Granger has caught a cold, and Miss Ashe writes that she must bring him a poultice. I would not go so far as to call her bold. I have too much respect for her father to go so far as that. I will only content myself with *eccentric* and say no more."

Mrs. Chattaburty's guests absorbed this tidbit with interest as they sat in their usual pecking order: Lady Babik lounging to the right of the fire; Mrs. Venable on the sofa, surrounded by a tangle of fabric and thread; Widow Turnbull seated furthest from the fire, trying to force a recalcitrant pair of hoops to do her bidding; Mrs. Chattaburty heading the small circle from a cow-hocked chair on the other side of the fire.

"A poultice for Theo Granger," Mrs. Venable murmured. She glanced significantly at each of her companions to gauge whether the suspicion in her own mind had popped into theirs as well. Lady Babik's soft features puckered into a thoughtful frown. Mrs. Turnbull pursed her lips and glared at her hoops. After a minute, the ladies' eyes turned upon their hostess, who declared roundly, "You are all mistaken. There will be no wedding bells in that quarter."

"I never thought there would be," said her ladyship promptly. "The Grangers are so amazingly red-haired and freckled."

"Miss Ashe and Mr. Granger would never suit," put in the widow.

Mrs. Venable, flushing with embarrassment, made an effort to defend herself. "He's quite set on having her, you know. He's told everyone as much. Why, he even confided the news to me Thursday last at the card party."

"But will she have him? That's the long and short of it," stated Mrs. Turnbull, who made up for her deficiencies of expression by her brevity.

"Well, she ought to have him, don't you think?" said the parson's wife as inoffensively as she could. "He is awfully eligible."

"You mean he is the only eligible catch within fifty miles in any direction," corrected Mrs. Turnbull.

"He is her age, nearly," observed Lady Babik, "and the lands they are to inherit lie handily adjacent. But if she continues to refuse him, he will find someone more tractable, and she will have to go to London to find herself a husband. And that is hardly likely, for Squire Ashe will never go to London."

"He would sooner dance a pipe in the town square," agreed the widow.

Mrs. Chattaburty, who had let the ladies speculate without the benefit of her guidance, now shook her head sagely. "Theo Granger will marry one day, I make no doubt, but Miss Mary Ashe will not be his bride."

Bowing their heads meekly at this assertion, the ladies waited for such explanation as their hostess would vouchsafe.

"It is not merely that the squire has quarreled with Mr. Granger. That would hardly constitute an obstacle if Miss Ashe meant to have the boy. No, it is clear to me that Miss Ashe does not intend to be any man's bride. She means to be a spinster."

At this, the ladies' heads snapped up. They gazed at Mrs. Chattaburty, awed by the profundity of her wisdom and the eccentricity of Miss Ashe.

"But no one *means* to be a spinster," said Mrs. Venable.

"I am afraid that you are a trifle innocent, Imogen," said Mrs. Chattaburty. "Mary Ashe is, as we have all agreed, eccentric. She is so precisely because she means to be a spinster."

"I do not pretend to guess what intentions may lurk in the mind of such a one as Miss Ashe," said Lady Babik, "but I do know that a young woman with such eyes and hair is capable of anything."

"Eccentric she may be, but as an heiress she may do exactly as she pleases," said Mrs. Turnbull.

"That is true," said Mrs. Chattaburty, her face turning more granitelike than ever, "but a woman has one and only one means of assuring her future—namely, marriage. If she has nary a farthing to her name, a husband will prevent her from starving entirely away or becoming a burden on her relations. If, on the other hand, she is as rich as our Miss

Ashe, a husband will see to the judicious management of
her wealth. In short, whatever her station, a woman cannot
fail to improve it immeasurably through matrimony."

"Moreover," added her ladyship, "it is one's duty to
marry."

Nodding in agreement, the parson's wife quoted her
learned husband. "Mr. Venable says that a woman assures
her place in heaven when she becomes a wife."

Mrs. Turnbull threw her hoops aside. "That is all very
well," she remarked, "but in my opinion, a woman assures
her place in this life when she becomes a widow."

Like a dour potentate, Theo Granger reclined on a daven-
port in the sunniest room of the house, his head and back
propped up on pillows and his throat wrapped in the softest
of handkerchiefs. His mother, weary with cosseting her
firstborn and receiving only petulance for her trouble, greeted
Mary's entrance with relief. Rising from her chair, she
made her excuses as quickly as decency would permit and
hied herself off to the cheerfulness of the nursery.

Mary sat down in the vacant chair, placed her basket on
the floor, and regarded Theo's pout. "You cannot be very
ill, Theo," she said, fluffing a pillow. "You are far too
troublesome, I think, to be really ill."

"If you have come merely to scold, then I wish you
hadn't come at all."

Mary took hold of her basket and stood up. "Good-bye,
then," she announced brightly. "I shall find a more grateful
object for my poultice. And as for the pudding I have
brought, I shall eat it myself."

"You have brought a pudding?"

"I have."

"Oh, Mary," Theo mourned. "You have no heart."

"What? Is it heartless to ride in such weather to bring
you these gifts? I declare, Theo, I could box your ungrateful
ears."

Theo fingered the edge of his blanket and glowered at the
far wall. At last he looked up to find Mary smiling at him.
After a moment, she sat down again.

"Why is it," she asked softly, "that sisters and brothers always wrangle? Do you suppose they are on such easy terms with one another that they may say perfectly horrible things with impunity?"

Theo grinned, a little ashamed of his petulance. Then he frowned once more. "But I don't want to be your brother," he complained. "I want to be your husband."

"So you've said, on more than one occasion."

"How can I persuade you that I am serious, that I have never been more serious about anything in my life?"

Opening her basket, Mary replied, "You can't."

She took out a small covered crock. "Ah, it is still warm," she said with satisfaction.

"We would deal extremely well together. Why, we've known each other forever and are as comfortable as can be."

"As comfortable as sister and brother," she said, dipping a spoon into the browned crust of the pudding.

Theo sat up and leaned toward her earnestly. "If we must begin as sister and brother, so be it. Many a marriage is built on far less."

Mary popped a spoonful of pudding into his mouth. "I am too old for you," she replied.

"Nonsense. You are barely two years older than I, and I am only twenty-four."

This gallantry was rewarded with a second spoonful of pudding. "In addition to my advanced years," Mary went on, "there is the matter of my disposition, which is crotchety, and my philosophy, which is cynical, and my eyes, which are beginning to sprout crow's-feet."

"You talk as though you were in your dotage! Your eyes are wonderful. And for pity's sake, put down that spoon. I am trying to talk seriously, and all the while you are treating me like an infant."

With an amiable shrug, Mary set the spoon in the crock. "Theo," she said in a low voice, "I will not risk losing my brother. I have need of a brother. I have no need of a husband."

"Brothers are nothing but a damned nuisance," he exclaimed. "Sisters as well."

"You may say so because you are blessed with three of one and two of the other. But I, who have no family at all save my father, am not disposed to disparage their importance."

"If it is family you want, then take a husband."

"I would, if I were the sort of woman who cared to marry, but I am not."

"Do you not wish to end the quarrel between our fathers? I daresay, the squire would be civil to poor old Papa again if he thought they were going to be related."

"I would give much to see that quarrel mended, for my father has been unaccountably obstinate about it. But I do not see why you and I should go to war in order to make peace between our parents."

"Why must you be so contrary? I vow, I think you say such things solely in order to plague me."

"If I wanted to plague, my friend, then I would marry you. But what I want is simply to be taken at my word, to be acknowledged as a rational creature who means what she says."

"Is it rational for a woman to refuse to marry?"

"Yes, especially when she is as old as I am."

Theo sighed irritably. "I will grant you," he allowed, "that for some females, age is an obstacle. But it is no such thing when you look as you do, and when there are vast holdings to be disposed of, and when I am here and so very willing."

"Have you ever stopped, Theo, and considered what we see and hear every day?"

"What in heaven for? We were speaking of marriage."

"I give you the Prince by way of illustration."

"In the name of mercy, the Prince! What's he to do with anything?"

"Only that he has treated two wives abominably."

"I don't see that at all."

"You don't see that he has exposed them to shame and ridicule, that he has paraded one before the nation as his mistress and accused the other of the vilest conduct—conduct, by the by, of which he himself is guilty?"

Theo deprecated these questions with a wave of his hand.

"If you are speaking of the Princess Caroline's by-blow, well I never heard the Prince had produced one. At any rate, that's nothing to the point."

"Nothing you say? His vagaries are excused, while hers are assumed—without proof—to be fact? I suppose if your wife displeased you, you would think nothing of replacing her and fabricating an excuse that would ruin her forever."

"I would do no such thing," he protested vigorously. "A gentleman has discreet ways of getting round a difficult wife."

Mary laughed. "The Prince's fault, then, is his lack of discretion."

"The only fault I accuse him of is extravagance. Apart from that, I do not reproach him; nor should you. In any case, you have done what you always do. You have turned the conversation from our marriage to politics, and I tell you, Mary, I am not to be so easily distracted from my purpose."

"I merely tried to illustrate what may come of turning perfectly pleasant young men into husbands."

He regarded her gravely. "I hope you do not speak this way in the company of others. Why, if I told my mother what your views are, she would be shocked."

"Then spare her and do not tell."

"I am very closemouthed and would not tell, and even if I did, I would tell exactly what I know, which is that you do not mean a word of what you say, that you profess outlandish opinions in the belief that eccentricity suits what you imagine to be your advanced years, and that you will come round at last."

Mary sighed, feeling that it was impossible to be believed in this case. Resolving to put the best face on it, however, she said, "Here is something to distract your mind from sore throats, princes, marriages, and all manner of disagreeable subjects." From her basket, she drew a slim folio.

Taking it from her, he brightened. "Sheridan. I am prodigiously fond of his plays."

"That is why I have brought him along. Now what part will you read? In your present condition, I should guess that Lydia Languish would suit you admirably."

"Not very likely," he retorted. "I shall be Captain Absolute, and I shall win the hand of the heroine in the end."

Mary made no rejoinder, reflecting that, after all, it was only a play and it was she, not Theo, who knew Captain Absolute's lines by heart.

Squire Ashe sat in his great chair by the fire reflecting on matrimony. As reflection always cost him considerable effort, he frowned. After a time, the furrows on his forehead smoothed, and he concluded that, taken all in all, one could say more in favor of the wedded state than against it.

He had adopted this philosophy late in life, having first spent his youth and then his middle age evading the snares commonly set for men of his sizable fortune. At the age of forty, he had disqualified himself as an eligible quarry by marrying a pretty young miss who, overcome by the honor of being Mrs. Hornbeak Ashe, discarded every wish or opinion of her own and adopted her husband's. In spite of this complaisance, the squire found cause to quarrel with his bride over the attentions of a military captain. He insisted upon feeling insulted for so many months that his wife was obliged to seek refuge with friends in the north country. Only the news that she was with child persuaded the squire to have her back again. She returned to him pale and hollow-eyed and lived some years in this condition until at last she fell into a morbid decline and died. She left her husband a full and prosperous henhouse, a bill from the bonnet maker's, and a black-eyed, willful daughter.

As a widower, the squire proved a good deal more amiable than he had been as a husband. He found himself the most sought-after gentleman in Burwash, nay, in all of East Sussex. On no account would he relinquish such a position of importance, and in the ensuing years he gave no thought to remarrying and providing his little girl with a mother. His ruminations on the present occasion concerned not his own matrimonial prospects but his daughter's.

These reflections had their beginnings in a remark he chanced to hear at a card party. Mrs. Chattaburty, who sat directly behind him at the next table, had leaned toward her neighbor and lamented in a whisper, "What a pity that Miss Ashe has turned out a spinster." So distressed was the squire at this remark that he had discarded an ace, to the disgust of his partner. Since that evening, he had been unable to shake off the memory of Mrs. Chattaburty's epithet.

Thus it was, that when Mary returned from her visit to Theo's sickbed, he broached the subject at once.

"Mary, my dear, is it not time you thought of marrying?"

The young lady's brows arched over her dark eyes. "On the contrary, sir," she said. "It is time I gave over all thought of marrying."

Puzzled, he begged an explanation.

"Surely you remember, Papa, that I shall be twenty-seven September next."

"And what of it?"

"When you were of marriageable age, would you have married a woman of thirty?"

"But why did we not think of this earlier, when there was still a chance of your catching somebody?"

"Because we are so very fond of one another's company and because we are perfectly comfortable just as we are."

"But I thought all girls took it into their heads to marry at one time or another."

Mary went to her father's chair and put her arms around his neck. "This girl has not taken any such notion into her head," she said. "And why should I, when I have everything I could possibly want? For not only do I have a dear father who spoils me dreadfully, but I also have the friskiest mount in the county."

He sighed and acknowledged to himself that he heard her words with relief. Having Mary as mistress of his household and heart was the closest thing to bliss he had been privileged to know. To welcome a husband of hers into their life would be to welcome an interloper. Far more welcome to him were her words of contentment.

He therefore thought no more about his daughter's spinsterhood until a week later, when a hale and hearty Theo Granger visited him expressly to ask in the most

petulant tones why Mary continually spurned his proposals
of marriage.

"It is unnatural for such a one as Mary to be a spinster,"
Theo exclaimed.

"That word again," murmured the squire.

As the two men entered the library, a high-ceilinged
chamber warmed by books and carpets, Theo advanced
upon a shelf full of sermons. Studying a particular title, he
said, "One would think she had some sense of duty." He
drew out the volume and fingered its pages as though it
added the sanction of divinity to his argument. "One would
think she had some sense of obligation to you, sir, and your
ancestors as well, for though they were in trade at the
beginning, they soon showed themselves English gentlemen
of the first water. To think that your blood, sir, your robust
Ashe blood, will never flow through the veins of another
generation! To think that all you have built will pass, in
time, into the hands of the Crown! Why, it is insupportable,
and I am amazed that she is insensible of it."

"It's not as if she would squander her fortune," the
squire grumbled. "It's not as if she had no skill in the
management of affairs."

"She will manage her fortune well," Theo allowed. "But
to what end, if there is to be no progeny?"

"If it pleases her to be unmarried, then let her be, I say."

"You may well say so, Squire, for you have all the good
of it. But what of her? What becomes of her when you are
gone?"

Now Squire Ashe was one of the most imperturbable
gentlemen in the nation. On this occasion, however, he
waxed almost fierce. Looking squarely into the eyes of the
red-haired young man, he challenged, "Are you saying that
I am going to die?"

"Very probably you will, sir."

"And that if I do, Mary will be all alone?"

"Unless she marries."

"And that if I die, she will have no one to fuss over and
no one to look after her?"

"Except, of course, if she marries."

Although the squire had no intention of dying, still he felt compelled to ponder this new view of the matter. After some time, he said, "I have always relied very heavily on my daughter. And I don't say I haven't been a trifle negligent in not urging her to marry. I don't say anything of the sort, young man."

As his tone defied contradiction, Theo remained silent. During the next quarter hour, the squire discoursed on fatherhood, and Theo nodded solemnly at every proof that as a father Squire Ashe had been possessive, dependent, and selfish. By the time the young suitor quitted Dearcrop Manor, he was able to congratulate himself on having brought his neighbor to a wretched sense of his failure as a parent.

Sitting once more in his great chair by the fire, the squire dwelt long and hard on the blame he bore for Mary's spinsterhood. These thoughts gave him a great deal of uneasiness, as a result of which, before Mary returned from her afternoon ride, Squire Ashe had made up his mind: His daughter would marry as soon as possible. The Ashe lands, as well as their gold, jewels, and shares on the Exchange would not pass into the hands of Hanover monarchs. Instead they would fall to a little son of Mary's, one whose rotund face and red cheeks exactly resembled his grandpapa's.

Furthermore, in the event of his death, his daughter would never know a moment's unhappiness. After all, had she not been at Dearcrop to pull at his beard and suck on his cravat after her mother had died, he might very well have perished with loneliness. He was obliged now, as her father, to return the favor, and in such a manner as to put an end to all the neighborhood prattling about spinsterhood.

He had no sooner settled on this plan than Mary swept into the room, still breathless from her gallop on the heath. Her father shifted in his chair, half listening to her describe the ride, and took the opportunity to observe her closely from the perspective of a man on the lookout for a son-in-law.

With each motion of her hand and tilt of her head his daughter displayed a confident grace. In this respect, as in all others, she was not a schoolroom miss by any means. Her figure was full formed, her voice commanding. Her smooth complexion—stark in contrast to the blackness of her hair and eyes—had none of the rosiness of youth. She wore her smart blue riding dress and plumed hat as though she thought no more of her appearance than of the caterpillar sleeping away the winter in her plum tree. This carelessness of hers, this total unconsciousness of self, spoke more than anything else of her womanliness. The squire sighed at these signs of maturity and wondered at the same time how he could possibly let her go. Feeling her kiss on his forehead, he preened himself on the noble act of self-sacrifice that he was about to commit.

"I hope you have not been dull this afternoon," she said, seating herself near him.

"Theo Granger paid me a visit."

"Then you have been dull. I ought to have been here to save you."

"Theo came to complain, and as he complained of you, I suppose it is well you were gone out."

"I can't imagine what he has to complain about. I have always been an unexceptional friend."

"That is his complaint. He wishes to be your husband."

"And so end our friendship forever."

"My dear, can you not consider him? I vow, I do not object to him as a son-in-law, at least not very much. I should patch up my quarrel with the father if you made up your mind to have the son."

"I never did understand that quarrel, Papa, and I think you ought to patch it up in any case. As for Theo, he would not like it if I complained to his mother about his relentless proposals of marriage, and I think it very wrong of him to speak to you about me. The next time he catches cold, he may pine in vain for puddings and poultices."

"Do you not think the two of you would suit? Or have you placed your affections elsewhere perhaps?" In appending this afterthought, he betrayed a tone of hopefulness.

"No such thing, Papa."

"Then why not take Theo?"

"Because I do not wish to."

"Then another fellow. Surely there is someone you like."

"I like a great many people, Papa. But I do not wish to marry them."

The squire sighed heavily and rubbed his beard. Addressing the ceiling of the parlor, he asked, "What is to be done?"

Mary rose from her seat to answer his exasperated question. "It is very simple, my love. We stop all this foolish talk of my marriage and direct our attention to something important, such as our dinner. Do you suppose we are to have the duck that cook dressed on Monday? I hope so, for I am starved."

On that, she left the room to change her dress. Her father remained in his chair, furrowing his brow and trying to formulate a plan; but after some time he gave it up. One could not, after all, persuade Mary to do what she did not wish to do, at least not without rousing her ire. Although the squire was not a timid man, and had even gone so far as to fight a duel in his salad days, still his daughter's wrath was a terrible thing to behold, and he would not for the world be the cause or the object of it. Once she took it into her head to be angry at a thing, she was implacable. Indeed, he could not imagine where she had come by such implacability, for her mother had been submissiveness itself. He wished there were some way of getting her married without her knowing it. But as that was impossible, given her astuteness and perspicacity, he concluded that the case was hopeless.

CHAPTER
TWO

Before the maid came in to dress her hair, Mary unlocked a pretty enamel box and drew out its contents, which consisted entirely of a few yellowed letters. Fanning herself with one of them, she sat down on the bed. She then gazed at the letter, seeing not its words but ocean waves overwhelming the shore at Brighton. She tasted the salty sea spray on her lips and felt once more the chill of an early summer morning.

Another year, she thought, she might have overlooked those sensations. That year, however, she had been eighteen and alive to everything. Her skin sensed the least change of temperature and wind; her eyes caught whatever darted in the air or the water; her breast rose and fell in rhythm with the sea; and her heart yearned for an object.

Mary knew now, but had not known then, that it might have been any object. As it turned out, it was a young parson, a tall, lean, grave gentleman who traveled from Sharpham each week to lead a few stragglers in prayer.

The first time she heard him, she felt a stirring that left her breathless. She closed her eyes, the better to absorb the power of his sound. Suddenly he stopped. Opening her eyes, she saw him staring at her with a light that penetrated her flesh. As soon as he saw her eyes on him once more, he resumed his discourse. Afterwards her chaperon, Miss Winkle, giggled and said she thought the parson was smitten with her.

Inquiries revealed that his name was Richard Hardie. He had taken on the pulpit temporarily, until its owner should recover from a noxious contagion that the sea air seemed to aggravate.

One afternoon, Mary spied Reverend Hardie near the subscription library, and to Miss Winkle's amazement, she ran off to speak to him. He started when he saw who it was that tugged at the arm of his coat. He looked at her, his fine head profiled against the storm-gathering sky. "You must never close your eyes," he admonished her.

"I can't help it," she explained. "I hear you most intensely when my eyes are closed. You seem to be by my side, and I imagine you are speaking just to me."

They walked for some time, followed by Miss Winkle, who sighed romantically at the sight of them. For many days and weeks they walked, and their conversation struck Mary as a mask for their emotions. The emotions were tumultuous; at least hers were. About his she could not say for sure. He was as elusive as the waves, drawing close, then receding, as though he were afraid that in coming close he had gone too far.

He declined to call on her and her father; nor would he permit her to introduce him to her friends. He would only preach to her on Sunday mornings and walk with her. His isolation bewildered her until Miss Winkle conceived the idea that he was too humble, too diffident to meet the family and friends of a young girl so evidently wealthy. Mary's heart went out to him then, and she told him that she loved him.

He leaned back against the cool stone of the church and sighed. "You mustn't love me," he said.

"It is too late for mustn't."

He looked at her numbly and then looked about him. When he saw that no one was near, he put his hands on her waist. "I don't want you to love me."

"Oh, but you do, you do."

He drew her to him with his eyes closed and his head shaking in resignation. "There's no help for it," he murmured.

Mary, exulting in the knowledge that she was loved, reached up to kiss his lips, but he stepped back and held her off. "You aren't thinking, my love. You aren't thinking about what may come of this."

"Oh, but I am. I am thinking that we shall be married, and then you will never be afraid to kiss me."

"Impossible."

"My father will not disapprove, not when he knows I love you."

"You are the undertow, pulling me along. I haven't the strength to stop you."

"Then give yourself up to me. Do not resist."

"Do you always have things your own way?"

"Yes. Always."

Miss Winkle's shrill call made them step quickly apart. Reverend Hardie excused himself and, seconds later, Mary heard his horse's hoofbeats as he rode out of the churchyard.

"I shall not ask a single question," Miss Winkle said with a simper. This noble promise was no sooner made than it was broken, and Mary was forced to spend the entire time of the walk back to town evading the chaperon's curiosity.

When they reached the main street, they met Mary's father strolling with an acquaintance. The squire turned to his daughter with a gloomy expression to say, "Why, my dear, Mr. Aycock has been telling me the most amazing on-dit. It seems there is a young parson, who is not the regular parson but only a temporary sort of fellow, who has been making up to one of our sweet little Brighton misses, while all the time he has a wife and three children in Sharpham."

Miss Winkle sighed and said it was a great pity that some young ladies were not better chaperoned.

"Perhaps it is mere gossip," Mary said in a shaky voice.

"Impossible," said Mr. Aycock. "I heard it from the vicar himself, who is now well enough to resume his pulpit. And none too soon, I'd say."

"Now, my love," said the squire, "if you know who this

young woman is, you must warn her at once. Oh, I suppose she will not listen—at any rate, not at first. Such a foolish girl will never listen to what is in her best interest. Nevertheless, you have a duty to make the attempt."

In reply, Mary earnestly begged to be taken home as she was fatigued to death. The others, all assiduity and attention, obliged at once.

The next day, a note, was brought to Mary's bedchamber. After some time, she worked up the courage to rip open the seal and read the spidery words dashed across the page. Addressing her as his dearest, Reverend Hardie appointed an hour and place of meeting for their elopement. They must marry at once, he wrote, as the vicar was on the point of claiming his post once more and banishing him to Sharpham forever.

Mary did not answer the letter. She kept to her room until the time of the assignation came and went. When she learned that Reverend Hardie had left Brighton, she placed his letter in the little box and vowed always to keep it by her as a reminder of her foolishness.

She smiled now as she looked at the letter and recalled the willful girl who had received it. She smiled to think how disastrously close she had come to being what everyone seemed to mourn that she was not—married.

Rising from the bed, she went to the glass. She could still see a remnant of that silly young girl who had thrilled to a sermon. She turned back to the enamel box and recalled two or three other young men who had wooed her as though she were a chest of gold. One of them had been an ensign, a very dashing fortune hunter indeed; another had been a Corinthian with a propensity to gamble; a third had been a nobleman with more blood and titles than scruples. Mary smiled at the letters from these gentlemen, for they had taught her a lesson equal in value to her considerable fortune, a lesson she would never be so foolish now as to forget. How fortunate she was that things had turned out so well. After all, she might have learned the lesson too late. She might have found herself shackled to a husband with complete power over her money and person.

She folded the letter along its well-worn creases and placed it back in the enamel box. For a moment she reflected wistfully that it might give her father some pleasure to see her married, and for that reason alone she ought to consider it. But she drove the thought from her mind; she had not escaped the clutches of the Reverend Richard Hardie and the others only to be delivered into the eager arms of Mr. Theodore Granger.

One of Mrs. Chattaburty's articles of faith was that good news—like bad—always travels in three's. As she sat in her boudoir and gazed abstractedly at the cloudy sky, she relished two excellent pieces of news recently handed her and speculated on the character of the third, which had yet to occur. The first of these tidbits had come from her daughter in Hoddesdon and announced the birth of a healthy baby boy. The second had come from her husband, a thin gentleman who always seemed to be blinking his eyes in bewilderment. Mr. Chattaburty had lately informed her that he meant to buy a new sow and would be gone the next two weeks in order to find one. It occurred to Mrs. C., as her husband sometimes called her, that the quest for a sow probably did not require two weeks' journey into the West and South. She took such satisfaction at the prospect of being at liberty, however, that she did not question him on the matter.

The third piece of news arrived later that morning, just after Mr. C.'s departure, and it came in the form of Squire Ashe's card brought to her on a salver. Mrs. Chattaburty could not but be surprised, for it was well known that there were two kinds of people in the world—those who paid morning calls and those who received them—and the squire placed himself squarely in the latter class. He not only abhorred going out in the morning, but he detested going out at all before his supper of boiled beef had been served and digested, and so his neighbors had formed the habit of coming to him in the daylight hours without ever expecting him to return the compliment.

Mrs. Chattaburty instructed the servant to say that she

would join the squire in the front parlor directly. She hurriedly straightened her white chignon and prayed that the poor light in the parlor would disguise the shabbiness of its furnishings.

Glumly, the squire cooled his heels, heedless of the furnishings, or, indeed, of anything else around him. All his concentration centered on the mission he had set out to perform and his many misgivings about it.

At the height of his desperation, he had resolved to seek out Mrs. Chattaburty, who, it was well known, understood the arranging of marriages better than anyone in Britain. But the prospect of laying before her his most private thoughts and feelings filled him with revulsion. He paced the floor of the dingy room with his chin on his chest and his eyes on the floor. When Mrs. Chattaburty entered at last, her guest's state was pitiful to behold, and she responded to it with all the condescension the genteel poor generally accord their betters.

Graciously presenting him with her hand, Mrs. Chattaburty modulated her voice so that her greeting should not prompt him to do what he seemed on the very verge of doing, namely, jumping out of his skin. "How very kind of you to pay me a visit, my dear squire," the lady intoned soothingly. "I am not insensible for the honor you do me, for I know you dislike morning visits."

"True enough," he replied miserably, "though I do not mind an evening at cards, especially where I am acquainted with everybody."

Inviting him to take a comfortable chair, one that hearkened back to the days of the last queen, Mrs. Chattaburty placed herself on the settee opposite her visitor. "My neighbors and I only wish that there were more occasions we could invent to lure you away form the charms of Dearcrop," she said cordially. Thereupon she looked into the most sorrowful pair of eyes she had seen since Mr. C.'s twin kids had been punished for vandalizing the chicken coops.

The squire was grateful for the lady's present softness; he had known her to be amazingly prodigious at times.

She leaned forward sympathetically, asking in the most

delicate tone whether something was the matter. "You know," she went on, "we have been acquainted these thirty years or more, ever since you first brought your little bride home. I remember I dandled Miss Ashe on my knee the very night she was left so tragically motherless."

The squire winced at the recollection.

"I do not mean to resurrect painful memories," Mrs. Chattaburty continued carefully. "My intention was only to remind you that we share a history, one which, I hope, may assure you that I am ever at your service."

Encouraged by this speech, the squire plunged headlong into his appeal, fearing that if he failed to plunge now he would never plunge at all. He summarized for the good lady his many fatherly concerns, in all of which his guilt and remorse were very much evident. He spoke of his desire to see his daughter married and himself provided with a grandson. He was willing, he said, to make the most advantageous settlements on a prospective son-in-law. He was also willing to welcome the gentleman into the bosom of his family with open arms.

But, he went on, there were grave obstacles standing in the way of his happiness. "To begin with," he told Mrs. Chattaburty in a whisper, "there is the matter of her age."

"She is twenty-six, I believe."

"Precisely so, and she is forever bringing it up, you know. She will never learn to leave a thing unsaid. Whatever pops into her head to say, that is what she says, and I suppose I am to blame for it, for I never taught her to do otherwise."

"Miss Ashe is certainly forthright."

"Tell me, in all candor, I beg you, is she too old to marry?"

"My dear sir," the lady replied indignantly, "a woman is not a stick of furniture or a particle of clothing to be discarded when she has reached a certain age. And I will tell you, sir, from my own experience here in this humble cottage, that even a stick of furniture and a particle of clothing may be put to very good use, despite its being sat on and worn for years."

A little confused by the lady's metaphor, the squire could only attempt to nod comprehendingly. "The question is," he asked, "who am I to get for her?"

"Theo Granger is not an object, I believe."

"Alas, no. I even offered to make it up with old Granger, even though he is completely at fault. But she will not have the boy."

Reminded of the squire's grudge against the elder Granger, Mrs. Chattaburty paused. The substance of the quarrel had long since been forgotten; yet Squire Ashe's umbrage over it persisted to this day. It recalled to her mind the quarrel that had driven the squire's bride north. Taken together, these incidents appeared to Mrs. Chattaburty as a warning.

Having received from the squire gifts of mutton, venison, and partridge, she did not now propose to relinquish future gifts by offending the giver. Indeed, the last thing Mrs. Chattaburty wished was to find herself in the squire's ill graces, for once locked in there, she knew, there was no escaping. Consequently, she held back, suggesting cautiously, "Perhaps if you made it plain that you wish it, Miss Ashe will accept Mr. Granger. It is well known that she will go to great lengths to please her father."

Squire Ashe colored and shook his head. "I will not ask her to marry a man she does not like."

Rubbing her hands together and gazing aloft in deep thought, Mrs. C. sighed. "You certainly do not make it easy, my dear squire."

"It is the very devil of a difficulty," he acknowledged. "That is why I have come to you."

The compliment, so instinctively and sincerely spoken, lent additional tilt to the lady's proud chin. It also lent her the courage she had lacked before, enough to say, "In truth, I never did think Theo Granger the man for your daughter, and you did perfectly right in coming to me. For one thing, you may count on my discretion. We shall not have it flying all over Sussex that you are on the lookout for a son-in-law."

Closing his eyes, the squire bowed his head in gratitude, inspiring the good lady to imagine gifts of lace and silver.

"For another thing, you may trust me to know how to deal with headstrong girls who have ideas of their own. As you may recall, sir, I have four daughters. They are each of them married, and to a number they have made me a grandmother several times over."

The squire's eyes opened wide, and he gazed at his formidable neighbor with admiration. She saw in that stare bushel baskets of apples, plums, and apricots.

Exulting, she pronounced in a voice redolent with triumph, "And finally, sir, I have the very man!"

The man was Lord Hugo Mallory, second Earl of Loudon, third Marquis of Lales-Allen. He was a distant cousin to Lady Babik, and, more significantly, a descendant of the eminent author of *Morte D'Arthur*. His lordship had ascended to the family titles only six months ago owing to a series of shocking coincidences: both his father and elder brother had died within the space of six weeks; four months later, the Marquis had been gathered to his ancestors, and in default of any nearer heirs, the title had devolved on Hugo Mallory.

Sadly, his lordship's late elevation had brought him precious little besides the responsibility for his father's gaming debts, his brother's snuff and tailoring bills, several encumbered estates, hunting lodges, and London houses, and an assortment of persistent creditors. It seemed he was ill-equipped by training and temperament to take on such responsibility, for he had provided for himself in the accustomed manner of second sons—by entering the military. Shortly after purchasing himself a commission, he had distinguished himself during the invasion of Mysore, as a result of which he had come to the attention of its revered commander. General Wellesley had taken a liking to the brave, striking young captain. He had appointed Sir Hugo his personal secretary and was pleased to find him as canny in administration as he was dashing on the battlefield. Wellesley had had him at his side during the war against the Mahratta chieftains and the capture of Gawilghur. Subsequently, he had insisted that Sir Hugo accompany him on his departure from India and his journey to Dublin as Chief Secretary of Ireland.

Sir Hugo's personal fortunes had risen with his mentor's, so that by the time he had arrived in Ireland, he was, though far from rich, at least solvent for the first time in his thirty-five years. He had, in fact, been the first Mallory in a century to find himself in such a charming condition. Lord Wellesley had regarded his protégé with an indulgent eye as well as a prudent one and had sent him out to flirt with the daughters of colonels and generals, so that he was known in various capitals for his exploits on the field of amour as well as the field of battle. It was known, too, that if Sir Hugo craved amusement, a new-fitted coat, fresh oysters, or a chance to wield his sword again for the honor of England, Wellesley had obliged him. In short, he had carved for himself a niche furnished with more pure pleasure than his extravagant, complaining relatives at home could boast. And as if that was not enough, he was said to have the most accomplished valet in Europe, a gentleman who understood the art of buffing one's boots with champagne and of slipping one young lady out of his master's quarters without catching the notice of the young lady just coming in.

Small wonder, then, that Lord Mallory considered his ascendancy as unappealing as it was unexpected. Small wonder too, that Lady Babik's gossip about her cousin's sudden acquisition of two titles and a passel of debts made Mrs. Chattaburty suspect that the gentleman might be amenable to an arrangement. The arrangement Mrs. C. had in view would not only eliminate Lord Mallory's financial straits with a single stroke, but would also supply her neighbor with the son-in-law he sought. Nor was it lost on the good lady that the successful completion of such an arrangement would enhance her reputation beyond anything.

As Mrs. Chattaburty told the squire all she had heard of Lord Mallory (leaving out, of course, his exploits on the field of amour), she was pleased to see the squire widen his eyes and drop his jaw.

"I have no doubt it can be easily done," she asserted. "You need only see your solicitor in London and arrange a meeting. I feel certain his lordship would listen to your proposal."

The squire's expression of delight began to fade, "London?" he repeated.

Mrs. Chattaburty now found herself repressing an emotion that greatly resembled annoyance. "Surely you can bring yourself to travel to London in such a cause as this," she declared.

"Do you know of someone else," the squire suggested, "someone who is exactly like Lord Mallory, except that he is handier to Burwash than London?"

"I know of no other."

"Pity." He shook his head in the manner of a man ready to throw up his hands.

"I cannot believe, sir," Mrs. C. said in vexation, "that you would hedge at a few paltry miles. We are speaking of scarcely any time at all—and on the Dover Road, after all."

Squire Ashe shook his head. "It is not possible," he said in despair. "It is just as I feared. There is always an obstacle. I suppose I shall have to give it all up."

Mrs. Chattaburty was distressed to see the blessings she had nearly tasted suddenly plucked from her hand. So distressed was she, in fact, that she could not bring herself to argue further. If Squire Ashe would rather stay at home than exert himself to achieve his fondest wish, then she would leave him to his despair, and heartily she wished him joy of it.

Oblivious to the schemes being hatched on her behalf, Mary directed the coachman to drive her to Littleton Vale and set her down at the door of a neat brick house, where Emily Hanks lived with her parents. She found Emily's mother in the sitting room entertaining Mrs. Venable and Lady Babik. The three women looked up when the footman ushered Miss Ashe inside. Lady Babik had been summing up for her hostess Mrs. Chattaburty's pronouncements on Miss Ashe. Mary's coincidental arrival caused the parson's wife to blush and Lady Babik to wonder if any part of the gossip had been overheard.

"Emily is above stairs," said Mrs. Hanks with a welcoming smile. "I shall tell her myself that you have come."

When she left the room, Mary turned to the others. The two ladies' conscious looks revealed at once that they had been talking about her. The idea amused her, and she could not resist remarking, "Pardon me, but I could not help overhearing as I came in something her ladyship was saying regarding a 'woman of means but no prospects.' Am I acquainted, by any chance, with this unfortunate creature?"

Mrs. Venable blanched and moved her lips as though she had hopes of producing a sound.

Lady Babik, who did not blink or blanch, lied smoothly. "We were speaking of Mrs. Turnbull, my dear. Her widowhood is sadly inconvenient, you know. Why, she could not visit us today owing to the loss of a wheel on her carriage and the snow has left the lane too muddy for walking. Heaven knows who will have it fixed for her. I refer to the wheel, of course. Only spring, alas, will mend the lane."

"Mrs. Turnbull's wheel must have mended itself, for I passed her on the way here, and she was trotting along at a cheerful pace."

"I am delighted to hear it," Lady Babik said icily.

"And I cannot agree with you about widowhood," Mary went on, "at least not as Mrs. Turnbull represents it, for she is the most independent woman I know."

"Oh, well, if it's independence you want, Mrs. Turnbull certainly has that!" her ladyship replied.

"Wouldn't you agree, Mrs. Venable?" Mary addressed the trembling woman whose lips still moved in an effort to form a word.

When no word came, Mary continued, "If being a widow is inconvenient, I think it is in this respect only—that a woman must first be a wife."

Mrs. Venable gasped, and Mary congratulated herself on having inspired that good woman to utter a noise. Lady Babik eyed her disapprovingly and observed, "I do not like being a tale bearer, Miss Ashe, but it is said you are forever speaking against marriage, that you have made up your mind to be a spinster, and that you are nothing short of eccentric!"

"You misunderstand me," Mary said. "I meant only that the loss one must suffer in order to become a widow must be one of the greatest misfortunes a woman can know, certainly greater than the loss of a wheel. My own father's loneliness has given me the deepest respect for a woman of Mrs. Turnbull's spirit."

Chastened, her ladyship hardly knew where to look. At last her eyes alighted on the parson's wife. "Mercy, Imogen," she exclaimed irritably, "Why are you moving your lips that way? I declare, you look ridiculous!"

Emily entered at that moment, reaching out her arms to her friend, and begging the ladies to excuse her for robbing them of Miss Ashe's company. The two young women dashed away to a small sitting room, where they customarily repaired in the knowledge that no one would interrupt them.

As a fire had not been lit, Emily gave Mary a shawl, and the two of them sat down. Taking one look at her friend's flushed countenance, Mary asked at once, "What has happened?"

"Only the most amazing thing," Emily blurted out. "I have received an invitation to visit Lady Baldridge in London." Her eyes shone as she awaited her friend's response.

Realizing that she was expected to rejoice at the news, Mary produced a smile.

"What is so remarkable," said Emily, "is that we met her ladyship only once, at Bath last summer. Mama said she had taken a fancy to me, but I did not believe it until yesterday when the letter arrived. It was so beautifully written, with a great flowing hand."

"Will you be going?"

"What a question! Of course I shall go. Mama says it is a great opportunity for me and one not to be missed."

When Mary did not reply, Emily looked at her in surprise. "Do you not think it is a great opportunity?"

Mary smiled. "It is a great one indeed for you, and for your mother, and most especially for Lady Baldridge, but it is quite the opposite for me. I shall miss you."

Emily blushed. "I shall miss you, too," she said warmly. "I shall write you every day."

Mary laughed. "Do not do that. I expect you will be busy, seeing London and flirting at balls."

Emily wished to protest, but as she had every intention of seeing London and flirting at balls, she only looked confused.

For her part, Mary was torn between wanting to share her friend's pleasure and wanting to keep her in Sussex. At no time would it have been convenient to part with the single young woman in the county in whom she could confide.

Although she was several years younger than Mary, Emily conversed intelligently, spoke fluent Italian, and sketched with a flair. And although Emily was as marriageable as a sprightly young miss with golden hair and no dowry could be said to be, she did not dwell constantly on the subject of husbands as other girls her age did. Instead, she shared Mary's pleasure in the changing seasons, in the good health of her loved ones, and in the duets they played by Mr. Purcell.

"You have caught me by surprise," Mary said at last. "I believed you to be content with your life here. I never imagined the prospect of seeing London would throw you into such transports."

"Oh, I have been content," Emily assured her. "It is only that I did not think I should ever see London. I try never to wish for what is not to be. But now it is to be, and I am free to dream as much as I choose. Don't you see?"

Mary was touched. "Yes, I do see. But why must you go now? Would not another season do as well?"

Emily pursed her lips thoughtfully. "Mama says I must go now, for when an opportunity such as this comes along, she says, it is a sign. She says London will provide me with a husband, that lady Baldridge will make certain of it, and to tell the truth, her ladyship said as much in her letter. Mama says all my hopes lie in this, for I am nearly twenty now, and if I do not marry soon, I shall end up a spinster like . . . ."

Here she broke off, and a rosy blush colored her fair complexion.

"Like me!" Mary laughed. "You need not falter at saying what everyone, including my dear father, is saying. Why should you falter? It is true."

Mary stood up and walked to the narrow window. Gazing out, she saw hills and dales covered with fallow brown fields, patches of snow, and graying mist.

Gently Emily asked, "Have you never thought of marrying?"

Mary turned to her with a smile. "I will confess to you, and only to you, that I am not as unnatural as some people are inclined to think. It has become clear to me, however, that marriage is not to be my lot. And, like you, I try never to wish for what is not to be."

"Perhaps if you were to go to London, you might feel differently," Emily suggested.

"My father will not go to London," Mary said, "and I will not leave him on any account. He very much depends on me, you know."

After a thoughtful pause, Emily ventured to say, "But there is Theo Granger."

Mary laughed merrily.

Emily frowned. "You should not laugh at him," she said in what for her was a stern voice. "He is as amiable a man as I have ever met."

"He has a great many amiable qualities, I am sure, but I have known him too long and too well to see them."

"It may be that you do not know him well enough," Emily replied with some heat. "You must see how handsome he is and how well he rides. His manners are easy and his conversation lively."

"You appear to appreciate his qualities well enough," Mary answered. "Perhaps it is you he ought to marry."

Emily blushed. The rosiness covered her neck and ears as well as her cheeks. "Mr. Granger is in love with you," she murmured. "The whole world knows it."

Sighing, Mary regarded her companion. "If I hear Theo mentioned once more as a husband, I vow I shall learn to dislike him heartily. Besides, we were speaking of you and the pleasures awaiting you in the capital. There are matters of moment to discuss in this regard, and if we do not give them our immediate attention, you will come upon the town without a bonnet or gewgaw to do you justice.''

Brightening, Emily said, ''I have seen a pattern of a worked muslin. You must tell me whether it will do me justice or no.''

With that, the young ladies made for the exit, and taking one last look at the bare room—the scene of so many contented hours and quiet confidences—Mary closed the door behind her.

She carried off the remainder of the visit with amusing high spirits, and when Mary parted from Emily, her friend believed that she participated wholeheartedly in her joyful anticipation. But by the time Mary returned to Dearcrop, she had lost her zest for pretense.

''Sending her to London as though she were a parcel of yard goods to be stitched up and sold!'' she muttered as she entered the sitting room.

''Is something the matter, my dear?'' Squire Ashe inquired, looking up from his reading.

She whirled on him with a fire of outrage in her eye. ''Why, nothing at all is the matter,'' she snapped sarcastically. ''Only that Emily Hanks is to make a Smithfield bargain.''

''Well, I am glad it is nothing,'' he said. Adjusting his spectacles, he resumed his reading.

''How can you say it is nothing?'' his daughter cried, startling him into looking up again. ''Is it nothing that my dearest friend in the world is to be taken from those who love her and set down in the midst of strangers who will regard her as merely one more damsel on the hunt for a husband? Do you call that nothing?''

''I think it has upset you, and therefore it cannot be nothing.''

Walking to the mantel, Mary rested her head against its cool marble. Her shoulders shook ever so slightly, giving her father the awful suspicion that she was weeping.

Stunned by this uncharacteristic display, the squire importuned her, ''Tell me, daughter, what has happened?''

''Emily Hanks is going to London.''

"London! I do not wonder you are beside yourself. It is enough to set anyone off. Poor Emily!"

Laughing, Mary turned to him. "It is not London I object to, Papa; it is her leaving. I will feel it, you know, and so will you, for you will have to take her place as my friend and companion."

Much struck with this responsibility, the squire stared at Mary. Recollections clouded his thoughts, bringing back to him with full force the worries that had occupied him these past weeks. At last he said aloud, "And what will happen to you when I am gone?"

"You are not leaving Burwash too?" she cried. "You detest traveling. Promise me you will always detest it."

"I believe I may safely promise," Squire Ashe replied. But so solemnly did he speak that Mary began to feel she had done wrong to unburden herself on the poor man. "I am ridiculous," she said, smoothing the folds of her skirt, "ridiculous and selfish. It is not enough that I care nothing for Emily's wishes and think only of myself. I must then go and pour out my sorrows to the most tenderhearted of men."

"You did well to talk to me," he answered. "If you had kept mum, then I should not be doing what I am about to do."

"Gracious, what are you about to do?"

"I must write to Mrs. Chattaburty," he stated resolutely.

"That is an ordeal, and knowing that you will enjoy it almost as much as you enjoy traveling, I shall leave you to it."

After smoothing the furrows on his forehead with her fingertips, she hurried up the grand staircase to her bedchamber. There she vowed to invent for Emily a gift of such beauty as to obliterate all her former selfishness.

CHAPTER THREE

"Hugo, you've got to help me," Charlotta said. As if to emphasize her distress, she smoothed back her flaming curls and formed her lips into a lovely pout.

Lord Mallory regarded her with a smile. "I knew it must be something catastrophic to bring you to my meager lodgings after so long an absence. I dared not hope you came just to see me."

"Ah, you are not mean-spirited enough to want me to beg," she replied softly. "I am depending on you to advance me a thousand. If you do not lend it to me, Binky is sure to find out what a muddle I have made of things."

"Binky would be most understanding, I warrant. And after all, what is the use of a husband if he cannot settle a muddle for you?"

Charlotta gave him a cold look. "There are certain things I would not wish Binky to know about. The thousand is one. You are another."

Hugo regarded her amiably. "It cannot be, my dear, that you are threatening me, can it? For if you are implying that you will go to Binky with details of your visits to me in India, then I must warn you, it will all be for nothing."

"You don't know Binky. He is very bull-headed, my dear. He has already fought two duels on my account."

"Then he is as empty-headed as he is bull-headed. But there is no use our going on in this vein, Charlotta, for I have heard it said—and I know too well its truth—that you cannot get blood from a stone."

She looked at him in disbelief. "Is it possible?"

"It is not only possible, it is so. You find me with pockets to let and no prospect of a recovery."

"But your inheritance. What of that?"

"I owe my present straits to it, thank you."

"You are talking nonsense, and I don't believe a word you are saying. This is merely your way of refusing me, and a shabby, vile way it is, too."

Laughing, he walked toward her and raised her hand to his lips. "You are magnificent, Charlotta," he said. "Your powers of deduction prove you are a worthy consort for Binky. Look around you and think about what you see—a threadbare carpet, a few miserable chairs, a fireplace that will not properly draw, a valet who must serve as butler and footman. Why do you suppose I live in such circumstances?"

Gazing at the chamber with distaste, Charlotta bit her lip. "You always said you would rather live in the worst hole in London that stay at Domville with your relations."

"Your memory is remarkable," Hugo observed. "Do you recall my ever saying that I preferred such rooms to a well-appointed, commodious house in Grosvenor Square?"

She frowned as she searched her memory, then shook her head.

"Excellent. I never have nor ever will say anything so silly. I live here for one reason only—because it is cheap."

Shuddering, Charlotta looked up at his handsome face, filled, just now, with amusement. "You don't look like a man on the edge of ruin," she said sullenly.

"I make it a point never to look like a man on the edge of ruin. And now, before I call Hawks to show you out, I am going to kiss you."

He had just taken her about the waist when Hawks entered to say, "Sir, there is a person here to see you who will not wait to be announced."

On the final syllable of this breathless statement, a small, red-faced fellow strode into the room waving a sheaf of papers in the air. Hawks instantly interposed himself between the stranger and Lord Mallory crying, "You cannot go in, sir."

"I am afraid the gentleman is already in," Hugo said pleasantly. He stepped in front of Charlotta to conceal her and invited the man to state his mission.

"I see your lordship is busy now, and I've no wish to disturb you and the lady there, sir, but I've bills 'ere for which I am told I must apply to you."

"Let me see them," Hugo replied. He studied the papers and then, seeing that they resembled a great many others of the same species, tossed them on a writing desk, saying, "I regret that you have suffered inconvenience at the hands of my late relations and can tell you only what I have told a host of other creditors, that I cannot pay you now, that if instead of being patient you choose to see me ruined or imprisoned, you will surely never see a farthing of your money again, and that if you do choose to be patient, I will pay you as soon as I am able."

The bill collector stared at Lord Mallory. "I don't know as I ought to say so, sir," he confided, "but gentlemen of your mold don't, in the general way, like to own up so easy. Perhaps your lordship would care to argue awhile, for form's sake, don't you know."

"It is very kind of you to offer," Hugo replied. "I am too well acquainted with the cousins and brothers of such bills, however, to pretend to argue."

"Most gentlemen like to say the bills are forgeries, which I swear to your lordship, they surely are not."

To his valet's horror, Lord Mallory answered, "I do not doubt your honesty, my good fellow."

"That's decent of your lordship. And I'll be honored to be patient for such a gentleman as yourself." On that he made his departure with Hawks at his heels.

"You see, Charlotta," Hugo said as he turned to her, "I am blessed with a great many visitors, and all in a cause similar to yours."

Irritably, she stamped her foot. "You ought not to promise to repay such people," she said. "If you recover your fortunes, you must think of your friends first."

"You are delicious," he said, looking as though he meant to claim the kiss that had been lately interrupted. "And are you still my 'friend,' as you call it? Will you hold my hand into the night and cheer my flagging spirits as you would have done once?"

"I'll do no such thing," she retorted. "You are horrible. First you refuse to lend me a few crowns, and then you laugh at me and tease me. You deserve no hand holding and no cheer."

She flounced to the door, her dress rustling and her head feather bouncing, and paused with her hand on the knob. Looking around at him for a brief moment, she dropped her flirtatious air long enough to say, "I wish I could help you, Hugo." Then, recollecting herself, she opened the door and was gone.

Hugo smiled, thinking that if given a choice, he would sooner face an enemy in battle than the parade of leeches who had frequented his lodgings of late. Walking to his desk, he picked up the latest bills and, adding them to the pile of others, began to rack his brain for a method of paying them. Hearing a noise behind him, he said, "Is that you, Hawks?"

A booming female voice replied that it was not. "Your butler appears to have gone out, so I took the liberty of peeking in."

Lord Mallory saw a large, buxom lady of prodigious mien. With a bow he invited her to leave whatever bill she had brought; he would give it his attention as soon as possible.

"I am not a bill collector. I am acquainted with your cousin, Lady Babik."

"I have never heard of her, but you are welcome. And since you have not come on a fiscal errand, I wish you will sit down and allow me to pour you a glass of wine."

She remained standing while he fetched the refreshment, saying, "Oh, but I *have* come on a fiscal errand!"

Handing her the glass he said, "It is too late. I have

already poured this out, and so you must drink it. But I would be pleased if you would do it sitting down.''

Unable to resist his lordship's smile, the lady complied.

He took a chair facing her and warned, ''It will do you no good, you know. There are at least a hundred tradesmen who have prior claim on my funds.''

''I have come to offer you money, not to ask for it,'' she told him.

He regarded her with interest. She appeared to enjoy her errand enormously. The pleasure of it softened her granite face. ''I must know the name of my benefactress,'' he said. ''And I must know why you are doing this.''

''I am not your benefactress at all. I am merely acting as the agent for a friend who is unable to come to you himself. He wishes to pay all your debts and to settle a sum on you which will guarantee your independence.''

Lord Mallory sat back in his chair. ''And what does he demand in return? If he proposes that I speak out against Arthur Wellesley, or that I sell Domville Castle, or that I forswear my kin and their debts, he may as well save himself the trouble. I will not do it.''

Mrs. Chattaburty gave him a look of approval. ''He wants you to marry his daughter,'' she replied.

His lordship raised a laconic eyebrow. ''She must be very ugly if he must buy her a husband.''

''You may judge for yourself, my lord.'' At that she handed him an oval miniature bearing the likeness of Mary Ashe.

He contemplated it for some time. Then, handing it back, he allowed, ''Very well, she is certainly not ugly, but she has a wicked look in her eye. I suppose she is quite mad.''

''Eccentric, perhaps, but hardly mad. She is a little beyond the usual age of marriage; that is all. Her father wishes to provide someone eligible for her before he passes on.''

''Is he very ill?''

''He enjoys excellent health.''

''You will forgive me if I find this highly improbable, albeit amusing. You arrive in my chambers unannounced, claiming to be the acquaintance of a relation I have never heard of, and bearing a proposal of marriage to a beautiful, eccentric young woman with a healthy and wealthy father.''

Mrs. Chattaburty put down her glass and rose. ''You are free to reject the offer, my lord. But if you are as much in need of assistance as I have been given to understand you are, and if you are the least bit curious as to the seriousness of the offer, I beg you will come to Sussex and speak with my good friend. Then you will see for yourself whether it is improbable or not.''

She set a slip of paper on the desk beside his sheaf of bills and without further conversation took her leave. Lord Mallory opened the paper. It bore a direction, a date, and a time a week hence.

Under no circumstances would it be possible for him to leave London so soon after settling here, he thought. He would have much to trouble him in the coming weeks, too much to permit a journey to Sussex in pursuit of an improbable hope. Folding the paper again, he set it down on the desk and noticed that Mrs. Chattaburty had left the miniature there. He smiled at this obvious ploy and studied the portrait once more. The lady's black eyes now appeared more mischievous than wicked. Her chin was lifted at a determined tilt, and her smile was full of play. Hugo began to think that, in defiance of reason, caution, and his devotion to bachelorhood, he had best go to Burwash and return the trinket in person.

Followed by a footboy who carried a beribboned bandbox, Mary stopped at the door to take leave of her father. As he appeared pale and nervous, she begged him not to fret on her account.

''I shall say good-bye to Emily with an easy heart,'' she assured him. ''You must promise to forget that silly display of mine.''

''Hurry or you will be late,'' the squire said.

''Ah, I see you are skeptical, Papa. You don't believe me capable of reversing my position so quickly. To tell the

truth, I have not reversed it. But I am reconciled and mean
to make the best of it."

"Do not delay, child, or she will be gone when you
arrive."

"I declare, you are in a great hurry to be rid of me."

"Not at all, my dear," he protested anxiously. "It is only
that I am expecting a visitor."

"And who is it that induces you to pack me off with such
unseemly haste?"

"It is merely a matter of business."

"Well, you may tell me all about it when I return."

"It is a trifle, I assure you."

"In that case, it will not take long to tell."

"Come, my dear. Here is the carriage."

The footboy handed the box up to the coachman, then let
down the steps for his mistress. Inside the carriage, Mary
peered through the window to see her father still hovering
by the door. She waved to him, but as his sights were set on
the approach that wound from the house behind a stand of
shrubs, he did not see her. Mary wondered what mysterious
personage had inspired such unaccustomed agitation.

It was with considerable disappointment that she passed a
carriage along the drive whose sole passenger proved to be
Mrs. Chattaburty. She could sympathize now with her father's uneasiness. That lady's visit portended a morning's
discourse on spinsterhood. With Mary at Hanks Cottage, the
poor squire would have to rely entirely on his own defenses.

As the carriages passed, the two women acknowledged
one another with polite nods. Mary had no sooner seen the
other carriage disappear from view than she remembered a
ring she had intended to bring to Emily. As luck would have
it, it still lay on a table in her bedchamber.

She ordered the coachman to pull up the horses and,
because the drive was too narrow to permit of his turning
the equippage around, she alighted, instructed him to wait,
and set off for the house on foot. Rounding the shrubbery,
Mary caught sight of Mrs. Chattaburty pacing at the entrance to the house, and, in hopes of avoiding her, darted

back out of sight. In doing so she collided with a broad, greatcoated chest.

It belonged to a blue-eyed gentleman who smiled at her as though he knew her. Steadying her by the shoulders, he said, "Do not apologize. I believe the coat is unharmed."

"Quiet!" Mary commanded.

She crept alongside the shrubs until the house came into view once more. Mrs. Chattaburty had come down the steps and was standing on tiptoe to facilitate an inspection of the drive. Mary felt the stranger come close beside her.

"What are we doing?" he whispered in her ear.

"Hiding."

"Excellent," he replied with relish. "You must permit me to assist you. I consider myself a proficient."

Mary could not help but look at him again, though the look in his eyes made her lower hers. "If you are going to laugh at me," she said, "I beg you will do it quietly."

"I can assure you I do not find hiding the least bit laughable. It requires the utmost agility and tact, and of late I have had numerous opportunities to improve my skill."

Noting the rakish angle of his hat and the sheen of his Hessians, Mary inquired, "From whom can you possibly want to hide?"

"Creditors, ma'amselle. Parasites. Would-be-borrowers. The sort of creatures who inspire one to cultivate hiding as others cultivate fine music or portraiture."

"Clearly you do not hide from your tailor, nor your bootmaker."

Snapping out a smart military bow, he thanked her. "I shall tell them their handiwork is much admired," he said. "Perhaps they may be persuaded to accept compliments in lieu of payment."

"I am afraid you cannot persuade me that you know anything at all about hiding, though I think you know a great deal about telling ridiculous tales."

"I have traveled many places, ma'amselle, and one thing I have learned is that nothing is too ridiculous to be believed. One may even believe the legend that beautiful maidens hide in the dogwoods of Sussex to enchant wayfarers with their magic spell."

Having uttered this gallantry, he peeked out of the shrub and asked, "By the by, from whom are we hiding?"

"Mrs. Chattaburty. She seemed to be watching for somebody. Is she still there?"

"I am afraid she is very much still there."

"Do you know Mrs. Chattaburty?" Mary asked.

"I had the privilege of meeting that lady one memorable evening."

"Do you suppose she intends to camp there? What can she mean by such behavior?"

"I do not know the lady well, but I would guess that if she meant to camp there, she would outlast the winter."

"Well, she will not outlast me. I will freeze here, if I must."

"I cannot permit that," he said. Stepping back from his observation post, he removed his greatcoat and folded it around her shoulders. He approved his handiwork and took up his watch again.

Mary observed him uncertainly. The gentleman had thrown her off balance, a sensation she had not experienced for many years. His sallies, his amusement, his impeccable cravat, his imposing height, his brown locks that curled à la Brutus under his hat, his seeming to know her, his knowing Mrs. Chattaburty, his blue eyes, his touch as he placed the coat around her—these things unsettled her. What was even more surprising, she found the sensation not at all unpleasant.

"Who are you?" she said. "What are you doing here?"

"My horse stumbled on the drive. I brought him to the stable, where he is being attended. One moment—I believe Mrs. Chattaburty has abandoned her watch and is going inside. Yes, that is precisely what she is doing. We have won!" He faced her with an expression of triumph.

"Who are you?"

"I must wait until we are properly introduced," he told her.

"What are you doing here?"

"I have business with Squire Ashe."

"I am his daughter, sir. You may tell me your business."

"I feel sure he will mention it to you," the gentleman replied, removing the coat from her shoulders and sweeping it over his own. "You will have to know sooner or later."

"Know what?"

"That we will have the pleasure of hiding together for many years to come."

With that, he walked toward the house and did not once look back. When Mary saw the butler open the door to admit him, she tried to recall why she was here in the first place. She stood in the patch of dogwoods and mayberries, shivering with cold, knowing she had returned home for a reason and wondering if the reason had been, in fact, to meet an enigmatic, blue-eyed gentleman who sent all other thoughts from her head. Slowly, she walked back to the carriage and permitted it to take her she scarcely knew where.

When he was shown into the drawing room, Lord Mallory saw two faces stare at him in surprise. The first belonged to Mrs. Chattaburty, whose stone countenance cracked into a smile. The second, he surmised, belonged to Squire Ashe.

"Thank heaven! You have come after all," Mrs. Chattaburty exclaimed.

After apologizing for keeping them waiting, his lordship allowed himself to be presented to the man who wished to be his father-in-law. At Mrs. Chattaburty's invitation, he seated himself on a chair not far from his host and looked about him.

Dearcrop appeared to be a fine old house, unlike Domville in its adherence to a single style of architecture and its cozy size, and far superior to his ancestral home in its neat, well-kept appearance. Its owner seemed equally fine, old-fashioned, singular, small, neat, and well kept, but he added to his style a frown of such proportions that Hugo doubted his welcome. As Mrs. Chattaburty inquired cordially after his lordship's journey, his accommodations at the Bear and Whale, and his difficulties in finding the manor, the squire receded gradually into the shadows of the drapery. By the time Hugo had answered all her questions, Squire Ashe had disappeared altogether.

His lordship concluded that the squire had changed his mind. Mrs. Chattaburty, however, explained, "Squire Ashe does not like interviews of this sort and wishes me to continue in my capacity as agent," and she proceeded to do so with spirit. Dispensing with preliminaries, she broached the business at hand. "Squire Ashe has asked his solicitor to draw up the agreements," she said. "If you will look them over, you will see how generous he intends to be to his son-in-law."

His lordship took the papers from her and perused them. When he looked up, he found the lady studying him anxiously. She pointed at the agreements, saying, "Of course, you will want to have your solicitor look them over as well. There is no cause for hurry."

"None at all," came a voice from the shadows.

"What I see here is more than generous," Lord Mallory said.

"Only in the payment of debts, the restoration of estates, and the settlements on yourself," said the voice from the drape. "Mary shall have her own fortune."

Addressing the drapery, Lord Mallory replied, "I would expect no less."

"Will you not sit with us, Squire?" invited Mrs. Chattaburty.

"I am perfectly comfortable as I am."

With an indulgent smile, Mrs. Chattaburty turned back to his lordship. "What is your opinion now, Lord Mallory? Do you still doubt the sincerity of the offer?"

"I believe you are perfectly sincere, madam. But I am afraid Squire Ashe has repented of the plan."

"I haven't," the voice stated.

"If he appears ill at ease, sir, it is only because he is fully aware of what is at stake," Mrs. C. declared. "But he has gained the most favorable impression of your character from everything I have told him."

"Everything?"

"Indeed, yes—your service under General Wellesley, your distinction in that capacity, your lineage. The squire is prodigiously fond of *Morte D'Arthur* and knows the Caxton edition by heart.''

"He knows a great deal more than I do, then.''

"Yes, of course, you know nothing about Miss Ashe as yet, and we will get to that.''

"I know only that she is a striking young woman who asks a great many direct questions.''

Squire Ashe stepped out of the shadows. "You have met her?''

"I have, sir. That is why I arrived late.''

"You said she had gone!'' Mrs. Chattaburty exclaimed to the squire.

"But she had gone! Heaven knows I hurried her as fast as I could.''

"I particularly said they must not meet, and here they have done exactly that!''

"I suppose we must give it all up now,'' the squire lamented.

Lord Mallory looked from one to the other with a smile. "I deduce,'' he said, "that Miss Ashe does not wish to meet me at this time.''

"She does not wish to meet you at all!'' Squire Ashe declared.

"Clearly she does not approve my history as her father does.''

"She never heard of you in her life!''

Distraught, the squire paced before his lordship's chair, completely forgetting his former reticence, and laying before the man he had hoped to catch for his daughter all the reasons why he ought to decamp on the spot, to wit: Mary knew nothing of the scheme he and Mrs. Chattaburty had concocted; when she found out, she'd be mad as a hornet; heaven knew what would happen when she did find out; she'd probably scratch all their eyes out; or worse, she might say nothing, just glare at him in that way of hers that made his cheeks hot.

Trying to quiet him, Mrs. Chattaburty cleared her throat several times and wagged her fingers in the air, but Squire Ashe was too rapt in contemplating disaster to notice.

"Forgive my obtuseness," Lord Mallory said, "but did you in fact just say that your daughter knows nothing of this arrangement?"

"You don't expect me to tell her, do you?" the squire demanded.

"Frankly, I assumed she had already consented."

"Nothing of the kind. Do you think she would consent to marry a man she has never seen?"

"I thought she was anxious to marry, and that you, sir, were anxious to provide for her. It was a natural assumption."

"Yes, yes, of course it was. But you see, Mary is not anxious to marry. It is I who am anxious on that head."

"Miss Ashe," said Mrs. Chattaburty in despair, "intends to be a spinster."

At that, Lord Mallory laughed. "Then she knows herself as little as she knows me."

Mrs. Chattaburty glanced at him closely. "You do not think much of her intention, I collect."

"I think she is one of the handsomest women I have ever seen, and at the risk of blemishing my reputation with you, I must confess that I have seen quite a few, of every shade, costume, and degree."

The squire looked at Mrs. Chattaburty. Then he beamed at his lordship. "You think her handsome? You do not think her awfully old?"

"My debts have made me poor, sir, but not insensible. You have a beautiful, intelligent, and amusing daughter, and, if I may be permitted to say what it is not at all in my interest to say, you might leave her to her own devices and she will find herself a husband."

"I'd just as soon it was you," stated the squire boldly. "That is, if you are agreeable."

Lord Mallory thought for a moment, then replied, "I might be agreeable, but I have a stipulation."

"You do not like the settlements?"

"I have no quarrel with the settlements. But you must tell your daughter who I am and why I have come."

Squire Ashe blanched. "I knew we should have to give it

up," he mourned. "We would have done better never to begin."

"Perhaps we might delay a bit," interjected Mrs. Chattaburty, "at least until Lord Mallory and Miss Ashe have had a chance to meet again. If she could but know him as an unexceptional gentleman, a friend of her father's perhaps, the announcement might be less likely to alarm her."

"That is it!" the squire agreed. "We must keep it a secret until you have had a chance to woo her."

"And suppose she does not like me?"

"I scarcely think that likely," Mrs. Chattaburty observed. "Certainly she will like you. And if she doesn't I shall make her have you anyway."

Mrs. Chattaburty gasped. "But you swore you would never insist on her marrying a man she does not like."

"I said that about Theo Granger," the squire explained. "Now we are speaking of Sir Thomas Mallory's descendant. That is an entirely different matter."

Lord Mallory smiled. He was accustomed to being pursued by daughters and feared by their fathers. The 'reversal amused him. Nevertheless, his pride forbade that he be forced on any woman.

"If I may be allowed to make a suggestion," he said. "I will extend my visit in Burwash in order to make myself known to Miss Ashe. If, at the end of a fortnight, she does not like me, I will accept my fate as gracefully as I may and withdraw, and if I must withdraw, I shall count myself fortunate for having made the acquaintance of two such agreeable friends as yourselves."

At this speech, the squire's jaw dropped. Turning to Mrs. Chattaburty, he said, "You did not tell me what an amazingly sensible gentleman he is. I am determined we shall have him!"

"Mary. Did you hear me?" Theo demanded.

She gazed at him, unseeing.

"I beg you will come inside. The carriage is gone and

Emily with it. There is no cause for you to stand here and freeze."

Docilely, Mary allowed herself to be led inside the cottage, where Mrs. Hanks had prepared a hot bouillon for the friends and family who had come to see her daughter off. Putting a hand under her elbow, Theo steered Mary to a chair by the hearth where she studied the flames in the fireplace and saw the face of a blue-eyed, smiling gentleman who appeared to recognize her. Racking her memory, she tried to recall where and when they might have met.

"I know you will feel the loss," Theo was saying. "Emily rode with you, did she not? And the two of you were prodigiously musical. Well, you need not repine, because I will ride with you from now on, as soon as the weather improves, for although you are content to brave the January air, I must be careful not to catch another chill."

Mary looked at him as though he were a phantasm.

"And as for the music, it is well known that I am tone deaf, but I shall be happy to listen to you play."

"I must go home," Mary said.

"So soon? You are not ill? You are never ill."

"Emily is gone. There is no reason to stay."

"Did you not hear me? I have been telling you how unnecessary it will be for you to miss her. I will amuse you, ride with you, do whatever you wish."

She smiled at him. "You are very kind," she said.

"That is your sister smile. I know it well and I detest it. It means you don't care a groat for my riding and amusing and listening."

"I have been inattentive. I am sorry."

"I may as well pack up and leave for London, too. And who knows, perhaps you will miss me if I do. And perhaps I may find a young lady there who will smile at me in an unsisterly fashion."

"It is a capital idea, Theo. You ought to speak with your father about it as soon as possible."

At this Theo sulked. Some minutes later, he handed Mary into her carriage and bade her good-bye with an admonition. "I shall go to London one day, and you will be sorry!"

When Mary returned to Dearcrop, she found her father wearing a path in the carpet of the drawing room. His face was flushed and beaming, and she could not recall when she had seen him so animated.

"Did you get Emily off?" he inquired with a broad grin.

"Yes, and I hope your business was equally successful."

"It was. It was."

"I am at leisure, Papa. You may tell me about it."

He stopped and his face fell. "I do not know what to say," he told her honestly.

"You had a visitor today. Who is he?"

"Lord Mallory. His ancestor is Sir Thomas."

"I see. And did you discuss *Morte D'Arthur*?"

"I cannot say we did, for we did not."

"Then perhaps you will tell me, Papa, what was his business here?"

Cornered, Squire Ashe squirmed and shifted about. He would not lie to his daughter; yet not for the world would he tell her the truth. At last, an inspiration seized him and he replied, "He is a relation of Lady Babik's, but you must not breathe a word to her of this."

"It is to be a secret? I am more bewildered than ever."

"Lady Babik has never met him. She knows him by reputation only. I shall introduce them and be the means of reuniting their family."

"Papa, you are one of the most generous creatures I know, but I have not known you to exert yourself in that quarter before. I confess, I am surprised, especially as you have always said that Lady Babik is a malicious tittle-tattle."

"Gracious, did I say that?"

"I am afraid you did. And I am afraid you were right."

"All the more reason why I should perform this act of charity, for that virtue is most blessed when it benefits those you hate."

"I do not mean to press you, Papa, and you need not go on if you do not wish to, but I am trying to understand your part in the affairs of Lady Babik and her long-lost relations."

"In point of fact, it is not only for Lady Babik's sake that I have taken an interest in this case. Lord Mallory is an excellent gentleman. It appears I am in a position to assist him in settling certain debts. It is a pity, these debts of his, for they are none of his doing." He followed this with an account of his lordship's life and adventures up to the present moment.

Mary could not help but be intrigued. It was not often that she met a gentleman who combined distinction and bravery with dashing good looks and amusing wit. "His history shows him to be a man of character as well as reputation," she said thoughtfully, "but I still do not understand why you should advance him the means of settling his debts. What is he to you?"

"Nothing! He is nothing to me. And I have not advanced him a groat at the moment, but even if I should, it would be with the expectation of repayment, for he is a very fine gentleman and not at all a rattlebrain."

"If you intend to discharge the debts of every pleasant, well-informed fellow you meet, we shall soon find ourselves in dreadful straits."

"I intend nothing of the kind! My plan, for the present, is to assist him by making the proper introductions."

"To his cousin, Lady Babik."

"Yes."

"And to Lord Babik, who may be induced to advance his wife's cousin a little of the ready?"

"A capital idea."

"And Miss Babik, who has just made her debut and would like nothing better than to marry a title?"

"Heavens. I was not thinking of that!"

"Dearest Papa, what have you been thinking?"

Squire Ashe regarded his daughter, then took her by the elbow and led her to the sofa. As they sat close together, he pressed her hands in his and said softly, "My dear, a man thinks of all sorts of things he never thought of before when he reaches a certain time of life. I have lived beyond my allotted three score and ten; I am at an age where I think of what lies ahead. I see that the road I must travel is not very long, certainly not as long as I wish it were. I see that there are deeds I must do now, while I am able, or I may never have the opportunity again. I see that I have had a good life and can render it a better one by doing what I can for others.''

Mary looked down at the wrinkled hands that held her own. ''You are not old, Papa. Your health could not be better. It is premature to think of these things.''

''I wish that were true. But I know I am going to die.''

Mary could hardly speak. She put her arms about the squire's neck and pressed her cheek to his. ''Oh, my dear father,'' she whispered hoarsely, fighting back tears.

Squire Ashe was profoundly moved by his daughter's ardent, affectionate hug, so moved, in fact, that he forbore to tell her that the prognostication of doom emanated ·not from any physician but from Theo Granger, the foremost hypochondriac in Sussex.

CHAPTER FOUR

The squire's preoccupation with his approaching death did not abate. Indeed, he spoke of it so often and with such relish that Mary began heartily to wish he would return to his old preoccupation with her marriage. Distressed at this new fixation of his, she cosseted his every sneeze and grew alarmed at the first sign of a cough, until he made it manifestly clear that he derived great cheer from anticipating his demise.

It rendered him sufficiently energetic to attend his lordship at The Bear, and Whale, to accompany him to Furringdale, where Lord and Lady Babik welcomed their long-lost relative with all due obsequiousness, and to join his voice with theirs in prevailing upon Hugo to remove to their mansion for the remainder of his stay in Burwash. Squire Ashe even went so far as to assist in the removal of his lordship's belongings from the inn, and certain though Mary was that he had managed to get in the way of the servants at every opportunity, still she noted with pleasure that he returned from his exertions without a single portent of catastrophe.

She cross-questioned him regarding Lord Mallory and his reception at Furringdale, and in response to her particular inquiry on the subject, he said he thought his lordship was much taken with Miss Babik. This golden-haired lass,

reported the squire, had greeted Lord Mallory with none
of the shyness customary in one so lately emerged from the
schoolroom. In fact, her lively spirits had set them all to
laughing—especially his lordship—when she had innocently
inquired whether cousins twenty years apart in age might be
allowed to marry.

On the very next day, Mary and the squire received an
invitation from Lady Babik summoning them to a reception
for her much-titled relation. Her ladyship expressed great
joy at the reunion that Squire Ashe had arranged, and she
promised to treat the entire county to dancing and supper in
consequence. The squire's pleasure in the forthcoming cele-
bration nearly exceeded Lady Babik's, and seeing how
much it raised his spirits, Mary looked forward to the event
with good cheer. If there was an additional motive for her
excitement, she kept it to herself.

When she entered on her father's arm, she saw a ballroom
that sparkled everywhere, from the high polish on the floor
to the chandeliers dangling from the frescoed ceilings.
Likewise, her neighbors sparkled, having braved the damp
cold and muddy roads to fill the room with their finery and
chatter. A trio of musicians played a gay melody at one end
of the room, while at the other, a table displayed a banquet
of cool wines, and a hundred delights with appetizing
French names.

All eyes turned on Lord Mallory, the tallest guest in the
room. Resplendent in a fawn coat and dark pantaloons, he
was surrounded by a circle of gentlemen who lapped up his
tales of India like champagne. Having delivered Mary into
the protection of Mrs. Chattaburty, the squire joined the
group of listeners.

Mary saw at once that the ladies were not as pleasantly
diverted as the gentlemen. The paucity of dancing partners
was a matter of some anxiety. Miss Babik wished aloud that
Lord Mallory would grow weary with recounting military
exploits and ask her to stand up with him, a hope shared by
every female within earshot. For a time it seemed as though
his lordship would grant the wish of one of them, for he
glanced frequently at the distaff contingent and made as if to

move in that direction. An eager question put to him by Theo Granger detained him, however, and before long he was induced to describe yet another battle.

"Lady Babik's guest of honor is remarkably charming," said Mrs. Chattaburty to Mary.

"The gentlemen appear to think so," she replied.

"What do you think, Miss Ashe?"

"I shall have to know him better before I may venture an opinion. And as it appears unlikely that I shall have that opportunity, I will say nothing at all."

"Do you not admire his bearing?"

"He is certainly very tall."

"His style of dress is exquisite, do you not agree?"

"His tailor has decked him out to perfection and deserves to be paid."

"There is an unmistakable look of nobility in his countenance. Brown eyes are so expressive, I think."

"His eyes are blue."

Mrs. Chattaburty smiled at this. "So they are," she said. "What an excellent thing your father has done—bringing cousins together."

"He has grown remarkably energetic of late. I hope he does not exhaust himself."

"He appears much taken with Lord Mallory."

"I have never known him to take such a fancy to anybody."

"How fortunate that his lordship holds your father in equally high regard."

"It is in his interest to do so. You see, my father means to persuade Lord Babik to help discharge his debts."

"That is unjust, I think. He would esteem him under any circumstances, for upon the completion of his removal from the inn, the first thing he would do was to sit down with Squire Ashe and listen to his recitation from *Arthur*."

Mary laughed. "My father exacts harsh payment for his kindness."

A deep voice behind her said, "Your father is incapable of doing anything harsh."

She looked up into Lord Mallory's blue eyes. In a trice,

he bowed to Mrs. Chattaburty and obtained Mary's promise
for the next set. As he walked off to chat with his hostess,
the ladies gathered about Mary to discuss the honor just
bestowed upon her. Hardly noting their sighs of admiration
or Miss Babik's pout, she followed him with her eyes.

When he returned to lead her down to the dance, she felt
the stares of the assemblage. The chatter died down, leaving
sentences hanging in the air. If Lord Mallory noticed the stir
he was causing, he ignored it. Mary, determined to follow
his example, put her arm in his. With her chin high and her
eyes looking straight ahead, she moved with him toward the
head of the line, disdaining to hear the whispered comments
on her emerald gown, her jeweled bosom, and her raven
hair.

Once they began dancing, everyone else followed suit.
The general noise and activity resumed, and Mary was able
to concentrate on the grace of her partner's steps. In silence,
they performed a number of turns and bows, and soon it
became evident that no one paid them any attention. Whereupon, Mary said, "I am afraid, sir, that you have inspired
the ladies of Burwash to hate India."

"And how have I managed that? I have never said a word
on the subject to any of them."

"That is precisely how you have managed it. Your tales
of that exotic land have kept the gentlemen from dancing.
Moreover, they have kept you from dancing."

"I trust at least one damsel was devastated as a result."

"Indeed she was. She fidgeted and complained until the
others grew quite out of patience with her."

"Well, I have made amends now."

"Rather you should say you have begun to make amends
now. The sight of a gentleman dancing always endears him
to those he has slighted. But you will not truly make
amends until you lead her down to the head of the set"

Lord Mallory looked surprised. "I thought I had just
done that," he said.

Mary flushed, then laughed. "It was not I who fretted and
complained, my lord. It was Miss Babik."

His lordship's eyes scanned the salon. In a moment they

came to rest on his young cousin, who danced with Theo Granger. "I am glad, at any rate," he said, "that you do not blame me."

"But I do."

"It appears I have a talent for provoking the ladies."

"I do not blame you for keeping the gentlemen from the dance but for confining your tales of India to them. I would have enjoyed hearing them myself."

"Perhaps I may have another opportunity of telling you everything you wish to know, though I must warn you, Miss Ashe, hearing what I have to say might astonish you."

Lifting her brows, Mary replied, "I do not think so, sir. I have read a good deal about India, and I do not think you can shock me."

"I never contradict a beautiful woman. Nevertheless, you must know that India is a seducer."

"And were you seduced?"

"Naturally. You would be, too."

"I assure you, sir, I am not easily taken in. My experience of the world, though not vast, has been sufficient to render me perfectly cynical. I do not believe more than a third of what I am told; nor do I swoon at the mention of suttees."

"India is far more subtle than that. Before long, you will find yourself decked out in a sari."

"I should like that very much."

He smiled, and after they parted to circle their respective lines, they rejoined hands to a new topic.

"Your father has been very kind to me. Did he tell you he assisted my valet in directing the removal here?"

"Yes, and I have no doubt his efforts cost you twice the time."

"His good will made it worth the while."

"He has taken a great fancy to you, Lord Mallory. I confess, I do not quite understand it."

"I collect, then, that you have not taken a similar fancy."

"I did not mean to imply that. I simply have never before seen my father bestir himself so energetically on behalf of anyone, excepting myself."

"Then you *have* taken a fancy to me?"

Mary's cheek grew warm. "You are quizzing me, sir."

"If my tone seemed to indicate that I was teasing, I regret it. We soldiers are a simple breed, better trained for bluntness than diplomacy."

"It is of no consequence."

"Ah, but it is. I must know whether you like me."

"It is not important whether I do or not. What matters is that Miss Babik likes you."

"Are you endeavoring to forward a match, Miss Ashe?"

"I understand it is you who are endeavoring to forward one."

"If military intelligence equalled the gossip of Burwash, I should fear for the safety of England."

"Do you deny that you came here expressly for the purpose of marrying your way out of debt?"

"I do not deny it. Since my arrival, however, I have conceived a much stronger motive."

"You admire the lady, then."

"I admire her very much."

Mary was not perfectly satisfied with this assurance. It gave her no pleasure to hear that he not only meant to wed Miss Babik, but that he also enjoyed the prospect. When the dance ended and he bowed, she wondered where she would find the patience to endure the remainder of the evening. She had already danced with the single most interesting person in the room. All that was left was to watch him pay his respects to others. Even now, as he bent gallantly over his young cousin's hand and led her onto the floor, Mary felt her impatience swell. Her discontent mounted as she watched them laugh together and swirl in time to the melody. Engrossed in this disagreeable occupation, she automatically accepted Theo when he claimed her hand for the next set.

Following the direction of her eyes, he observed that Lord Mallory seemed an excellent fellow, and it was a great pity he had been forced to abandon his service to Wellesley.

"I cannot pity a gentleman who has come into two

honorable titles and the lands that attach to them," Mary said.

"He thinks nothing of the titles," Theo replied. "He is not a bit proud, you know, nor does he have the least idea of his own importance. He speaks of his former career only, and with a vast deal of homesickness, too, it seems to me."

"Perhaps when he has concluded his business here, he may return to service."

"Business? He did not say he had business here. Indeed, at this moment, he seems to have his mind on something far different."

When Mary looked at Lord Mallory again, she was forced to agree with Theo. His lordship appeared to take a decidedly unbusinesslike interest in whatever Miss Babik was rattling on about. She heartily wished his lordship had the grace to be as bored as she was.

Theo concluded aloud that Miss Babik certainly knew the manner of entertaining a fellow, and seeing Mary scowl at this, he added, "As for me, I prefer women who have a great many more years to their credit."

"Your proficiency in the diplomatic line," Mary answered, "would qualify you for soldiering."

Theo, who took this as an encomium, affected a tender expression and, thinking to repeat his late success at gallantry, went on to opine that though some might dangle after green girls, he himself admired maturer ladies with more to recommend them than mere youth and beauty.

As this did not in the least mollify Mary, and as Lord Mallory was now standing up with Miss Babik for a second time, she turned on her companion with a steely eye and said, "If this is your notion of making love to me, Theo, I think we had better dance."

The dance seemed interminable and insipid. As soon as the music stopped, Mary seized the opportunity to send Theo off in search of a bit of refreshment. Moodily, she stood by a column and surveyed the company, which streamed in the direction of the champagne. Lord Mallory moved in the opposite direction, and, joining Mary at her column, he said, "You are engaged to Mr. Granger?"

"Who told you that?"

"Miss Babik took her oath that you were on the brink."

"Miss Babik gives every promise of following in her mother's footsteps."

"You disapprove of the young lady, I collect. Do you think I should give up my suit?"

"You should attend to your matches, and I shall attend to mine."

"Then there *is* to be a match with Mr. Granger."

"It apparently matters little what I say. My neighbors will always have it otherwise."

"I do not know you well as yet, Miss Ashe, but I doubt you are the sort to marry in order to please your neighbors, though I suspect you are not above marrying in order to *dis*please them."

"You read my character aright, sir. And since you do not like mincing words, I will tell you what I have told Theo and the entire world—I shall never be Mrs. Granger."

"In that case," replied his lordship with a smart bow, "may I call on you soon?"

Lord Mallory called the very next day, and by the time the sun was high over the bare oaks and rolling hills, he had proved himself as intrepid a horseman as Mary had ever met. The chill winter air, replete with droplets of ice and occasional blasts of wind, merely spurred him on.

When they dismounted to inspect a churchyard, he noted her attempts to breathe some warmth onto her fingers. Instantly he remarked on the thinness of her gloves and took the business of warming her hands into his own. He looked up from his work to study her face, which told him that she was as content to have him chafe her hands as he was to do it. She confessed she ought not to have ridden so far with frozen hands. He replied he would have turned back at a word. And they both felt how fortunate it was that she had ridden as far as she had with frozen hands, and that they had not turned back.

Subsequent days brought a round of visits and parties, each one more charming to Mary than such occasions had ever been in the past. She attributed their charm to the fact that his lordship's attentions to Miss Babik were no more than what an uncle may owe a flirtatious niece. His attentions to her, on the other hand, were such that everyone remarked on them.

Naturally, Lady Babik could not refrain from making certain pungent observations. Sitting with Mrs. Venable and Mrs. Turnbull by Mrs. Chattaburty's fire, she declared, "I never thought I should see a woman of her age set her cap for a title."

"What has age to do with it?" asked the magistrate's widow, tasting her bread and butter. "He is as handsome a fellow as I've seen since Henry Crowe was brought before the bench and hanged."

"I never thought Miss Ashe was particular about titles," Mrs. Venable put in.

"You are dreadfully innocent, Imogen," remarked her ladyship.

Mrs. Chattaburty answered complacently, "Clearly he is the one who has set the cap."

"Nonsense," insisted her ladyship.

"I believe Harriet may be right," said Mrs. Turnbull, "for they stood together for a full hour at the card party, and he could not take his eyes off her."

"And the squire dotes on him," added Mrs. Venable irrelevantly.

"You all disappoint me," exclaimed lady Babik, "and especially you, Harriet, for you have always showed good sense regarding Miss Ashe and were the first to point out that she is eccentric."

"I am still of that opinion," Mrs. C. replied, "But I have also observed that his lordship's inclinations run strongly to eccentricity."

"As a gentleman of breeding," declared her ladyship, "his inclinations must run to the charms of youthful modesty."

"They have promised to be at the vicarage tonight," said Mrs. Chattaburty, "and then you may see for yourself where the gentleman's inclinations lie."

Lady Babik did indeed see for herself, and she disliked

what she saw well enough to cut Harriet Chattaburty at the next party and to prattle to her neighbors more than ever of Miss Ashe's impossible black hair.

In contrast, Mary liked what she saw well enough to set out for the dressmaker's in Burwash. There she endured with happy docility the measurings and pinnings of Miss Trimble, who gaped at the bold red fabric and the bright gold frogs Miss Ashe selected. The seamstress could not refrain from remarking that Miss Ashe's new walking suit would resemble the most striking of General Wellesley's uniforms. As this was precisely the effect Mary hoped to achieve, she turned contentedly to the matter of a new ball gown. Eschewing the muted colors she had favored in recent years, she chose a purple of the finest silk.

"Gracious!" Miss Trimble exclaimed, "how that color makes your eyes to shine."

The source of that shine entered the dress shop just as Mary was leaving. He did not notice her at first, being preoccupied with parting the window curtains a fraction of an inch and peering outside.

"Why, good afternoon, Lord Mallory," Mary greeted him.

"Quiet!" he replied.

Looking round then, he saw who it was he had addressed so rudely and endeavored to rephrase his request more tactfully. "I would be much obliged, Miss Ashe, if you would converse *piano* rather than *forte*." Then he returned to the window, keeping close to the wall so that he could not be spotted from the outside.

"Why, sir, I believe you are hiding," she whispered.

He smiled and looked at her. "If you recall the circumstances of our first meeting, you will not give me away."

"I would not be so ungrateful. In fact, I will return the favor you did me and help you as best I can. Unfortunately, I have no greatcoat to throw over your shoulders, and even if I had, it would stretch across no more than half your back."

"You have an accurate memory."

"Had you forgotten that part of it?"

"I haven't forgotten a thing."

"Well then, let's get to it. From whom are we hiding?" She approached the window and looked into the street, which bustled with activity in the winter sunshine. Standing close to her, he looked as well.

"We are hiding from my cousins," he whispered.

"A great pity," said Mary solemnly. "I understand it perfectly. Nevertheless, it is a great pity."

"That I must hide from my hostesses?"

"That you must hide from your betrothed."

Turning from the window to face her, he replied, "On the contrary, it is vastly amusing."

"I suppose it will amuse you to marry a woman from whom you must hide."

Taking her hand in his, he answered, "I would much rather marry one who would hide with me."

As Mary did not blush when she met his eyes, and as she did not withdraw her hand, he raised it to his lips, upon which they heard a prodigious sigh emanate from the breast of the enchanted Miss Trimble.

Lord Mallory called at Dearcrop Manor the next morning to leave his card and a package for Miss Ashe. No, he informed the butler, he would not stay to visit but would certainly do so when he returned on the morrow. The neatly wrapped box was delivered into Mary's hands in the breakfast parlor, along with a letter from London.

"What a windfall for you," the squire exclaimed. "I do not think I have ever received both a letter and a package in the same day."

"Perhaps you will some day," said his daughter as she broke open the seal on the letter.

"I do not have many days left in which to do so," announced the squire cheerfully. "If they do not hurry, they will not arrive until after I am dead."

"If you continue in that vein, Papa, I shall be forced to place an order for your shroud."

"No need for that, my dear. I have already seen to it." With the expression of a man who knows his affairs are right and tight, he sawed off a piece of smoked fish and savored it sweetly.

"Emily Hanks sends you her love, Papa."

"How does she get on?"

"She does not write the letter, Papa. She positively sings it. She is that delighted with London."

"Her voice is quite charming. Do you suppose she would sing a Psalm for me at the church when I am gone?"

"Shall I ask her when next I write?"

"By all means. I have chosen a pleasant one, you know—nothing about smiting enemies and that sort of thing."

"You would not smite an enemy, even if you had one."

"Yet I can be firm when my mind is made up."

"You have certainly made up your mind as to this dying business, Papa, and you are certainly firm in your plans for the event."

"Be sure to write Emily about it. What else does she say?"

"Only that Lady Baldridge has invited me to visit with them in London. It seems Emily has told her all about me. She appears to regard me as a challenge and would consider it a feather in her cap to marry off someone as ancient as I am."

"You are not going?" her father cried.

"I have too much to occupy me here."

Her father asked delicately what occupation she had.

"Well, for one thing, your funeral arrangements."

"No, no," he insisted with a wave of his hand. "I am arranging all that myself. It will be time enough for you when you have your own funeral to look after."

Mary laughed and asked him, "Have you not noticed, Papa, what a good many parties and what pleasant company we have enjoyed these past two weeks?"

"Have you enjoyed them, child?? I am very glad."

"Now what do you suppose is in this package?"

"Why, look at the crest on the seal."

"It is Lord Mallory's."

Ripping open the wrappings, she uncovered a thickness of

filmy cloth. She pulled the fabric from the box, revealing long, wide strands of the most exquisite blues, greens, and violets.

"I am sure I have never heard of sending a lady a bolt of cloth. Perhaps it is a military custom or a habit his lordship acquired in Ireland. They do things very oddly there, you know."

"It is a sari, Papa."

"Aha," he said, not because he had ever heard the word before and knew what it meant, but because he perceived his daughter attached particular meaning to it. If there might be anything out of the way in the gift, the squire was disposed to overlook it. He knew only that Lord Mallory had thought to send it and that Mary had never looked so delighted with any gift in her life.

"Thank you for remembering," Mary said to Hugo the next day.

As soon as the butler left them alone, he replied, "You wear it beautifully."

"I wasn't certain I had it quite right." She stood up from the sofa and inspected the folds of the sari. "It seems a trifle lumpy in parts. I know you will probably laugh at me."

He could see very well that it was lumpy in parts, but he did not laugh. Indeed, as he looked at her, his expression grew serious. "There is something you ought to know, Miss Ashe," he said, "and I would like you to know it before we proceed any further."

Surprised at his grim tone, she begged him to speak out.

He paused, evidently trying to frame the words, and then told her, "It would be better if you would wrap the end over the other shoulder."

Mary attempted to follow his instruction. When her fumblings only made matters worse, he was forced to come to her rescue. As she had tangled the end of the blue scarf into the folds of the violet one, and as he was continually distracted by the sight of her neck and the fragrance of her hair, the adjustment took considerable time. Mary waited patiently until he finally worked the cloth loose. Drawing it from her left shoulder, he laid it gently across the right. In the process, he glimpsed her black eyes smiling into his, and his troubled expression deepened.

Instinctively, she touched his arm. "What is the matter?"

Stepping away, he assured her there was nothing amiss. "It seems a little close in here, don't you think?"

Slowly she approached him, her head tilted a bit to the side. "There *is* something the matter, only you will not say so."

Hugo moved to the mantel where he studied the intricacies of a china bowl, saying, "I wish your father had spoken to you. There is a great deal he can tell you. I am not sure you will approve. Indeed, I wish he had told you from the first."

"What do you think I ought to know?"

"For one thing, I have not lived these past years in a monastery. I am sure you will recall that I have lived in quite another sort of setting."

"Of course, I recall. If you had lived in a monastery, you would not have sent me a sari."

"Exactly. And I think now that I should never have sent it. It was improper. I repent it heartily."

"You merely took pains to gratify my expressed wish. If there has been any impropriety, it has been mine, parading before you in this perfectly ridiculous way."

"I wish you had not worn it."

She moved nearer to study his profile. In his turn, he studied three little blue figures in a blue boat.

"I have offended you and I am sorry for it," she said. "I understand completely. After what you saw in India, you no doubt have difficulty keeping your countenance. Indeed, it must take all the force you are master of to keep from laughing at me."

"It takes all the force I am master of to keep from kissing you."

After Mary absorbed this, a feat that seemed to take a month's time, she replied, "Well, I wish you would kiss me. Anything is better than having you frown so."

His frown did not soften, but because his lips were

pressed to hers, she did not know it. She flung her arms
about him and lost herself in sighs, assuring him that he had
not distressed her by this display. He therefore sought out
her neck and indulged in the luxury of tasting it.

All at once, Mary felt herself gripped by the shoulders.
He held her away from him and looked at her with that same
serious expression. "You must speak to your father at
once," he said to her.

"Gladly," she replied. "But please do not look so grave.
He will be overjoyed, I assure you."

He seemed as if he would kiss her again and stepped
close to touch her cheek. Something clouded his face,
however, reversing his intention, and in another moment, he
was gone from the room.

Exultantly, Mary reviewed what had just passed. "Speak
to your father at once!" he had told her. How gallant of him
to appear anxious about his success. She smiled, thinking
how little he needed to be anxious on that head.

Certainly she would speak to her father. She would not,
of course, tell him that Lord Mallory was in such a case that
just seeing her in a sari caused him to lose his equanimity.
She would not mention her delight in the poor man's
desperate state or allude to her own equally desperate one.
She would merely inform the good squire that chance had
now provided her with a husband in the person of his
lordship, and she made no doubt her father would welcome
the news so gratefully as to postpone all funeral preparations
in order to make arrangements for a wedding.

Among the charms of Dearcrop Manor was a room that
faced west on the main floor. It was too sunny and too small
to be used for company, and as it housed many treasures
belonging to the squire's late wife, it had come to be called
the Mother's Room. Standing by the French doors, which
looked out on a rose garden were Mrs. Ashe's harp, cello,
and pianoforte. Nearby lay her sewing baskets, embroidery
frames, sketch pads, music sheets, and household account
books. They sprawled casually on the tabletops and mantel-

piece as though their owner would be in to claim them within the hour.

Scattered among these treasures were mementoes of Mary's childhood: a cleverly carved spinning top, a marionette with twisted strings, a doll whose porcelain head hung onto its body by a thread, and an earless and eyeless furry creature that bore the vaguest resemblance to a bear. Among these homely comforts, the squire kept a humidor full of tobacco in case he should feel like a pipe in the evening. By the humidor sat his monograph on the Arthurian legend, a work that he had been composing for twenty-five years.

To this cozy chamber Mary now repaired with her father.

"Is that a new gown?" the squire inquired as he sat down. "It is highly original. I declare, I never fancied the French style very much and think it very odd that we should be imitating their fashion while fighting their emperor. I like that gown of yours much better."

Still standing, Mary turned about. "It is the sari Lord Mallory sent yesterday morning, Papa."

"Ah, yes, the Irish cloth. It is most becoming, and I trust you have thanked him."

"I did so not an hour ago, and he asked me to speak to you."

"Did he? Well, you may tell him for me that I wish to place my order for a sari."

"He is going to visit you, Papa, to ask for your blessing. We are going to be married."

Mary was concerned to see her father turn bright red. He grasped the arms of his chair and inhaled until his chest puffed high. For a moment, it appeared to her that he was on the verge of activating his funeral arrangements. She drew close and peered down at him, whereupon he startled her even more by jumping up and capering about the room. From the sprightliness of his dance, she deduced that he was pleased.

"A fortnight!" he crowed. "He said a fortnight, and a fortnight 'tis."

"I knew you would be happy, Papa."

"Happy? Happy? I may die in peace, at last."

Mary laughed. "We will have no dying, Papa. I am depending on you to see to my wedding."

The squire paused in his jig to embrace his daughter. "I shall have only one thing left to wish for," he murmured. "I wish to see a grandchild."

"Then you do like Lord Mallory, Papa?"

He held her away, his eyes bulging with tears. "Like him?" he cried. "Like him? Why, I picked him, didn't I?"

"I know you took a great fancy to him."

He led her to the sofa, a confiding tone in his voice. "I did fancy him right away, as soon as Mrs. Chattaburty told me who he was and what a pickle he was in. Of course, I did not believe it would come to pass, certainly not when I heard I must go to London. But then Mrs. C. said she would go in my stead. Of course, we did not think he would come. Mrs. C. had her doubts, so naturally I thought it was all up with us. But then he did come, and he liked the arrangements as well as we could have hoped."

"You arranged for him to come?" She sank down onto the sofa.

"I cannot take the credit, my dear. Mrs. Chattaburty thought of the match to begin with and arranged it all."

"Mrs. Chattaburty has been arranging a match for me?"

"But Mrs. C. cannot take all the credit, my love, for it was his lordship who said if he could not win you in a fortnight, he would give up the suit."

Mary grew thoughtful. "It has been two weeks since he arrived in Burwash."

"Two weeks to the day!"

"Lord Mallory is certainly punctual."

"Yes, and you love him in the bargain. Now you can see why I am content to die."

"I see much that I did not see before."

"You must not look so serious, child. There is nothing more to fret about. It has all come to pass, just as Mrs. Chattaburty said it would, though I despaired a thousand times."

"You are very happy, Papa?"

"*Happy* is too paltry a word for what I am."

Here Mary paused to withdraw her hands from his. Smoothing the filmy cloth of the sari, she asked, "But what if something should still go awry? What if it turned out that his lordship and I did not suit after all? Would you be dreadfully disappointed?"

The squire's jaw fell as he contemplated this conjectural disaster. "I should not recover, of course," he stated. "But that is mere web spinning, for everything has gone off just as it should."

"I do not think so, Papa."

He screwed up his face in puzzlement. "What can be lacking, daughter? The gentleman wants to marry you. You want to marry him. I want the two of you to marry. The two of you want me to want you to marry. Mrs. Chattaburty wants the two of you to marry. Except for Lady Babik, the whole world wants the two of you to marry. Nothing stands in the way."

"That is not true. There is a very great obstacle."

"You must not worry about the arrangements, my dear. We have already agreed on the terms of the marriage. You shall have your own fortune, and he shall have his, so that there will be no awkward dependency on either side. His lordship was in total agreement and has not a greedy bone in his body. Once his debts are paid and his settlements made, he agrees you ought to be free to do exactly as you wish."

"Then I wish to change my mind."

The squire beheld her in disbelief. "Nonsense," was all he could say when he found his voice.

"It is done. I have changed my mind."

"You cannot change your mind!" Squire Ashe exclaimed. "You cannot bring me in here—not in the Mother's Room— and tell me that you have gotten yourself engaged and then, in the very next breath, declare that you have gotten yourself disengaged."

"I deeply regret your disappointment, Papa. And I know how silly I must appear to you—announcing my betrothal and then immediately withdrawing the announcement. But I did not understand the circumstances. Now that I do, I have no choice but to vow never again to see Lord Mallory."

"What on earth is there to understand, except that I shall be the most miserable corpse in the churchyard when I anticipated being the most satisfied?"

"Only that his lordship does not love me."

"Why would he send you such an outlandish costume if he did not love you?"

"To woo me, Papa, or rather, to woo my riches. No doubt it is all the same to him."

"Of course it is all the same. You are an heiress, my dear. Do you suppose he could afford to love you if you were not?"

"You wished to buy him for me, just as you once bought me my pony and my phaeton."

"Well, you have had a precious deal of happiness from them both, have you not?"

"That is not the point."

"Aye, I can tell by your tone that it is not the point. The point is there will be no grandson to know what sorrowful old man is buried under my headstone."

"I beg you, Papa, think for a moment of my future. What will my life be with a man who does not love me?"

"And I beg you, daughter, think for a moment of why I went to all the trouble of finding a husband for you and paying Mrs. Chattaburty's way in London, and getting the gentleman up here, and installing him with Lady Babik, and sending papers back and forth to solicitors. Why, I ask you, have I done all of that?"

"You believe that once I am married you will be able to die with a clear conscience."

He was surprised but pleased. "You have said it very nicely. Indeed, I could not have done better myself. And so let there be an end to this discussion."

"Will your conscience be clear, Papa, if you have co-erced me into marriage with a man I do not wish to marry?"

"You do wish to marry him. You told me so not five minutes ago."

"That was then. I do not wish to do so now."

"And have you stopped loving him so soon?"

Lowering her eyes, Mary shook her head. "In a matter of weeks, I shall be wholly indifferent to him, I assure you."

"Are you so fickle as all that?"

"I am not fickle. I am only well practiced in schooling my heart to do my head's bidding."

"I fear your head is full of flax and wattles. As your father, it behooves me to insist that you do what is in your interest."

Mary regarded her father defiantly. "You mean to force me?" The icicles on her words made the squire wince.

In an ameliorating tone, he pleaded, "Let us not talk of force and such medieval nonsense. Come, let us be on our old terms, and you will see that being a marchioness will amuse you greatly."

On this he attempted to take hold of her hands once more, but she held them rigid and rose grandly from the sofa. He cowered at the sight of her looking down at him, calmly furious, stonily rebellious. He nearly declared his surrender.

"Did it amuse Guinevere to be a queen?" she asked in an arctic voice. "'Was her high position sufficient to keep her from falling in love with her husband's first knight, bearing his child, and precipitating all of Camelot into tragic wars?"

"Do you invoke *Arthur*?" cried the squire, his resolution restored and his blood rising.

"I do, because I know of no other way to tell you what becomes of women who are forced to marry for convenience—the convenience, that is, of their families, their husbands, their nations, certainly not their own. They become as desperate, wicked and foolish as Guinevere, and I will not be one of them."

"Is that what you think of Guinevere?" he said in horror. "I cannot believe my own daughter could so misread Sir Thomas!"

"Please, Papa, you must tell his lordship that I cannot entertain his proposals and that he must leave Burwash as soon as possible."

"I will tell him," said the squire looking his daughter square in the eye, "that the marriage will take place as soon as possible, if he still means to have such a headstrong, eccentric girl as you are.''

Because Mary had never failed to get her way with her father, she did not know precisely how to respond to this firmness. In days to come, she thought, she would have a better chance of persuading him to relent. For now, there was but a single prudent course of action open to her. Immediately seizing upon it, she burst into tears and ran out of the room.

CHAPTER FIVE

Mary spent the next several hours closeted in her bed-chamber. A hundred times she thought to remove the pretty enamel box from its secret place and reread the letters that had been her insurance against folly. Each time she dismissed the idea with scorn.

Safety, she saw, had been a chimera. She had deluded herself into thinking her heart could never be wrung in that way again, and in her delusion she had grown full of pride, imagining herself invulnerable, too wise to be fooled. Such thinking had trapped her; she had fallen in love again with a fortune hunter. Admittedly, this one was not encumbered with wife and children as the first had been. Nor was he as obvious or indelicate as the ones who had followed. Still, they were as alike as the Roman twins raised by a she-wolf.

Although she wished to cry, Mary in fact found herself laughing—bitterly, despairingly, but laughing nevertheless. In her besotted state, she had utterly misread Lord Mallory's distress, attributing it to desire inspired by the sight of her in a sari. Now it was clear that his conscience had pricked him, as well it might, and that he had every reason in the world to fear for the success of his suit.

For a moment, she entertained the idea of letting her father do as he wished with her. Her own efforts had proved futile and ridiculous. Perhaps she would do better to give herself over to those who were so certain they knew what was best for her.

Before her eyes there rose a picture of life as Lady Mallory, and she tried to imagine herself busy with furnishings, neighborly gossip, and balls. In the end, though, it would not fadge, for the only picture that presented itself as real was the image of an awkward, stiff Mary Ashe, longing hopelessly for the love of her husband. It was an image that filled her with revulsion. She might be spoiled, eccentric, willful, silly, and perverse, but she was not able to exist on fantastic hopes or crumbs of affection.

Coming full circle, she arrived at the determination to remain unmarried. Consequently, she sought out her father to see what might be done toward softening his position. As she entered the hall, she found him on the point of leaving the house. His face was so white and hard that she feared he might be ill, and his eyes fixed themselves everywhere but on her face.

"You are going out?" she asked softly.

"I mean to call on his lordship."

"What will you tell him?"

"Everything, I suppose. That you love him but do not love him. That you wish to marry him but do not wish to marry him. That as you do not know your own mind, I must know it for you."

Seizing his hand, Mary pleaded, "Do not go, Papa. Stay awhile yet so that we may talk."

He looked at her hand and drew his own away. "I must not stay," he said hoarsely. "If I do, it will all be up for certain. You will talk me out of everything, and when you do, I shall be the most miserable of men."

"Is it preferable that I be the most miserable of women?"

"You will not be miserable. A marchioness—the wife of such a one as Hugo Mallory—cannot be miserable."

"I beg you, Papa, do not choose him over me. Until he arrived, nothing ever came between us. Now he is a wall keeping us apart."

Sadly the squire shook his head. "He does not divide us, my child. You do that."

Mary turned away, too full of emotion to expostulate further. She had lost more than a lover this day, it seemed; she had lost a loving father as well, and the realization stung her as nothing else had done. Her body trembled with silent tears, and the full magnitude of her loss completely overcame her. For an instant, she felt her father's comforting hand on her shoulder. Then she heard the door open and close, and when she looked around, she saw that he had gone.

Wearily, she climbed the stairs and returned to her chamber. Her grief had exhausted her, and she wished she might sleep. As she tossed on the counterpane, she turned alternatives over in her mind, seeking some recourse, some haven, some friend who might help or at least soothe her.

Theo would take her part, she had no doubt, but his solution would be to offer himself in lieu of Lord Mallory. If she was going to be unhappily married, she might as well be so to his lordship, she thought. No, she could not depend on Theo.

Of all the women in the county, only Mrs. Chattaburty had the strength of character to defend her, but as that lady was in league with her father, she could not seek refuge in that quarter. Besides, Harriet Chattaburty did not approve of her. No, she could not count on Mrs. C.

There was, in fact, no one in Burwash on whom she could depend. Her one friend, her only true friend, resided in London at present, the charge of Lady Baldridge. Mary had always known that she would miss Emily, but she had never guessed just how desperately she would need her.

The thought gave her a headache. She sat up and rubbed her temple, and then it occurred to her that it was the height of folly to lie there longing for her friend when she might, within a matter of hours, have all the comfort and security of her company.

Furringdale, with its stolid brick front and bare approach, presented a gloomy face, and in his present frame of mind, it suited Squire Ashe admirably. He was shown into the sitting room, where Lady Babik sat with her daughter, Mrs. Chattaburty, and Lord Mallory. His entrance interrupted Miss Babik in a demonstration of how her new little pug could dance. She held him upright by the paws and sang a little tune, while the small creature squealed and did his best to thwart his mistress's intentions.

"Oh, dear!" exclaimed Mrs. C. when she beheld the Squire's pallid countenance.

Lady Babik and her daughter, thinking the exclamation denoted some impropriety on Pug's part, searched the carpet for a stain. Finding none, they began to greet their visitor, until they too were struck by the old man's appearance.

"You are ill," said Lord Mallory. He led the squire to a chair and poured him out a glass of wine.

"Indeed, I am not well," Squire Ashe confessed.

"And Miss Ashe," inquired Mrs. Chattaburty anxiously, "how does she do?"

In reply, the squire groaned. Little though it was, it was revealing enough for Mrs. Chattaburty. She had groaned many an answer in response to inquiries regarding her own daughters and knew full well the implications of that sound.

"I was afraid of that," she said gravely.

Taking in that dire tone, Lord Mallory deduced that Mary had spoken to her father. Evidently the squire had kept his promise to tell the truth. The outcome, he guessed, had answered his worst fears.

"I am sorry to hear that Miss Ashe does not do well," said his lordship quietly.

"She looked perfectly well yesterday at the bonnet maker's," threw in Miss Babik, who snuggled Pug to her cheek in an ecstasy of adoration.

"Indeed she did," sniffed her ladyship. "I declare, she looked positively rosy for her age."

"Well, she is in a sad case now, I'm afraid," said the squire.

"Perhaps she would like a visitor to cheer her," said Miss Babik. "I shall take Pug along to show her his tricks."

The squire shook his head. "Oh, she would not like that at all."

A little miffed, Miss Babik shrugged her pretty shoulders and clapped Pug's front paws. "I'm sure I would not wish to thrust Pug upon her if she would not like it."

"Perhaps Lord Mallory might cheer her," suggested Mrs. Chattaburty.

She glanced at the squire significantly, and they both looked at Hugo.

"If you think it might do any good, I'd like nothing better than to call on Miss Ashe," he told them.

"Oh, we cannot possibly spare you, cousin," cried Lady Babik. "If you leave now, we shall sit an odd number at supper, and I detest odd numbers at supper."

"We usually sit only three to supper, Mama," said Miss Babik. "Just you and myself and Papa, so I wonder you make such a fuss."

"Have you forgotten, my love, that you were to show his lordship your skill at portraiture? You promised to do his head, did you not?"

"Shall I get my sketchbook?" Not waiting for a reply, Miss Babik ran out of the room to fetch it.

Taking advantage of his mistress's exit, Pug squeezed himself under the sofa and refused to come out, despite her ladyship's stern order. Mrs. Chattaburty evinced a strong interest in capturing the creature, and insisting that she and Lady Babik kneel on the carpet to coax the shivering thing out of hiding, she left the gentlemen at liberty to talk.

"May I go to her?" Hugo asked the squire.

"I don't think she would receive you."

"We have managed badly, very badly. We ought to have told her at the very first."

A tear streaked the old man's cheek. "She would have done just as she does now. It was doomed, you know, from the start."

"What does she say?"

"What does she say? She talks gibberish. She even invokes Guinevere, saying tragedy befalls the woman who is forced to marry where she does not want to."

Hugo pulled a chair up to the squire's. "I will tell you, Squire, I thought she did want to. I believed she loved me."

"And so she does. But she thinks you do not love her, that you love only our arrangements, and the silly girl is too proud to take you on those terms."

"I don't blame her. I would not have me on such terms either."

"But you do love her. I know you do. Well, you do, don't you?"

"What does it matter, if she thinks I do not?"

"You must go and tell her you do. You must go at once. When she knows you love her, then everything will be well again."

Hugo contradicted this as gently as he knew how. "It is too late for that. She would think I was saying so from a mercenary motive."

"I don't care about your mercenary motive," declared the squire. "Once she is married, she will be happy. I am certain of it. Oh, why will she not simply do as I wish? Why will she insist on having her own way?"

Hugo grew thoughtful. "You recall my saying that if she would not have me, I would give up the suit. I shall leave Burwash as soon as I am packed."

The Squire jumped up and exhorted him in a piteous voice not to go. "I tell you this notion of hers is only temporary. She loves you as sure as the robin lays eggs. And as soon as she remembers that—that she loves you, I mean, not the eggs—she will forget that I have interfered in her life. Her anger at me may make her forget that she is angry at you."

"I have come between you then."

"You have done only what I asked. The fault is not yours. You must speak with her and make it right again."

"It will do no good," Hugo insisted. "If she believes I am a fortune hunter, nothing I can say now will change her mind, and nothing you can say will persuade her to have me. I cannot see her pressed or forced against her will. I can, however, leave her in peace."

"Aye, and what about me?"

"I hope we may visit again, Squire Ashe. I have enjoyed our many talks. You tell me more about my esteemed ancestor than all my relations together."

Hanging his head sorrowfully, the squire sighed. "It is a grievous day for me. I have never quarreled with my daughter, not like this, and now you are going away. I have lost a son and a daughter in a day. My only comfort is that I have my shroud in a cedar chest and my marker ordered at the stonecutter's."

"I have got you, you vicious scamp!" hissed Lady Babik, causing the gentlemen to look her way. She rose from the carpet with Pug in her arms, and, vowing to speak to her daughter about his egregious manners, she ran out of the room to dispose of the rascal.

Mrs. Chattaburty, still on her knees, scanned the gentlemen's faces. "Where do we stand?" she asked.

Lord Mallory approached and handed her up while the squire responded, "We are no better off than we were before. Indeed, we are a good deal worse, for I doubt she will forgive any of us, and my only hope is that I will die and not have to endure her reproaches for very long."

Walking to the squire's side, Mrs. Chattaburty said firmly, "You must return to Dearcrop at once, neighbor, and you must tell your daughter that the whole matter is to be forgotten. Perhaps then she will have liberty and leisure to reconsider."

"I cannot do that," he replied gloomily. "I cannot give up his lordship. He ought to have been my son-in-law. I cannot forget that. It was my dearest wish, you know. And so, I shall return to Dearcrop to await the Grim Reaper."

"You must not talk in this way, Squire," Mrs. C. advised. "It is morbid. You must try to look on the bright side."

"But I do," he explained. "I do not fear death. On the contrary, I welcome it."

Mrs. Chattaburty looked pleadingly at Lord Mallory, her stone face cracked in anxious lines.

"Promise me, Squire, that you will not die," his lordship

said, "at least not until I have made it up to you in some way."

"I do not know why I ought to make any promise of the kind when I have made such a hideous muddle of everything."

"Because it would please me," Hugo said. "Next to marrying Mary, it would please me more than anything."

Sighing mournfully, the squire went against his better judgment and promised.

Mary set out on horseback with a carpetbag full of clothes and a boot full of sovereigns. She knew by heart every inch of the way that led five miles west from Burwash to the Tunbridge Wells road. As a result, even though the twilight hid many twists and turns along the path, she reached the town in excellent good time to consider riding as far as Mickleham.

The inn at Mickleham appeared warm and commodious, but just as she was about to dismount, she heard a shout of voices go up in the public room, and it occurred to her that weary and chilled though she was, she would be better off with something a good deal quieter. She set out toward Limpsfield then, along a road much less familiar than those she had traveled thus far. Thankful that she had thought to wear woolen gloves, she resolutely turned her thoughts from a time when she had worn such thin ones that her hands required much chafing to restore their blood.

Several times she passed carriages along the way, and each time she pulled down her broad-brimmed hat and lowered her chin into her cloak. In this manner, Mary made her way to Limpsfield, conjecturing as she approached its suburbs that it could not be more than a few hours before dawn. She yawned sleepily and wondered how she might manage to secure a bed for the night at such an hour without causing an uproar.

The answer presented itself in the form of a stable. It stood to the east and just a little behind a tidy inn. As all was quiet, Mary guessed that the publican and his guests had gone to sleep; thinking it high time she did likewise, she tied her mount to a stall and gathered together some hay for a bed. As she laid herself upon it, she felt a few straws prick through the thickness of her cloak. Apart from that, she thought her makeshift bed would do very well until morning. She snuggled into her cape, bone tired, but not too tired to contemplate what she had done and what she was about to do.

Time and distance, Mary thought, ought to bring about reconciliation with her father. Before long, he must permit himself to see her point of view. Emily and Lady Baldridge would surely do their possible to effect a reunion. And what the elements of time and human effort could not accomplish, the habits of a lifetime, recollections of intimacy, a wish to restore fondness and laughter could not fail to do. Such were her ruminations until sleep claimed her at last.

A noise startled her awake. She could not tell how long she had slept or what the hour was—only that it was pitch dark and that loud, angry voices grew louder and angrier. Realizing that the voices were coming close, Mary jumped to her feet. At that moment, a tiny black shadow streaked across the stable and disappeared into the darkness. Creeping into a corner, she saw a lantern appear at the door, which creaked wide open, admitting the owners of the voices. Other lanterns appeared, revealing the presence of four men and a woman, all of them crying in tones of outrage, "Come out of there, you rapscallion!" and "You're done for now, you thief!"

"Are you sure he ran in here?" one of them demanded.

"I saw him with my very own eyes," a female voice said.

The figures scattered with the lanterns. Mary saw whiskered faces, sinister in the dim light, and then felt herself seized and pulled roughly from her corner.

Immediately she was surrounded by narrow eyes. They were, she saw, as stunned as she was.

"Who the devil is she?" one of them shouted.

"Must be an accomplice," another answered.

"But he is still at large and right here, I warrant."

Except for her captor, who held her with hairy hands, the strangers scattered again to search. At last the woman came forward, half dragging, half carrying a lad of about nine by the scruff of his collar. This item of clothing was so ragged and thin that it separated from the rest of him to set him free. He dashed off in the direction of the door and disappeared, leaving the female holding a dirty collar in one hand and a dressed goose in the other.

The men lit out after him but returned some minutes later empty-handed.

"No matter," said the woman. "We have the goose back, and we have the accomplice."

"She looks awfully fine to be an accomplice," Mary's captor observed.

"A lady is as a lady does," the woman replied. Then, addressing Mary, she demanded, "What've you to say for yourself?"

Removing her hat and smoothing her hair, Mary replied coolly, "I require a bed for the night, if you please. I have taken the liberty of seeing to my horse, and now I must see to my supper and my rest."

She then detached herself from the hairy fingers that gripped her arms. Haughtily she marched toward the inn, the others following dumbly in her wake. She paused at the door to allow it to be opened for her, then proceeded inside to the main room. "As soon as you have lit a fire in your best bedchamber, I will retire," Mary announced.

The others stood frozen, staring at her. To bring them to life, she reached into her boot and withdrew a coin. Prying open the woman's hand, she placed the coin in her palm and closed the fingers over it, saying, "If you do not bestir yourself, my good woman, I shall be forced to seek lodging elsewhere."

The company sprang into action, and within minutes Mary found herself installed in a neat little room with a bed and a candle. She was congratulating herself on her presence of mind when she heard the key turn in the door locking her inside, and the woman's voice whisper to her companions, "And there she will stay until the justice of the peace arrives!"

* * *

"She is gone!"

"Good heavens, Squire," said Lady Babik. "Are you here again?" She smiled indulgently at her guests so that they might think it the most natural thing in the world for her neighbor to burst into her drawing room shouting at the top of his lungs. In addition to Lord Mallory and her family, she entertained sundry Chattaburtys, Hankses, Venables, and Grangers.

"I tell you she has gone!"

Lord Mallory and Theo Granger came to him at once.

"I will get my horse," said his lordship.

"Who is gone?' asked Theo. "Is it Mary?"

When Hugo went out, the squire explained to the company that Mary had run away, leaving behind most of her belongings and a note.

"It is nothing," Lady Babik apologized to the company, which gaped in astonishment. "She is only a very eccentric young lady and runs off and does just as she pleases. But it does not signify."

"Why should she run away?" Theo asked.

"She does not wish to marry his lordship," cried the squire.

"Marry his lordship?" Theo exclaimed. His eyes bulged and in another moment he stomped out of the room after Lord Mallory.

Mrs. Chattaburty begged the squire to collect himself. "Surely you do not wish to alarm your neighbors for nothing," she warned him. "Get hold of yourself, sir, before you make yourself and your daughter the subject of talk. She may only have gone to visit a friend—Mrs. Turnbull, perhaps."

The squire allowed himself to be led to the sofa and fed a glassful of ruby port. "You are very good to say so, Mrs. Chattaburty," the old man lamented, "but as you can see, she has left this note. She has gone to stay with Lady Baldridge, whom she never met in her life."

The assemblage gathered round to read the paper that he held out to them, and as it passed from hand to hand, Mrs. Venable speculated that Lady Baldridge would decline to take a runaway under her protection, Mrs. Hanks declared it would be a very fine thing for her daughter to be reunited with her dearest friend, and Miss Babik wished that she, too, might have the opportunity to visit London.

"What a ridiculous thing for her to do," declared Lady Babik. "Without meaning to offend, Squire, only such a conceited, headstrong girl as Miss Ashe would imagine that his lordship means to offer for her. I am sure I do not let any cats out of any bags when I say we all know to whom he means to make his proposals."

At that, Hugo entered and made a hasty excuse to his hostess. To the squire he said, "Where do you think she has gone?"

Mrs. Chattaburty handed him Mary's note, and after perusing it a moment, he said, "I will bring her back, Squire Ashe, I promise you."

"Bring her back a bride or do not bring her at all!"

"You are angry now. You do not mean it."

Wiping away a tear, the squire affirmed that he meant every word.

Theo, who had flung open the door, now voiced his protest. "If he tries to force her, sir, he shall have me to deal with!" So saying, he clenched his fists and pointed them at Hugo.

The squire looked at the two men, at the faces of Lord and Lady Babik, at his ogling neighbors, and at the stern granite face that aimed darts of disapproval his way. "I will not have her back!" he vowed. Then he threw his hands up in the air, crying miserably, "Damn, I wish you would all go to London!"

Court convened in the main room on the morrow. The justice of the peace, hauled from his bed without breakfast, arrived sleepy-eyed and grumpy. Shortly after he seated himself at the far end of a very long table, Mary was brought before him.

Her guard had attempted to bind her hands and lead her by the elbow, but she treated him to such a withering look that he thought better of it. In the end, he marched behind her armed with a broomstick.

The room was packed with curious spectators, causing Mary to wonder who remained in the town to look after the shops and farms. Breaths of admiration went up as she removed her cloak and flung it into the guard's abdomen, revealing a velvet riding dress of deep rose. Imperiously, she faced the justice of the peace, who swallowed hard and pulled out a chair for her. She seated herself in the grandest manner and awaited the inquisition.

"What is your name?" the justice of the peace asked meekly.

"Why are you detaining me?" Mary asked.

"Are you acquainted with one Jeremy Little, age nine?"

"What evidence has been brought against me?"

"I wish you would answer my questions, ma'am, so that we may end this as quickly as possible and allow you to continue your journey."

"I wish you would answer my questions, sir."

"You must confess, ma'am, that there is good reason for us to be holding you. A robbery has been committed. You were found hiding in the stable, a lady with no carriage, no attendants, and no companion to vouch for you. It is suspicious, to say the least."

"I had nothing to do with your robbery, and as the stolen item has been retrieved, I see no reason for you to prosecute me or anyone else. As for my unusual manner of traveling, I will tell you this—I am running away."

"Aha!" the woman who had captured the lad's collar and the goose declared. "I thought as much. There's enough of them that's come to my house as I knows the look of 'em."

"You are the landlady?" Mary addressed her coldly.

"I am," the woman said, drawing herself up proudly.

"Then I am obliged to inform you that you have bed-bugs."

This announcement caused the onlookers to giggle, exclaim, hoot, and make such a racket that the justice of the peace was compelled to bang on the table with a tankard and shout for quiet. The landlady, who glared at Mary, was restrained by the guard.

"The question seems to be why you are running away," the justice of the peace said with an obsequious smile.

On this, Mary looked down at the hands folded primly in her lap. "It was either that," she said at last, "or be forced into a tragic marriage." On this she looked under her lashes at the justice of the peace, who clucked sympathetically.

Once again a clamor arose. Some argued that women ought not to be compelled to marry against their will. Others maintained as loudly as possible that if women were not forced to marry, they would never marry at all. A pair of laborers nearly came to blows over the issue, while a large contingent of villagers complained about the difficulty of securing dowries and the inconvenience of raising female offspring.

As no amount of banging the tankard appeared to have any effect on the crowd, the justice of the peace sat back in his chair and enjoyed the view of Mary's profile.

The company was brought to order at last by the arrival of the hairy fellow who had captured Mary. Under one massive arm he carried Jeremy Little, who kicked and squalled mightily.

"That's 'im," the landlady said. "That's 'ow 'e repays my kindness to 'im, by stealing my goose."

The captor stood uncertainly near Mary's chair. As no one gave him permission to set his quarry down, he continued to hold onto it, while its kicking and squalling continued unabated.

"Who are his parents?" the justice of the peace inquired.

The crowd volunteered the information that Jeremy had no parents, that Mrs. Dalrymple, the landlady, had rescued him from the workhouse and put him to use at her inn, that he was a vicious lad who had been caught stealing food before, and that he might as well be hanged now as later.

Mary, who had observed Jeremy since his entrance, now stood up and told the justice of the peace, "That child has been beaten."

Those closest to Jeremy inspected the little body that squirmed under the great arm. But as he was covered with dirt and straw, it was impossible to ascertain what was Jeremy and what was not.

"You may set him down now," Mary said, and there was something in her voice that inspired the hairy fellow to obey at once.

Jeremy looked as though he might run away again, but seeing a wall of faces surrounding him on every side, he burst into tears instead. Mary lifted his face by the chin and displayed it to the onlookers. Among the streaks that ran from his eyes and nose, amid the smudges of dust and mud on his cheeks, there were bloody traces of the lash.

"You've been whipped, Jeremy," Mary said.

"I stolen a bread."

"Why did you steal a bread?"

"I uz hungry."

"Does not Mrs. Dalrymple feed you?"

"She says I am a thief and must steal to eat."

"So you are just following her orders, is that it?"

Here the boy dug a toe into the floor.

"You know it is wrong to steal, don't you, Jeremy?"

"It's wronger to starve," he replied.

"Mrs. Dalrymple, you will get this child some breakfast at once," Mary declared.

Purple with rage, the landlady demanded, "Who is the justice of the peace 'ere?"

Immediately, the justice of the peace replied, "The lady does very well, I vow, but it will be necessary to incarcerate the boy until we can settle this."

Putting her arms around Jeremy, Mary stated, "You will do nothing of the kind."

Pained, the justice of the peace was about to insist when Jeremy smiled brightly up at his protectress and assured her that incarceration was a very fine thing, for a fellow always got something to eat.

"In that case," Mary said, "you may incarcerate us both."

This created the biggest stir of all. The townspeople

divided into several vociferous camps, from those who decried the coddling of criminals to those who celebrated defenders of the helpless. So great did the pandemonium grow that Jeremy clapped his hands over his ears, and the guard had to prevent the landlady from pulling Mary's hair. The justice of the peace climbed onto the table to call for order, while a number of his neighbors threw whatever came to hand at his head. Scuffles broke out here and there, and a man of the cloth attempted to quiet the proceedings by singing a hymn.

In the midst of this uproar, the door opened, and a number of spectators were pushed to one side. Lord Mallory entered with Theo Granger.

"Mary! Thank heaven!" Theo cried.

"Ah, there you are, Miss Ashe," his lordship said, "and surrounded by admirers, as you deserve."

Chapter Six

Theo stood in front of Mary, facing the crowd with a hand on his sword and a threat in his eye. The onlookers, in their turn, observed the new arrivals with curiosity and impatiently awaited the outcome of the morning's entertainment. They threw catcalls at the justice of the peace and disparaged the cut of Theo's fur-trimmed cloak.

Lord Mallory drew the justice of the peace aside, and when he had heard his account of the proceedings, he whispered a request. The justice of the peace bowed to his lordship and set about shooing the oglers away. They departed with grunts of disappointment and many backward looks at the fashionably dressed strangers. Following the last of them out of the room, the justice of the peace left the newcomers to the offices of the landlady.

This good woman Lord Mallory now addressed with marked courtliness. "Justice Steward tells me that you are Mrs. Dalrymple. I beg you will excuse our extraordinary entrance. A woman of your stamp and sensibility must be greatly distressed by the disruption of your household order. You must accept my apologies."

Mrs. Dalrymple stared. Never in her life had such a tall, handsome gentleman greeted her so civilly. Noticing that she had grown speechless, Lord Mallory proceeded to introduce himself, saying her inn had been the happy site of a reunion between himself and Miss Ashe, daughter of the squire of Dearcrop Manor.

The woman flushed and hoped they would excuse her for mistaking Miss Ashe for a thief. Lord Mallory graciously replied that it was the most natural mistake in the world, given the steely look Miss Ashe tended to wear and the circumstances of her arrival at the inn.

He then walked with her into the hall, giving polite directions for a lavish breakfast.

"Theo!" Mary cried, when they had gone. "Will you help me?"

"Do you need to ask?"

"Thank heaven. I did not know whether I could depend on you."

"You wound me, Mary; I declare you do. There is nothing I would not do for you."

"Bless you, Theo. Will you take Jeremy and have him washed?"

For the first time, Theo looked at the filthy urchin who clung to Mary's skirt. Appalled, he asked, "Have him washed, you say?"

"They have beaten him. If his wounds are not cleaned, he may die."

"My brothers never died when they got muddy."

"I beg you, Theo."

"I don't like to be washed!" Jeremy cried, looking as if he would run away again.

"Jeremy!" Mary said with firmness. "Do you mean to repay my kindness by defying me? Do you not know that I will take care of you and do what is best for you?"

Jeremy grimaced as he looked at her stern face. "But must it be washed?" he cried pathetically.

"It must."

Sighing, the child gave himself up to Theo, who held his neck at arms' length and averted his face in order not to smell him. "Are you sure this is what you want, Mary?"

"I am."

"Could I not call out his lordship instead?"

"If you do anything so silly, I will never ask you to do anything for me again."

Like Jeremy, Theo sighed and gave himself up. As he escorted Jeremy out of the parlor, he passed Lord Mallory at the entrance. Theo bestowed one of his most menacing glances on his lordship, and received an answering chuckle.

The door closed, and Mary saw that she was alone with Hugo. She immediately thought of making her exit but upon reflection realized she had nowhere to go. Besides, she was starved and longed for the breakfast his lordship had ordered. She therefore seated herself majestically in her chair and fixed her eyes straight ahead.

For a considerable time, Lord Mallory said nothing. He paced behind her chair, came toward it two or three times as if to say something, and then resumed his pacing once more. At last Mary broke the silence.

"Let us not be awkward, Lord Mallory. It is foolish to make a fuss over the circumstances that bring me here. We are both out of the schoolroom too many years to stay on our high ropes forever."

"I cannot be easy, Miss Ashe," he said. He had his back to her and his hand on the mantel. "Though you may not think so, I am not accustomed to having young ladies flee the protection of their friends and family in order to escape my addresses."

"Do not flatter yourself, sir. I am not running away from you."

He turned and looked at her. Then he took a step toward her. "Then my addresses have not been entirely repugnant to you?"

"Oh, but they have. I merely meant that I was running away from my father, who has temporarily lost his reason."

"I see."

"I am certain that when you take me back to him, he will have repented. You cannot stand between us for long, sir."

"You are not going back to Dearcrop."

Mary rose from her chair and stared at him.

Hugo continued, "I have asked Justice Steward to send for your carriage, trunks, and maid."

"Why are you not taking me to Dearcrop?"

When he did not immediately reply, she approached him and asked urgently, "Why must I go to London?"

When he still did not answer, she buried her face in her hands. It had come over her now that she was no longer a runaway. In a trice, she had been transformed into an exile. "He does not want me back," she murmured.

"I'm sorry."

She hardly heard him. He came to her and lightly touched her shoulder. "I wish I knew what to say to you."

At the sensation of his touch, Mary whirled on him. "It will be the most horrid journey you have ever taken, sir! I'll see to that. I shall make you earn whatever my father has paid you."

"I've not taken a penny from him."

Searching his blue eyes only made her angrier, for she suspected he was telling the truth. She looked away in order to keep from softening. "Then how do you intend to pay for all this?" she asked, sweeping her arm to indicate the entire room. "I have had the finest bed the inn affords, and I intend to eat a substantial breakfast. Moreover, there is the matter of little Jeremy. I intend to take him under my protection, which means that Mrs. Dalrymple will have to be paid off. Of course, the boy will have to be properly fed and clothed, and no doubt his bath and the resulting damage to the tub will have to be taken into account."

Lord Mallory laughed. "If you are endeavoring to embarrass me, Miss Ashe, I must tell you, it won't do any good. The Mallory tradition forbids that I pay any bills of any kind whatsoever. Indeed, if I paid a farthing, the blood of my ancestors would rise up and declare me an imposter. Should Mr. Granger's pockets be in a condition similar to my own, you will have to produce the blunt yourself."

He leaned his elbow on the mantel and regarded Mary complaisantly while she returned his look with one of scorn. Thus Theo found them as he entered the parlor to announce that Jeremy was scrubbed. "I hope his bellowing did not give you a fright," he said.

Observing the two of them as they glared at one another,

he went to Mary. "What has he been saying to you? It
would give me great pleasure to kill him, you know."

"Theo, I want to leave this place. You will take Jeremy
and me to Lady Baldridge, and, if you care for me at all,
you will take us at once."

"If I care for you at all? Why am I here if I do not care?"

At this, she buried her face in his shoulder. When he
finally managed to overcome his surprise at this display, he
patted her on the back and made comforting noises. Peering
up from Theo's shoulder, Mary saw Lord Mallory turn his
head away.

"I'm afraid I cannot let you take her, Mr. Granger,"
Hugo said.

Theo's hand clapped his sword. Pushing Mary gently
aside, he assumed his customary look of menace and inquired why the deuce not.

"Imagine, if you will, Lady Baldridge's response to your
arrival—unannounced, unchaperoned, unattended. You arrive on horseback with no one to vouch for your respectabil-
ity but a tiny ragamuffin. You tell her ladyship that Miss
Ashe has run away from her father. What do you suppose
she will say to that, after she has recovered from her faint?"

Theo screwed his brow into a knot. "It would be a devil
of a pickle," he concluded.

"Worse than that," his lordship suggested. "Should
Squire Ashe's daughter arrive in London with only yourself
as escort, she would be forced to marry you to avert a
scandal."

At this, Theo smiled broadly. "That is a capital idea!
What do you say, Mary?"

Mary replied acidly, "I say that if gentlemen were as
profligate with their money as they are with their proposals
of marriage, we should all be ragged little Jeremys."

"But I cannot take you to London. Damn, we shall be
stranded here till we die."

"Not that long, I trust," Lord Mallory replied. "Only
until Miss Ashe's carriage arrives."

"His lordship has taken it upon himself to send for
my maid and my things. As I am not welcome at my

father's house, I must go to Lady Baldridge, and in the proper manner. Is that not so, my lord?''

Hugo looked at her without replying.

"I have the oddest premonition," Mary continued, "that it is likely to be a catastrophic journey. Indeed, Lord Mallory, I should not be at all surprised if it were the most troublesome journey you have ever made in your life.''

"I should not be surprised either," answered Hugo, "and it would be worth every bit of the trouble, too. Unfortunately, Mr. Granger will have to be the beneficiary of your premonition, as I will go on ahead directly after breakfast to prepare her ladyship for your coming.''

The door opened then to admit the fellow with the hairy arms, who pushed before him a clean and rosy Jeremy. Seeing that his benefactress beamed approval at his appearance, the boy tugged shyly at his forelock and wondered what to do with his arms and legs.

"Master Little," Lord Mallory addressed him gravely. "You must bow to the lady." At that, he demonstrated a modest, graceful nod of the head and clicking of the heels. Jeremy essayed to imitate him three or four times and then could not forbear asking, "When do they bring in the vittles?''

Owing to Lord Mallory's preparations, Mary's arrival in Green Street insured a hearty welcome. Emily ran down the front steps as soon as she heard the first sound of wheels on the cobblestones. Bobbing up and down, she tried to refrain from exclaiming until the footman had handed her friend out of the carriage. But when she saw who the gentleman was who followed her, she could no longer contain herself.

"Mary!" she cried through tears, looking all the while at Theo.

Solicitously, as though she were an invalid. Theo escorted Mary toward the house. She stopped to smile at him and begged him to see to Jeremy. After only a few smothered oaths, Theo went back to the carriage and availed himself of the boy's collar, by which he steered him in Mary's direction. Jeremy kicked and squalled as usual, but he was too

awed by this magnificent surroundings to infuse his protests
with their customary energy. When he followed Emily and
Mary inside the house, he declared he must certainly be at
Windsor Castle, and when he beheld the haughty grandeur
of Brumbie, the butler, he was sure he had stumbled into the
presence of the King himself.

"Her ladyship awaits you in the drawing room," Bumbrie
announced, opening the doors with a flourish and ushering
the newcomers into a large salon papered with red flock and
peppered with sundry pieces from Mr. Wedgewood's
warehouse.

Jeremy and Theo fell back at the sight of an immense
female on a white sofa. Mary approached, curtsied, and
tried not to gape at the woman who was to be her protectress.

The folds of Lady Baldridge's chin flowed into the folds
of her bosoms. These, in turn, billowed into the folds of
her pink skirts, from the bottom of which peeped two
exquisitely small shoes. On top of her mounds of powdered
hair, she wore an equally small and exquisite lace cap. As
she gave Mary a smile of welcome and held out her hand,
she displayed outsized jowls and capacious underarms. The
warmth of the smile and the handshake completed Mary's
first impression of Lady Baldridge. She knew she would
never gaze on that ample, benevolent soul without thinking
of pillows and featherbeds.

"His lordship was right! You are perfect. And those black
eyes! I vow, they will enchant the Prince himself." With
such encomiums did her ladyship greet Mary, who sat down
beside her and introduced Theo and Jeremy.

These two gentlemen, daunted by the sight of so much
soft pinkness, produced hesitant bows.

"Bumbrie," said Lady Baldridge, "you must take the
little one to your Missus, who will find something useful for
him to do. Miss Hanks, you must take the big one and keep
him occupied while I speak with Miss Ashe."

At the word, Bumbrie fixed Jeremy with a stern eye and
marched from the room. His small charge followed adoringly.

Emily removed with Theo to a seat in a bay window
overlooking the square and asked him how he did.

He replied offhandedly that he did extremely well and then belied the assertion by exclaiming, "This business of Mary's has me in a state, I can tell you."

"What business is that?" Emily inquired.

He looked at her. "Do you not know? Didn't his lordship tell you?"

"I know nothing out of the way, and his lordship said nothing. What has happened?"

"Only that he so disgusted Mary by his proposals that she was forced to run away. I knew no good could come of her refusal to marry me."

Emily looked in consternation at her friend, but seeing her laugh with Lady Baldridge over some little joke, she became easy again. "Do not worry, Mr. Granger," Emily vowed. "We shall look after her." She turned to face him again and found him staring at her.

"You are all grown up," he said irritably.

"I suppose I am," she apologized.

"Are you not awfully chilly in that?"

She inspected her dress, with its short sleeves and open neck. "Lady Baldridge assures me it is the current style, even for this time of year."

"I assume the London gentlemen have told you how beautiful you are and have quite turned your head."

Emily blushed. "They have not turned my head."

"Well," he said, "you certainly have grown up."

"Where will you stay in London, Mr. Granger?" Emily inquired.

His eyes, which slowly met hers, wore an expression so forlorn that Emily feared she had somehow offended him.

"I haven't the least idea."

Meanwhile, Lady Baldridge regaled Mary with a detailed account of what she might expect for dinner that evening and for breakfast on the morrow. The good lady took such pleasure in pronouncing the names of the meats, the sauces, the jellies, and the tarts that Mary began to think herself quite starved. But these were not the only delights in store for Mary in Green Street, her ladyship assured her, for she boasted a cellar unequaled in the world for its store of French wines.

"I acquired them during the time of the revolt. I knew then there would be no getting much out of those rackety fools once they had cut off the heads of everyone they could lay their hands on. And so I sent my husband over to rescue every bottle he could discover, and though he caught a dreadful sneezing cold crossing the channel, I declare, he never did a more heroic deed in his life. When he died, I thanked him for it, because, you see, he knew less than nothing about keeping a cellar, and it was all up to me."

"You are very kind, Lady Baldridge. I did not anticipate being so kindly received."

"Nonsense. When Hugo told me you were coming, I could not have been more delighted, for I have been inviting you in Emily's letters for an age now. I have told Mrs. Bumbrie to prepare extra sweet cakes against your coming."

"You are acquainted with Lord Mallory, I collect."

"He did not tell you? I have known him forever. His aunt was a dear friend of mine until she lost her hearing and one had to shout into her trumpet to be heard. The exertion made me perspire like a horse, and so I was glad when he resettled her at Domville."

"Did Lord Mallory explain why I come to you in such haste, with so little advance warning?"

Her ladyship smiled conspiratorially. "He said only that you had quarreled with your father and needed a place to wait it out until he sent for you again. But I am no fool, my dear, and though I am very large, I do not waste my time tying myself up in corsets. No, I can see very well that there is a gentleman in the picture."

When Mary blushed, Lady Baldridge went on, "It is clear you want to marry, and your father does not approve of the gentleman. You therefore did what every woman of spirit would do, my dear. You packed off to London, and your father's loss is our gain. I have a mind to write him and tell him so, in fact."

Mary could not help but smile at her champion.

"Not only that," declared her ladyship boldly, "but

whenever you wish to procure a special license, you have only to drop a word to me, for I have the means of getting you one on short notice. Then you and Mr. Granger may marry to your heart's content, and I shall make your wedding breakfast with a baron of beef and a mountain of strawberries."

Mary's initial impulse was to correct the mistaken impression. It occurred to her, however, that there was no harm in Lady Baldridge's thinking that Theo was the gentleman in question. She therefore said nothing and listened complaisantly to her hostess describe Emily's debut at Almack's.

"She was absolutely lovely," her ladyship said with a sigh, "and I was not ashamed of the London bucks, I can tell you, for they liked her very well, and she had partners for her dances and a great many beaux to talk to."

Mary turned around on the sofa to look at Emily and saw her friend doing her utmost to cheer a disconsolate Theo.

"What is the matter?" Mary asked. Emily and Theo approached the sofa, and as soon as Theo had done complaining about filthy orphans who had beds while he himself had to put up in the park, Emily informed them of Mr. Granger's predicament.

"Goodness, I forgot!" Lady Baldridge said with a giggle. "Help me up."

The three young people, one at each arm and the third at her back, hauled Lady Baldridge to an upright position. Steadying herself, she walked with many swishes of her gown to a delicate table ornamented with a fine bowl. From the bowl she took a piece of paper and handing it to Theo, she said, "That is where you are to stay, Mr. Granger."

He read the direction, and as it was not a number and street he recognized, he looked at her, puzzled.

"It is a lodging house, I'm afraid," apologized Lady Baldridge, "but his lordship insisted on putting you up."

"Lord Mallory?" Theo exclaimed.

"Yes, indeed."

Mary looked skeptical. "Why would he accommodate Theo?"

"Isn't it obvious?" her ladyship asked, laughing, her rolls and folds quivering under her gown. "He told me he and Mr. Granger have a vast deal in common, by which I understand him to mean that he intends to stand up for Mr. Granger at your wedding."

Assessing the shock on the faces of her listeners, Lady Baldridge wagged a plump finger in the air. "Did you really think to pull the wool over my eyes, you rogues? I can smell a scheme in the air as well as I can smell a pork pie abaking."

Emily, who was the first to recover her voice, asked Mary, "Is it true? You are to be married to Mr. Granger?"

In a single voice, Mary answered "No," Theo answered, "Yes," and Lady Baldridge hoped they would notify her when it was time to order up a wedding cake.

Theo arrived at Hugo's lodgings in Lady Baldridge's curricle. When Hawks admitted the young man to the dingy sitting room, Lord Mallory greeted him with a clap on the shoulder.

"How kind of you to accept my invitation," Hugo said.

"I don't know that I had any choice."

"I suspected you had nowhere else to go. You were so busy with Miss Ashe's affairs that you did not see about your own."

"First thing tomorrow, I will seek lodgings for myself."

"You will stay here, Mr. Granger."

"I will not be obliged to you, sir. Your behavior to Miss Ashe has been such that I have all I can do to be civil."

"Perhaps a bit of refreshment will facilitate your efforts." On that, Lord Mallory filled two glasses from a decanter. "It is a creditable medoc," he said, sipping, "not, of course, what Lady Baldridge will offer Miss Ashe, but serviceable nevertheless."

Grudgingly, Theo took the proffered glass and drank, whereupon his lordship refilled the glass.

Hugo settled himself into a threadworn chair and invited his guest to make himself at home. "You will like it well enough here," he said, "especially as I shall charge you nothing for your bed. Speaking of which, you will have to make do with mine. This chair will do for me until I leave.''

"You are leaving?''

"In a short time, I shall return to Dearcrop.''

Theo frowned. "I think you like making up to the old squire.''

"I like it very much. He is as good a man as I've met since Arthur Wellesley took me under his wing.''

"Well, it's no use. She won't have you, even if he will.''

"Very true. But Squire Ashe deserves to hear that she is safely installed in Green Street, and he may want the company now.''

Theo shook his head. "You are a deep one, Lord Mallory. Still, I cannot bring myself to accept your hospitality." So saying, he poured himself another glass of medoc.

"Perhaps in the morning you will change your mind.''

"I do not change my mind so easily as that.''

"Nor does Squire Ashe. Still, I hope to persuade him to take his daughter back.''

"Let me presume to advise you a little, sir,'' Theo said, slurring his words a trifle.

"By all means. And let me persuade you to take a little more wine.''

Holding out his glass, Theo lowered his voice to say, "Do not think you can persuade him to do anything, your lordship. He is as stubborn as she. The acorn does not fall far from the oak, I daresay. Were they not so stubborn, I should have married her long before this.''

"Then she is not only stubborn, Mr. Granger, but she has execrable taste.''

"Do you really think so?''

"I do. I only wonder that you did not see it yourself and set your sights elsewhere.''

"I don't know where I might have set them, except perhaps on Emily Hanks.''

"Ah, yes, the fair-haired child staying with Lady Baldridge.''

"Do you know, Lord Mallory, I too thought she was a child. Then I came to London and found her not a child at all!''

Hugo looked grave. "Why, you are right. She is a young woman. It is a pity that she is not taller."

"She is tall enough."

"You are right again. I only meant that she ought to wear more becoming colors."

"I take my oath, that apricot made her shoulders shine."

"I stand corrected. But don't you think she smiles too much?"

"On the contrary, I was distressed to see her look so troubled, especially when I said I should probably have to return to Sussex soon."

"Now why should that trouble Miss Emily Hanks?"

"I wish I knew."

The valet brought the gentlemen their dinner, and as it was plain fare, it was well they had the medoc and Miss Emily Hanks to dwell on. They had just finished dining when an urgent knock sounded at the door, and Hawks, winking and rolling his eyeballs upward, whispered there was a lady to see his lordship.

"There is no use trying to be discreet," Hugo said. "I cannot very well stash Mr. Granger in the closet. Nor will I meet with the lady in the stairwell. Be so good as to tell her I have a guest and, if she will leave her card, I will return the visit as soon as I can."

The valet left to do as he was bid, and in another moment, Charlotta flew into the room. Aside from her flaming red hair, there was not a spot of color on her person. She wore a dress of black crepe and a heavily veiled black hat.

"He is dead, Hugo!" she announced breathlessly, leaning against the doorjamb and looking ready to faint.

Lord Mallory rose, took her by the hands, and made her sit down.

"Lady Melrose is evidently distraught," his lordship said. "Otherwise she never would have been so careless of her reputation as to come to my poor rooms. Isn't that right, your ladyship?"

"Binky is dead, Hugo. Do you know what that means?"

"I know that you ought to quiet yourself." He found

some strong wine and poured a bit of it out for his visitor. Theo helped himself to a glassful too, and as he drank, he studied the vision of beauty who sobbed on his lordship's chair.

Kneeling at her feet, Hugo prevailed on her to sip. It appeared to calm her, so much so that she was able to relate the details of the duel that had dispatched her husband.

"I suppose you were fond of Binky, in your way," Hugo said.

"I detested the brute!"

He stood up and smiled. Walking to the desk, he folded his arms and shook his head. "You never fail to delight me," he said.

At the same time, Theo drew closer to have a better look at the magnificent widow. He brought the decanter with him.

"He left a paltry ten thousand," Charlotta cried. "That's all that is left. It cost a pretty penny to bury him, you know, and then there were all the debts to pay—the milliner, the dressmaker, the jeweler. How could he leave me in such a lurch, Hugo?"

"Ten thousand," Lord Mallory said. "That's a great deal. It's ten thousand more than I've got."

"You do not expect me to live on ten thousand, do you?"

Charlotta dabbed at the veriest trace of a tear with a lace handkerchief and, indicating the gawking Theo, inquired, "Who is that?"

"Permit me to introduce Mr. Theo Granger of Sussex."

She looked at him under her lashes and smiled sadly. "Forgive my appearance, sir. I am sure I look a fright."

"I believe I have never seen anyone look as you do," breathed Theo.

"Gracious, am I that frightful?"

"You are divine. May I offer you more wine?"

As he poured it out, Theo inhaled her perfume. Shutting his eyes at that fragrance, he splashed a spot on her dress. He straightened, horrified at his clumsiness. Simultaneously, Charlotta rose, and in the process, her face came alarmingly close to his. Theo gulped, apologized, and caressed the decanter. Charlotta, assuring him it was only the merest stain, found his eyes and held them for some time.

Hugo came forward now to inform her that Theo was on the brink of engaging himself to a young lady from Burwash.

"You ought never to marry," Charlotta mourned, "for it will only break your heart."

Theo, who looked as though his heart was breaking then and there, nodded his head. "You may be right," he said hoarsely.

"Of course, I am," she said with a smile, "but that never made a handsome young man listen to good advice before, and I doubt it will do so now. You wicked fellows take it into your heads to have your way, and you persecute us until you do."

"Persecute? I never meant to persecute her."

"Ah, naturally not. You only thought of your own desires, I warrant."

"By God, I did! I have been a selfish beast."

"I don't doubt it. Now, you must mend your ways, Mr. Granger, and when you have released the poor creature from your thrall, you may come and visit me."

She handed him her card and rustled to the door.

"What did you come to see me about, Lady Melrose?" Hugo asked. "Or have you forgot the reason for your visit?"

Charlotta giggled. "Why, I did forget. But now you remind me, I wanted you to know that you are free to visit me whenever you like. And you, Mr. Granger, I will expect to see you very soon."

When Theo vowed he would come on the morrow, Lord Mallory remarked, "I'm afraid you will be too occupied with seeking lodgings."

"Did you not invite me to stay here?" Theo asked.

"I've done a great many ill-advised things this past month."

"Well, then you will come!" Charlotta said.

"We will both come," Hugo said. At that, he escorted her out and down the stairs to her barouche. He returned to find Theo standing by the fire, holding the decanter and wearing a daft expression.

"If you mean to stay," Hugo said, "you will be so good as to render me a favor in return."

Absently, Theo nodded.

"I see you are not the least bit curious to know what the favor is, and I could ask you for your birthright just now and be sure of getting it." Then, taking the decanter from him, he looked hard into Theo's face. "You will be my spy, if you please."

This succeeded in startling Theo awake.

"You will call in Green Street with great regularity and see how the ladies do. Then you will write me at Dearcrop Manor with a report on Miss Ashe's health and activities. I shall frank the correspondence, of course."

"You want me to spy on Mary?"

"Yes."

"Whatever for? She can take excellent care of herself. Lady Melrose was right. I have foisted myself on Mary every bit as much as you have done. No wonder she has refused us."

"Do you suppose Emily Hanks can take care of herself as well?"

"Emily?"

"A different story there, I suspect."

"I shall look out for Emily, I assure you."

"And you will look out for Miss Ashe as well?"

"Very well."

"Then all that remains is to see who the deuce will look after you."

CHAPTER
SEVEN

Every day Mary wrote to her father. Every day she asked what had come for her in the post. And every day brought no word from Dearcrop.

Seeing her friend unhappy, Emily made a number of shy attempts to draw her out. That strategem failed, causing Emily to enjoin patience on herself until such time as Mary desired to take her into her confidence. Lady Baldridge was not so scrupulous, however, and made it her crusade to cheer Mary. Consequently, she herded the two young women to Covent Garden, the museum, and the subscription library. In the mornings she took them on visits; in the evenings she took them to card parties. And when none of her schemes succeeded in softening Mary's grave expression, she ordered her cook to serve up buttered crab.

Mary often asked Theo what news he could give her from Burwash. He wrote frequently to his parents, usually with a request for funds, and each week he received a letter in reply. But the young man had furrowed himself into such a preoccupation that he had scant attention for Mary's questions. He sought many a tête-à-tête with Emily, and then, when he had succeeded in getting her off in a corner, he gazed about him as though he had forgotten why. Mary began to suspect that Theo's forgetfulness betokened an awakening fondness for Miss Hanks.

In Sussex she had been too close to events to see how very fond of him Emily was. Now she could not overlook the girl's flushed cheeks and exultant smiles whenever he walked into the room. Nor could she ignore the manner in which Theo returned Emily's long looks or the custom he had adopted of telling her how very grown up she was. Observing the two together as they bent over a piece of music at the pianoforte or strolled a lane in the park, Mary felt comforted. Theo was a very good young man, she thought, and Emily was the best young woman in the world. It gave her pleasure to imagine them married, settled in a cottage hard by Burwash, and living the life they were meant to live. If she could see those imaginings become fact, it would almost compensate her for what she herself had lost.

But Theo gave little promise of granting Mary's wishes. His leavetakings were always made abruptly, with vague excuses that he had promised to meet A Certain Party. So frequently did he mention this Certain Party that Mary began to wonder if there were someone besides Emily who had brought Theo to his present state of distraction. For a time, she observed his oddities with amused curiosity. Then, as he grew too muddleheaded to give her coherent news of Dearcrop, she grew irritated.

Lady Baldridge came upon the two young ladies in the sitting room one day, busy with their drawing books. After pausing to consider Mary's frown, she taxed her with worrying overmuch about Mr. Granger. Before Mary could answer, she was assured by her ladyship that Theo's preoccupation was only temporary at worst.

"I've seen it often," Lady Baldridge said. "A young man from the country comes to town, and therein lies the tale." Here she winked significantly, causing Emily and Mary to look at each other in bewilderment.

"What tale?" Emily inquired.

"Why the tale of his education. Depend upon it, children,

there is a lady in the case, a lady who will end by teaching him the ways of the world."

As Mary hoped the lady was Emily, and as Emily assumed it was Mary, they did not dispute Lady Baldridge's conclusion. Instead, Mary corrected the misapprehension under which her hostess labored.

"It is not on Theo's account that I am uneasy, although I do not enjoy seeing him behave like a lunatic. My concern is for my father, who does not acknowledge my letters. I hope he is not ill."

"Aha, but he is," declared her ladyship, "and stubborn pride is his illness. You must marry your young man, my dear, and then your papa will be forced to have you back."

"There has been too much forcing of late."

"Well, fathers, husbands—it's all one, you know. And you may take as much time as you like making it up with him or marrying yourself into an establishment of your own, for I am very glad to have you here. I vow, it is the liveliest thing in creation to have two young ladies to share my table and to lift me from my chair. But depend on it, Miss Ashe, there is a lady in the case, and you must learn to be grateful for it."

At this juncture, Emily took up Mary's drawing and studied it closely, whereupon Lady Baldridge assumed a stern look. "If you wish to look at drawings, Miss Hanks," she said, "I will take you to an exhibition, though I can't abide the tedious things except for the watercolors with the apples and pears. I vow, I could pluck them off the canvas and eat them on the spot. But we have to look to our amusement now."

She declared the weather sufficiently warm to bundle them all off to the Pall Mall. There the three of them would seek out the linen-draper's and find themselves the makings of new ball gowns. Her ladyship apologized for not riding with them, saying that Mary might take herself and Emily in the phaeton and four, while she followed in her coach. It discomfited her ladyship to have to squeeze her bulk into a carriage in order to accommodate other riders. How much more delightful to spread herself out at will and leave the young ladies to their confidences and giggles.

The young ladies neither confided nor giggled as they rode, but Emily did mention to Mary that her drawing had struck her as remarkable.

"I hope it is," Mary said. "It is for my father."

"The physiognomy is familiar, but I cannot place it."

"It is Arthur. He has just dislodged Excalibur and is mighty pleased with himself."

"I ought to have known. Squire Ashe is so very fond of the Camelot legends."

"You must not call them legends, Emily. My father would have it that they are as real as you and I."

"And so I wish they were." Her pretty face then frowned as she thought to state, "But the head is familiar for another reason. I feel as if I've seen him before. It is something about the width of the shoulders, perhaps, or the gleam of a laugh in his eye."

"No one sat for it, I assure you. I imagined the face and the shoulders. Indeed, I hardly thought about it but just let my pencil wander where it would."

"Still, I cannot escape the feeling that I know him."

As Mary maneuvered a difficult turn, she said, "I wish I knew Theo. He has grown so odd these past weeks. One cannot talk to him without his jumping up or staring off into space."

"I think he is troubled."

"You are very kind to fret over him. I only wish he deserved it."

"He is very good, you know. Just yesterday he brought me a piece of music he had found."

"That is the one deserving quality he's demonstrated of late—his attention to you. It took him long enough to wake up, but now that he has, I can almost forgive his earlier obtuseness."

Emily blushed. "He has been awfully kind."

"Stop saying that, my dear Emily! You must learn to take a gentleman's attention as no more than your due."

"So long as I continue to be your friend, I am certain of receiving every consideration from Mr. Granger."

"Nonsense. You receive it on your own account. Nevertheless, I pray you will be my friend forever, for if you cast me off too, I shall be reduced to desperate action."

Emily appeared distressed at this assertion. "You would not do anything extreme?" she cried.

"Oh, wouldn't I? I have half a mind to do it now."

"I beg you will consider, my friend. There is no difficulty so dreadful that it cannot be endured."

"A wise sentiment, Emily. I suppose I shall not buy a castle in Scotland after all, and though I had visions of haunting the moors in a hooded cloak and muddy boots, I suppose I shall go instead to the Pall Mall and deck myself out for a ball."

The draper's, one of the most fashionable in London, afforded Mary the opportunity to distract herself with brightly colored bolts and stylish patterns. She and Emily studied the tippet and bonnets of the clientele, peered at the dresses on the headless forms, and marched back and forth between the glass cases until they had made up their minds. They had no sooner named their selections than her ladyship arrived to change their minds. With the draper and a line of factotums in tow, Lady Baldridge filled the spacious rooms with her massive presence. For Emily, she chose a white sprig muslin embroidered with pearls. For Mary, she selected a deep blue silk. And for herself she bought a flowered red and orange, whispering to her young ladies that such patterns hid all sorts of sins and permitted her to go forth in the world without a corset.

They had sent their boxes to Lady Baldridge's coach and were on the point of making their exit, when her ladyship gasped and summoned the young women's attention. Following the direction of her hostess's pointed finger, Mary spotted Theo Granger and a red-haired beauty dressed in black. The two bent close together over a piece of cloth at a table, while behind them, Lord Mallory looked about him and yawned. When he saw Mary and her companions, he smiled and approached.

Lady Baldridge glowered as he kissed her hand. Then she reprimanded him severely. "Hugo, you have not taken up with Charlotta Melrose again?"

"You have found me out, my lady," he replied. "While Miss Ashe looks after the orphans, I look after the widows."

"That sort of thing may do very well abroad," Lady Baldridge replied, "but in London there is still such a thing as morality."

"I hope you are right," he said, "and I look forward to meeting with some of it very soon."

"Do not pretend to toadeat me while all the time you are laughing," she said. "And now you may say your hellos to the young ladies while I see what Mr. Granger can possibly be thinking of."

Mary watched her hostess descend on the two at the table, then turned to meet the eyes of Lord Mallory. He bowed to her and to Emily, and asked how she got on in London since they had last met. Emily, studying his lordship's face intently, replied vaguely, and then thought to ask why Lord Mallory had not visited in Green Street since announcing Miss Ashe's arrival in town.

When Hugo replied that he was uncertain of his welcome there, Emily looked from his face to Mary's. Mary, meanwhile, had turned to inspect a bolt of violet-colored fabric displayed on a rack. She drew the filmy gauze over her hand, hoping the sight of her so engrossed would dissuade his lordship from seeking any conversation with her.

"The color suits your hair," he remarked to her. "It lacks only blue and green filaments draped over your shoulder."

"I do not wear saris any longer, sir," she said.

"I'm sorry to hear it. You look most becoming in a sari."

"I look a fool."

"No one would dare mistake you for a fool, Miss Ashe."

"There was a time, I think, when you mistook me for one."

"If I did, then I was the fool."

Mary began to move away when a word detained her. "I have just returned from Burwash," his lordship said.

"Perhaps your visit explains why my father has been too busy to answer my letters. Is he well?"

"He has a sore throat." When Mary looked alarmed, he added, "It is only a cold. I expect he will recover soon."

"I mean to send him a drawing of Arthur. It is possible he will like it enough to reply."

"I hope he will. Perhaps I may bring it to him. I return to Dearcrop in a fortnight."

"Do you do everything in fortnights, my lord?"

"Not nearly as much as I would like. But will you allow me to take the drawing?"

"It is not finished yet. There is the chance it will turn out badly."

"Nothing you send him turns out badly, I assure you."

"He reads my letters then? I was afraid he destroyed them unopened."

"He reads them again and again."

"But he does not answer."

"He is proud, like his daughter."

"Mayhap he does not need a daughter now that he has adopted a son."

Lord Mallory grew serious and replied, "Do you really believe I have replaced you?"

"I only know that I send him letters and hear nothing in return."

Lord Mallory looked grave and even the approach of Lady Baldridge with his companions could not succeed in rousing him from his brown study.

While the introductions were made all around, Mary inspected the magnificence of Lady Melrose, who clung to Theo with an air of ownership and declared in a breathy voice that she did not know what she would do without her compassionate friends to squire her about.

"As a widow," she said, "I may go everywhere myself, but I am unused to it, you see, and am so grateful that Mr. Granger has taken pity on me."

Because it was Theo who looked pitiful, and not the alluring Lady Melrose, the listeners said nothing. Lady Baldridge, however, frowned a great deal, and in another moment she blurted out, "What in heaven's name are you doing looking at greens and purples, Charlotta? have you forgotten you are a widow now, or does that tidbit interest you only insofar as it inspires young men to pity you?"

Charlotta laughed at this and smoothed back a flaming red curl. "I shall not wear widow's weeds forever, Lady Baldridge. And I shall not wear them at all when Lady Miselthorpe gives her ball."

"You cannot go in and out of widowhood at will, my girl! It will not do. If you turn up at Miselthorpe House, it had better be in black. And then you had better not dance."

"Poof. I shall dance, for everyone knows me too well to expect I will behave in a proper way, and I shall not disappoint them."

"I had no opinion of your husband, getting himself killed in a duel, and I have no opinion of you, Charlotta Melrose. But if you will not think of yourself, have consideration on this gentleman." Turning to Theo with a wagging finger, she added, "If I were you, Mr. Granger, I would look to my reputation."

Then, with a significant glance in Mary's direction, she barged through the shop, elbowing customers out of her way. When the young women caught up with her outside, she declared that Theo Granger deserved spanking for taking up with Charlotta Melrose when he might have the likes of Miss Mary Ashe. Mary and Emily begged her ladyship to tell them if Theo was truly in any danger.

"He is in very great danger of making a cake of himself," Lady Baldridge said. "I shall not advise you to alarm yourself over it, however, Miss Ashe, because Hugo looks after him, I expect, and when Hugo is absent, well, the lad must have his education, you know. I said he had found a lady to teach him, and I was right. I could wish it were not Charlotta Melrose, for what she has to teach will make him a rackety fellow, and London already has them in abundance. Nevertheless, it does not do to make an uproar over what nature decrees. I for one intend to be philosophical, and if you will take my advice, Miss Ashe, you will assume an air of tolerance and not come down too hard on the poor boy."

"But your warning to Mr. Granger," Emily said. "Did you not say his reputation will be ruined?"

"Of course I did. One has a duty to reproach silly young people who will always go their own way and not care a groat for society's claims."

"Did you not mean it?" Emily asked.

"Of course I did. I always mean what I say, especially when I am standing on a point of morality."

"I am afraid you have us at a loss," Mary explained to her ladyship. "Emily and I are so new to town that we require your guidance in this. How are we to be fearful of our friend's reputation and morals, and at the same time be philosophical and tolerant?"

Lady Baldridge screwed her rosy bow lips into a moue. "I can think of only one answer to that," she said at last. "You must acquire the skill of holding two contradictory opinions at once. After a few more months in London, you will catch the knack of it."

When they had deposited Lady Melrose and her bandboxes in Portman Square, the gentlemen repaired to Hugo's lodgings. There they fortified themselves with warmed-over mutton and an indifferent burgundy. As conversation was all the dessert at hand, Theo squared his shoulders and addressed his host.

"My father has sent me funds, your lordship."

"Well done, lad. You are to be congratulated on having a parent who sends funds instead of begging them."

"He says I am to give you as much of it as you will take."

Hugo's eyebrows lifted. "I am fortunate indeed to meet with so many fathers anxious to foist money on me. I only wish their daughters liked me half so well."

"My oldest sister is not yet ten but she told me she likes you almost as well as she likes her parrot. As for my father, he says it is worth every farthing to have me off his hands and looked after by a gentleman of the world."

"I'm afraid I haven't looked after you nearly so well as

he thinks, else you would not dangle after Lady Melrose like a fawning puppy.''

From his vest, Theo drew a packet that he handed to Lord Mallory. ''There it is, sir, and I give it with thanks, for you have been as good as my father says, when you might easily have borne me a grudge. You must allow me to say, if I was rude in the matter of Miss Ashe, I beg your pardon.''

''Do you still love her?''

At this question, Theo looked abashed. He frowned at the packet, which his lordship made no move to take, and laid it on the table with a troubled sigh. ''Perhaps I do not allow boyish passion to rule my head as I was wont to do in the past,'' he said apologetically, ''and perhaps I do not persecute her in regard to marriage as I once did, but I shall always worship Mary.''

''Brave lad. And what about Miss Hanks? Do you continue to admire her as well?''

Theo's brow contracted, and he looked distressed. ''Miss Hanks has certainly grown up. Indeed, I am tempted to say she is the loveliest young woman I have ever met in my life. I fear, however, that I do not deserve the esteem in which she holds me.''

''I fear you may be right. Which brings us to Lady Melrose.''

At the mention of Charlotta's name, Theo's cheeks flamed and he fell into a trance. When he recollected himself again, he confessed, ''I love her to distraction.''

''I hope you mean to leave one or two pretty damsels for the rest of us poor fellows.''

''I have the greatest respect for Mary,'' Theo explained, ''and the greatest admiration for Miss Hanks. But Lady Melrose commands my adoration.'''

''If that is truly the case, lad, you will not dance with her at lady Miselthorpe's ball.''

Observing Theo's face fall, Lord Mallory gathered that the young man had counted on having his two dances with the red-haired widow.

''I am not so spineless as to be put off by Lady Baldridge's warning, you know. I do not care a fig for my reputation.''

"Naturally not. A bold, hotheaded fellow such as yourself sneers at the tongue-waggers and gossips. Still, you do, I am certain, care a fig—or possibly even two figs—for Lady Melrose's reputation."

While Theo's eyes opened wide, Hugo continued, "You see, Charlotta grew up in all manner of foreign places where military gentlemen were plentiful, but, alas, ladies of quality were scarce. If she is careless of her reputation as a result of her education, it is up to us, her friends, to protect her."

Theo pushed back his chair and stood up. "You are right," he said staunchly. "How could I have been so selfish as to promise myself a dance with her?"

"When blood rises up and demands a dance, it is difficult to quell it again. I understand completely, lad."

With a look of gratitude, Theo picked up the packet once more, saying, "I beg you will take this, sir."

Hugo put up his hands and protested. "You must not give me money, my friend. It will only cause trouble. As soon as I have a little of the ready, I am constrained to decide which of my creditors will have it, and as I feel too much sorrow for those who will not be paid, I think it best that I owe all of them equally. No, no, Mr. Granger, you must keep your blunt and save me much grief."

"I cannot do that," Theo asserted, "for my father said to turn it over to you, and turn it over I shall. But if you do not like to have it, perhaps I may give it to your landlord, and thereby do my share toward the leasing of these rooms."

"If you are so determined to give away your funds, Mr. Granger, you may certainly pay my landlord. But if you have any heart to spare from your three beautiful ladies, then I beg you will keep some money to buy a bottle of decent champagne."

Mary did her best to concentrate on Mrs. Siddons, who declaimed Lady Macbeth in the most scarifying manner. Try as she might, however, she could not prevent her gaze from wandering to the gallery, where the spectators sat open-mouthed, and from thence to the boxes, where the cream of the *ton* sat craning their necks, and from thence to Emily, who looked fixedly down at her hands in her lap.

Just as her gaze wandered, so did Mary's thoughts. She pinched her bare arm in order to force her attention on the great actress, who now strove desperately to cleanse her hands. Despite numerous heroic pinches, though, Mary's mind persisted in summoning up the beauteous face of Lady Melrose. In vain did Mrs. Siddons curse the red spots on her palms; Mary thought only of red hair.

It seemed to her that Lady Melrose might be playing a deep game, one that permitted her to shoot longing glances at Lord Mallory, while, at the same time, clinging to the arm of Theo Granger. Lady Melrose would emerge the winner of the game, Mary felt certain, and she feared that Emily would be the loser. Should the girl imagine that Theo's tendre for the widow was not merely a passing amour, she would be crushed. In truth, Mary could hardly persuade herself that his foolishness would pass in time, for she knew his regard, once won, was not easily lost again. His persistence in her own case indicated that it could easily withstand every effort to drive it off.

These disquieting thoughts inspired her to linger in the box after the play to say to Emily, "Do you realize that I have been here six weeks and we still have not had one of our chats."

"I do know it," Emily replied, "but the want of it has not prevented me from sympathizing with your difficulties. If it will not pain you, you must permit me to tell you how much I grieve for you in this estrangement from your father."

This heartfelt candor stopped Mary's breath for some time, so that she could not immediately respond. When she did at last reply, she said, "Tell me what you know of my difficulties. And then you may tell me, if you please, how to get out of them."

"Mr. Granger has told me what passed between you and the squire. I see, though you are careful to hide it, what it has cost you. I am also indebted to Mr. Granger for what I know of your flight from Lord Mallory."

"Theo is mighty communicative for a coxcomb."

"You use the epithet because you are angry with him, but you ought not to be."

"I will not be angry with him if you will not."

"Why should I be angry? Lady Baldridge has explained the situation aptly, I think."

"Oh, Emily, I am so relieved to hear you say so. I was afraid you would think he had formed a real attachment to Lady Melrose."

Emily grew rather pink at this reference and said quickly, "I confess, I wish she were not so beautiful."

"I would like her infinitely better if she squinted."

"You are as beautiful as she, only you do not flaunt yourself in an insinuating manner. Mr. Granger must see the difference in time."

"I do not care whether he sees it or not. I have had enough of his scrutiny to last me a lifetime."

Shocked, Emily stared. "You are joking."

"I do not joke about Theo. He has been far too provoking."

"But you are going to marry him!"

"I've told you before, my love, I have no intention of marrying him."

"But all this talk of your betrothal—Lady Baldridge speaks of it as a fait accompli. So did Mr. Granger when he brought you here. Indeed, he said it was merely a matter of time before the two of you were married."

"Lady Baldridge speaks as she does for the simple reason that I am not yet ready to disabuse her. It gives her pleasure to think I am on the brink, and I see no point in depriving her of entertainment just now. Besides, if she were to discover the real reason why I fled Burwash, it would be Lord Mallory this and Lord Mallory that. I would never hear the end of his sterling qualities, and she would shower me with special licenses. As for Theo's relentless courtship, I am grateful to Lady Melrose for relieving me of it. In that respect, she has performed a great charity. But I can assure you, Emily, it is you he loves and no one else. He simply does not know it yet."

On this, Emily produced a stream of tears.

"I thought you would be pleased."

Sobbing, Emily shook her head. "But you must love him," she cried. "He is so sweet and so earnest. You are only pretending to be indifferent because you know how much I love him."

"You will think me awfully obtuse, my dear friend, but I do not love him and never have, except as a brother. And even then I've had my moments of wanting to pull his hair."

"And Lord Mallory?"

This innocent question flustered Mary. She felt the heat rise to her face. Then, as a cool anger filled her, she replied, "I feel toward him as I feel toward any fortune hunter, for that is all he is.'

"I'm sorry to hear it," Emily said, genuinely distressed. "I like him, and I did think he looked something like the Arthur in your picture."

Mary blinked at her friend. "I shall certainly destroy the picture if he does."

"I cannot help but pity him, even if he is a fortune hunter, for it seems to me that he looks at you softly and his voice grows very low and grave when he speaks to you."

"One must be mindful of the forms in a linen-draper's shop, you know. It would not be seemly for him to renew his hateful addresses in such a place, nor for me to rail at him like a fishwife, much as I'd like to."

"Do you hate him as much as that?"

"How else can I feel when he has come between me and my only blood relation, my dearest father, with whom I never quarreled until Lord Mallory insinuated himself into his affections? It matters not that I have refused him. My father persists in wanting him for a son-in-law, and his lordship persists in making pretty speeches to me."

"Poor Mary," Emily said. "Persecuted by two gentlemen you don't love."

Mary smiled at this. "You will oblige me by taking one of them off my hands."

"Very well," Emily said kindly, "and perhaps Lady Melrose will take the other."

CHAPTER EIGHT

Mary alighted from the hackney coach and took a breath of evening air. Emily stepped down next and did likewise. Although Lady Baldridge had instructed them to await her in the cloakroom at Miselthorpe House, the young ladies could not help but linger outside awhile, for the slight breeze that billowed their wraps bore the unmistakable stamp of spring.

Her ladyship's carriage was a little delayed by an accident that had befallen the red and orange flowered gown. It had stuck in the door of the carriage, wedged there by a substantial hip, and the footman had had all he could do to push Lady Baldridge inside. In the process, the fabric of the skirt had torn. Her ladyship had positively refused to get out again in order to have the tear mended, claiming that she had already gone to a vast deal of trouble over that incorrigible door and would have nothing further to do with it until she reached her destination. She insisted that the young ladies go on ahead, for calamities far worse than this had struck her now and again, such as the afternoon at Pimlico when she had sunk into a mud puddle up to her knees, and it would take only a second for her maid to come to the carriage and stitch her up.

The fragrance of the spring breeze cheered Mary. Each breath infused her with new hope that all would be well soon. It would not be long before her father sent for her, before her aching for home would be soothed.

Taking Emily's arm, she walked up the steps and was admitted to the house by a toplofty footman in Moorish costume. The cloakroom proved as ornate and exotic as the footman, being festooned with all manner of etched brass and ebony carvings. Their capes handed over, the two young women watched the ladies and gentlemen who squeezed round them, all engaged in removing wraps and admiring the strange decor.

A clamor announced the arrival of Lady Baldridge. Looking into the hall, Mary saw her hostess inspecting the footman from head to toe through her glass. Mounted as it was on a long, golden stick, and topped as it was with gold-leaf horns, the glass seemed to point at the footman like a weapon. He eyed it with terror and trembled when her ladyship asked him what in the name of mercy he thought he was supposed to be in that outlandish dress.

Seeing Mary then, Lady Baldridge came forward and invited the crowd in the cloakroom to stop gawking and make her some room. She then divested herself of her wrap and beamed warmly at her charges. With one on each arm, she glided to the ballroom, and as she waited to be announced, she whispered to them that they must not be amazed. Lady Miselthorpe was evidently in a Moorish mode, which promised to be every bit as tiresome as her late Chinese and Egyptian modes.

The hall was already filled with guests, dancing and talking to the strains of the fiddlers. Wearing a bejeweled turban, Lady Miselthorpe approached to greet the new arrivals in a florid manner. At the same time, Mary noticed three familiar faces on the far side of the room. Lord Mallory and Theo, flanking Lady Melrose, lounged by a pillar. Her ladyship was dressed in black, and her hair was demurely covered by a cap. Mary wondered if Lady Melrose would dance, and it soon appeared that she would not. Her companions regaled her with conversation that made her exclaim, gesture, and laugh, but they did not lead her out.

Instead, Theo left her side and made his way through the crowd; after greeting Lady Baldridge and Mary, he begged Emily to favor him with a dance.

Mary opened her fan and studied her friends as they swirled around the ballroom, and it seemed to her that Emily was prettier than ever, that Theo betrayed a fascination with the girl's delicate face, and that he had shed much of his country bumpkin air. Before long, they began to talk in what Mary thought was a most eager and urgent manner. She could not tell what Theo said or what Emily replied, only that he suddenly raised her hand to his lips and planted three kisses on it.

Never in her life had Mary imagined she would feel such a tenderness for Theo as she felt now. Certainly she had never felt it in the days when he plagued her to marry him. But now he had apparently—and at long last—come to his senses. Now he had opened his eyes and heart to Emily. In consequence, Mary instantly forgave him all his past stupidities.

She was enjoying the scene with a full heart when Lady Baldridge wondered aloud why on earth Theo had asked Emily to dance instead of Mary. Her ladyship expressed indignation at the insult, while at the same time she cautioned Mary not to work herself up into a jealous snit over it.

At the end of the dance, Theo returned to his companions across the floor. Mary observed with pleasure that Emily, breathless and pink-cheeked with exercise, watched him go with regret.

Turning to observe the threesome on the far side once more, Mary saw that it was now Lord Mallory who left his companions and came toward them. He too led Emily onto the dance floor, and as Mary observed them, she could see her friend stiffen at each remark his lordship made. Although Emily was too shy and kind to be rude, still, she was, to Mary's eye, more distant than was her habit. Her face was serious, her lips pressed together thinly, and the moment the dance ended and his lordship escorted her back to Lady Baldridge, Emily whispered an apology to Mary.

"I could not help accepting him when he asked," she explained. "Indeed, I do not know how to refuse such an imposing gentleman. But I assure you, I did not answer above half his questions."

"It is not necessary for you to be cold to him on my account," Mary told her. "I expect it gave you a vast deal more pain than it gave him."

"But you must know, I did not enjoy one minute of the dance."

"I derive no comfort from that knowledge, Emily. You must enjoy every dance and refuse those dances you will not enjoy."

"I promise to do so from now on."

Mary noticed that Lord Mallory had now returned to Lady Melrose's side, permitting Theo to cross the room once again. It dawned on her that the gentlemen took turns keeping the flaming-haired widow amused so as to keep her away from the dance floor. And as Lady Melrose was engrossed in entertaining the dandies and tulips who flirted with her, she did not appear to pine for dancing in the least.

Theo now led Mary onto the floor with Lady Baldridge's "It's high time" following them. For some minutes, they absorbed the music and movements in silence. Then, when the steps enabled them to be more at leisure, Mary said, "London agrees with you, I collect."

"Very much so. Lord Mallory looks after me."

"You have changed your mind about calling him out, then?"

Looking chastened, Theo said, "I was an ass. He is the noblest gentleman I know."

"That *is* a turnaround. May I ask how it comes about?"

"I only threatened what I did because I thought he was poaching my deer, so to speak."

"You don't suspect him of poaching any longer?"

Theo did not answer this right away. He looked about him, licked his lips and inhaled deeply. Finally he said, "The deer does not belong to me, never has and never will."

"I wish you would not refer to me as a four-legged creature. We have been friends too long to speak in metaphors."

He grew a little pink in the cheeks. "Metaphors help cover my shame, however."

"What on earth are you ashamed of?"

"Why, that I've thought better of our engagement."

"There is no engagement, never has been, never will be."

He smiled a trifle, still looking distressed. "I did not think I should ever be so disloyal."

"You are not disloyal, my brother; you are sensible. And as Lady Baldridge says, it's high time!"

So delighted was he at these words that he stopped dead in his tracks, causing a number of swirling couples to bump into him. Aware that he had caused a bottleneck, he re-sumed dancing immediately. "Do you mean that, Mary?"

"Heavens, how little you know me, Theo. Not only do I mean it, but also I am pleased as I can be. I know why you have finally decided to behave rationally. There is a lady behind it."

His eyes went wide and the expression of shame crept back over his face. "You are not angry?"

"Angry? She is the loveliest, sweetest, most generous creature I know, and except that she loves you to distraction, she is a most intelligent creature as well."

Again he stopped the traffic of the dancers. Staring at her in surprise, he said, "In truth, she is all those things you say, and more, but I hardly know what to do about it."

"You seemed to know what to do well enough when you fancied yourself in love with me. Why, you dolt, you propose marriage to her, six or seven thousand times a day."

"I cannot do that."

"Ah, I had begun to think you were turning into a gentleman of some character. Now I find you are the same bumbling fellow who used to fall out of the apple tree every time we climbed it."

"Do you really think I ought to?"

"As soon as possible."

"No, no. There is no hurry. We cannot marry until she is out of mourning."

It was Mary's turn now to induce the dancers to collide.

She did more than just stop waltzing, however; she marched off the floor and availed herself of a glass from the tray of a passing footman. As it was champagne and not lemonade, she was forced to occupy some time with coughing. All the while, Theo murmured that he hoped she was not going to be sick to her stomach, and to do what he could to prevent such a calamity, he thumped her on the back.

"What have I done?" she cried when she could speak.

"You've drunk a little champagne is all. The fit will pass."

"Have I just urged you to pay your addresses to Lady Melrose?"

"Yes, but Mary, I must tell you, I do not intend to rush into anything."

"You don't?"

"As I said, she is in mourning and is certainly not prepared to receive my addresses. And besides that, I have a good deal to do before I can present myself to her in the character of a husband. I must talk with my father, for one thing, begin paying attention to the management of the farms and the house, and learn what income will be required to insure Lady Melrose's comfort, for while she is the most adorable woman I've ever met, she is rather expensive."

Mary sighed in vexation. Theo had still not come to his senses after all. He meant to offer for a silly flirt when he might have had a woman worth a hundred of her. Exasperated, she glowered at him, until it occurred to her that his determination to wait could not fail to work to the good. He meant to give himself time, and in that time he might yet prove himself a rational man.

"I am proud of you, Theo," she said as brightly as she could. "This patience of yours bespeaks great good sense on your part."

Lowering his eyes modestly, he thanked her. "His lordship has taught me a vast deal about the world, Mary. I won't make an ass of myself this time, I promise."

"I believe you are right. And I shall school myself to be patient. There is much to do in the coming months, and you must be sure to spend every moment you can with Emily and me, so that we may assess your progress. Meanwhile, you will say nothing to Lady Melrose."

"His lordship advises me to keep mum for the present, and I value his opinion."

"I could be grateful to him, if I did not have a father in Sussex."

"You ought to be grateful, Mary. Indeed, I am amazed that you spurned his offer."

"You should not be amazed. I spurned yours as well."

"But, as you see, I do not mind it any longer, whereas his lordship is in the most woeful straits imaginable, and if he does not find some money soon, he will have to look elsewhere to marry it."

"He may look elsewhere with my blessing. I am not some dividend from the five percents, you know."

"Now don't get on your high ropes. I wish you would be pleased with me again, as you were when we were dancing. I vow, I have never been in your good graces as much as that."

Mary bowed her head and allowed him to lead her back to the floor.

Later, as she watched Theo rejoin his companions, she observed Lord Mallory excuse himself to Lady Melrose and make his way across the room. His tall figure moved determinedly through the crowd, which seemed to make way for him instinctively, owing perhaps to his height and his military bearing. He wore a slight smile, a smile Mary associated with his mischievous moods, and she guessed he was on the point of asking her to dance. It would amuse him, she thought, to challenge her in such a manner.

But he did not ask her to dance. He asked Lady Baldridge instead.

"Are you bosky?" her ladyship replied to his gallant invitation.

"I am no such thing. I am merely in a dancing frame of mind."

"Then ask Miss Ashe. I vow, you appall me, Hugo Mallory, asking a woman of my proportions to do a set. What do you take me for?"

"I take you for one of the best dancers in London. You know very well that is what you are. This reluctance of yours says you merely want coaxing. Well, I shall say whatever it will take to gain your promise. I shall begin by complimenting you on your gown. How cleverly the headfeathers match."

Lady Baldridge retorted, "You are quizzing me, Hugo, and your punishment is that I will indeed dance with you." Thus she extended her hand and permitted him to lead her forward.

Mary refused an invitation from a captain so that she could watch Lord Mallory spin her ladyship round the floor. His lordship had been right; Lady Baldridge proved an exceptional dancer. For all her bulk, she was light and graceful. The flair of her gown revealed a pair of tiny, beautifully shod feet, which fell in rhythmically with Lord Mallory's steps. It was not long before his lordship assayed a number of intricate moves, every one of which Lady Baldridge executed flawlessly. Mary asked Emily if she were not amazed at their hostess's grace and found her friend wiping away tears with her handkerchief.

"What is it?" Mary asked. "Did one of your partners crush your toes?"

"Please do not make me laugh now. I want to be unhappy."

"There is not a wish of yours I would not grant if it is in my power to do so. But it is not in my power to let you be unhappy. Tell me what has made you cry."

"Mr. Granger is to marry Lady Melrose."

"Did he tell you that?"

"Yes. I spent an entire set listening to him praise her. Oh, I wish she were not so beautiful."

"What did you say?"

"What could I say? I wished him very happy and said I thought Lady Melrose was the most fortunate woman in the world."

"Is that when he kissed your hand?"

"You saw that? I could not stop him, you know. It happened so quickly."

"It would have been a pity to stop him. You deserved kissing for that generous sentiment. But I promise you, Emily, he will never marry Lady Melrose."

"How do you know that?"

"Because he intends to wait until he has money enough, which I doubt is possible in her ladyship's case, and Lord Mallory advises him to wait. By the time she is out of mourning and he may safely ask her, he will have realized that it's you he loves."

"You are very sweet to say so. I only wish it were true."

"I do not say it out of sweetness, Emily. I have too little of that commodity to waste it where I am insincere. No, it is the truth."

Smiling desolately, Emily shook her head and refused to be consoled. "I'm afraid I must take Mr. Granger at his word. If he says he loves that woman and means to have her, I must believe him. What I cannot do, however, is watch him woo her. As soon as we return to Green Street tonight, I will write my mother to say I am coming home."

"You will retreat and leave the field undefended? I thought you had more spirit than that, Emily."

"I regret that I have disappointed you," the girl said miserably. "Nevertheless my mind is made up."

Mary shook her fists and wondered how it was that so many people would not heed her. She knew absolutely and passionately that these two young people were meant to love and marry each other. Why could they not see it? Why could they not put aside all this fussing and nonsense and admit they belonged together? If she were a mother instead of a friend, she would do her possible to make them see their own best interests. She might even arrange for them to marry each other on the spot and leave them to discover their true feelings afterward.

Lady Baldridge hardly puffed at all when Lord Mallory escorted her back. Most of the crowd gazed at her with admiration and surprise, while she, ignoring their stares, scolded her dance partner.

"I suppose that will teach you, you puppy."

"It teaches me to ask you again."

"Well, I dance only once in ten years. You must cool your heels for a decade. Meanwhile, you must ask Miss Ashe."

Hugo looked hard at Mary until she was forced to bend her eyes on a festive lantern. "Miss Ashe does not wish me to ask her," he said.

Lady Baldridge was puzzled at first, and then, as she recollected something, nodded vigorously. "Yes, yes. I suppose she is tender of Mr. Granger's feelings."

"What the deuce does Mr. Granger have to do with it?" his lordship demanded.

"Why, they are engaged."

"I understood there was no engagement."

"Well, I don't know why you should think that. I trust you are wrong, else why does Miss Ashe permit me to go to all the trouble of procuring a special license? And, indeed, I had better hurry up about it, for while she is disposed now to be philosophical in the face of Mr. Granger's attentions to Charlotta Melrose, still it must pain her to see him behave so disloyally, and who knows how long her patience will hold?"

"Are you certain they are engaged?"

"Gracious, Hugo, of course I am certain. I have spoken of the matter to her a hundred times at least, and Miss Ashe has fallen in completely with my idea of a special license. What is it to you, anyway?"

Here Lord Mallory's face hardened. He looked across the room, where Theo stood basking in Lady Melrose's chatter. Then he looked at Mary, who again averted her eyes.

"Still, I do not think Mr. Granger would mind it if you danced with his betrothed. I hope our civilization has progressed beyond that sort of jealousy."

"Civilization has progressed to where we mask our savageries behind ingenuousness. We make pretty speeches, we declare our passion for one lady and then offer for another, and, above all, we lie about it."

"What a very gloomy thing to say, Hugo. If you mean to be so gloomy, I wish you would take yourself off."

With a slight bow, his lordship obeyed.

Moments later, he returned with Theo and Lady Melrose. After a few awkward cordialities, during which Lady Baldridge complimented Charlotta on her black crepe gown, Lord Mallory asked Emily to dance and Theo asked Lady Baldridge. Absently, Emily went out to the floor with his lordship, both of them looking as though they had lately joined a funeral procession. Lady Baldridge positively refused to dance with Mr. Granger or anyone else, but she did allow the young man to lead her to the table and fill her plate and glass to overflowing.

Alone with Lady Melrose, Mary asked if she, too, cared for some refreshment. Her ladyship replied she would rather sit with Miss Ashe in a nearby corner. Mary saw that Lady Melrose intended a tête-à-tête, and as she wished to glean everything that might assist Emily, she acquiesced.

As soon as they were seated, Lady Melrose asked, "You are engaged to Lord Mallory?"

Mary laughed. "According to Lady Baldridge, I am engaged to Mr. Granger."

"Which is it, Miss Ashe? Surely, you do not mean to have them both?"

"Do you?"

Charlotta smiled broadly. "I like you, Miss Ashe. You are not timid; nor are you unintelligent. Will you answer my question?"

"Yes, I will, your ladyship, only first you must tell me what on earth made you ask it."

"I am very skilled in certain ways of the world. I know, for example, when things are not what they seem. My blood pumps and it won't rest again until I have possessed myself of the truth. It is apparent to me that you and Lord Mallory hardly speak to one another, that when you do you are just barely civil, and that you will go to virtually any lengths to avoid meeting one another's eyes. I conclude that you are engaged."

Mary flushed. "We are not engaged, Lady Melrose. If we appear ill at ease, it is because I blame Lord Mallory for coming between myself and my father."

"How has he done that?"

"I prefer not to speak of it."

"It is scandalous?"

"It is painful."

"Let me tell you a little about myself, Miss Ashe. When my mother died, my father brought me with him to his various military stations in Europe and Asia. There I learned to be spoilt by gentlemen. I learned I might cajole them into doing whatever I wanted by seeming to be empty-headed and dependent, and this pleasant state of affairs continued until my father decided it was time for me to marry. He selected my husband for me out of the hundreds of officers who drank and fought with him. The man he chose was Lord Melrose, a charming, simple fellow with a neat little fortune completely at his own disposal. I liked Binky well enough, but I was already in love with someone else. This gentleman and I had enjoyed a number of walks, dances, and quiet talks together, and I knew I loved him. You have surmised by now the gentleman's name, and so I will not weary you with repetition. When I told my father who it was I wished to marry, he was distraught. He could not permit me, he said, to marry where there was no provision and no security.

"These difficulties notwithstanding, I would not have married Binky, save for one thing. Hugo never asked me to marry him. Indeed, he never even intimated that were he in a position to do so, he would offer for me. He was kind, he was gallant, he was ardent, he was amusing, but he was never serious."

"Perhaps he wished to marry an heiress."

"I choose to ascribe a nobler motive to him, Miss Ashe. He had nothing to offer me, and he is not the sort of man to offer marriage where he has nothing to give. Well, I married Binky, and I suppose I was no more unhappy than most women are when they marry someone they do not love, until I went with him to India and met Hugo again. We flirted at dinners. I sent him gifts and wrote him letters. Once or twice I visited him in his tent. In short, I did everything I could to compromise myself. You see, a gentleman of his sort always feels obliged to protect a woman who appears on the brink of ruin. And he was protective. He was kind, he was gallant, he was amusing, but still he was never serious. And, in truth, how could he be? I was married now. He might indulge himself in a playful kiss, but he would never go beyond that.

"Now, however, everything has changed. Hugo is a marquis, and I am a widow. I cannot claim that Binky left me wealthy; I am unused to practicing economy and have picked away at his fortune considerably. Still I have a great deal more than a competence and certainly more than what sustains Hugo at present. What I have will help him out of his difficulties, and, I assure you, I will turn every penny of it over to him with a glad heart. In short, nothing stands in the way of our marrying now. Nothing, Miss Ashe, except you."

Mary, who had listened with rapt attention, bristled at this. "I do not stand in the way of anything," she declared. "I wish you would marry him and pack him off to Europe and Asia once more!"

"You may pull the wool over Lady Baldridge's eyes, Miss Ashe, but you cannot fool me. It is Lord Mallory who interests you, not Mr. Granger."

Her breath coming hard, Mary collected herself before speaking. "As you have been so kind as to favor me with your history, Lady Melrose, permit me to reply in kind. I too lost my mother when I was but a girl, and like you, I was raised by my father. It would be less than honest to say that my character did not suffer somewhat as a result. I was spoilt. I did not imbibe a respect for forms, as most young girls do. And I had things pretty much my own way. Nevertheless, I was not able to control my destiny, any more than you were. More than once I gave my heart only to find that I had to patch it back together again. More than once I had to school myself in the art of overcoming an attachment. Having learned my lesson well, I am prepared to ignore any feelings I might once have cherished for Lord Mallory, and I am content to let the world consider me engaged to Mr. Granger."

"That is all well and good. Still, it is you who stand in the way."

"You have no grounds to say so. I give Lord Mallory no encouragement, no reason to think that I would welcome his addresses, no indication at all that I can bear the very sight of him."

"I know. That is the difficulty in a nutshell."

"You are impossible to make out. Would you have me throw myself at him?"

"Yes. It would disgust him, and he would put you out of his mind entirely."

"I might agree with you, Lady Melrose, were it not for the fact that he is after my fortune. If I threw myself at him, he might catch me, I fear, and then you and I should both be miserable."

Charlotta bit her lip and thought a moment. "Your fortune is certainly a consideration," she said at length. "But it is not the basis for his fascination. I believe he may be enchanted because you hate him."

"If that is so, then why do you not make it a point to hate him as well? By your reasoning, he would then fall instantly in love with you."

"The possibility certainly occurred to me. However, he is so used to my loving him that I would not carry it off with any degree of credibility."

"In the same way, Lord Mallory is so used to my hating him, that he would suspect something was amiss if I suddenly loved him. In any case, I could not pretend any such thing. It is out of the question."

"Yes, I see it is a pickle. We may devise something yet, however, for if it is Hugo's absence you require, I would be delighted to assist you in any way I can."

"I am not averse to striking a bargain that will keep Lord Mallory out of Sussex."

"Since you will not resort to strategems, Miss Ashe, you have no choice but to send him packing, and you must do so as quickly and cruelly as possible."

"I will do it tomorrow, only you must give me something in return."

"If I have it to give, it is yours."

"Mr. Granger."

Charlotta looked puzzled. "What could you possibly want with him, as you do not mean to marry him?"

"It may be useful to say I do, however. Lord Mallory once believed that Theo and I were engaged. He may be brought to believe it again. It will make my dismissal of him all the more convincing."

"Well, I shall certainly miss Mr. Granger, for he is a dear boy and fetches my books and my shawls whenever I ask. Still, if I must give him up, I shall. I have given up at least a dozen splendid gentlemen and know how to do it tenderly. He is a sweet boy and I would not want to render him inconsolable."

"No, no, your ladyship. There will be consolation aplenty, I assure you. You must send him packing, and as quickly and as cruelly as possible."

With somber looks, Emily and Lord Mallory walked from the floor. As they approached, Mary stood up.

"You must be tired, Emily," she said. "Wouldn't you like to rest yourself a moment?"

Emily sat down, looking everywhere but at Lady Melrose. In another moment, Theo and Lady Baldridge returned with the news that the aspic was runny, but the strawberries were not to be missed. Lord Mallory turned to Mary then and asked if she had a mind to try a strawberry. Laying her hand on his arm, she permitted him to escort her to the table.

He watched her as she studied the banquet, which was replete with heaping piles of fruit in exotic inlaid bowls of brass and porcelain. "I would have invited you to dance, Miss Ashe," he said, "only I thought you would not like it."

"It's well you did not ask, my lord. Otherwise I might have missed chatting with Lady Melrose."

"Was it a pleasant chat?"

"It was most enlightening."

"Charlotta is many things. I had not thought enlightening one of them."

"She informs me that your friendship with her is of very long standing."

"Lady Melrose has become acquainted with a great many gentlemen over the years."

"So she tells me. But she appears to hold you in higher esteem than all of them."

"Did she say so?"

"She said as much. I wonder you do not turn such a situation to your advantage."

"Advise me, Miss Ashe. How should I do that?"

She gave him an arch look and availed herself of a strawberry. "I do not have to advise you, sir. You know well enough how to ingratiate yourself with heiresses." She bit the tip off the plump berry and savored its sweetness.

Reaching for a piece of fruit, he held it in his hand and contemplated it. "My knowledge is of no use to me whatsoever, I'm afraid. If it were, I would be married to an heiress by this time."

"You must not despair, my lord. There is always hope, you know."

He scanned her face. "Is there?"

Mary evaded that intent look by allowing her glass to be filled by a footman. Seeing that she ignored his question, Lord Mallory inquired after Jeremy.

"He has been adopted," Mary replied. "The housekeeper cossets and hugs him until he sets up a howl."

"As I recall, he is a great howler."

"The only thing Mrs. Bumbrie will not do is permit him to steal food. Poor Jeremy. He seems to enjoy stolen crusts more than a handful of legitimate tarts. But the lady will have none of it, and he must resign himself."

"What will become of him?"

"I had hoped to take him with me to Dearcrop, only I do not know when I will return."

"I go tomorrow."

After a pause, Mary asked, "Will you call on me before you leave, my lord? I would have a word with you."

"Will you give me your drawing to take with me?"

At this reference to her depiction of Arthur, Mary blushed. "I have destroyed it," she said. "It was ill-drawn."

"Perhaps you will do another."

"I fear it would turn out just as poorly. No, I merely wish to speak with you before you see my father."

"If you do not mean to entrust me with a drawing, then perhaps you mean to give me a message."

"Why, yes, I do."

Her saying so provoked a grave look. "A message announcing your engagement to Mr. Granger, I collect."

"My engagement to Mr. Granger?"

He leveled a stern look at the fruit. "These strawberries are not what I hoped. They have been sugared over because they are not fully ripe. Indeed, I find them bitter." Then, stopping Mary's hand in the act of picking up a berry, he said, "Lady Baldridge means to procure a special license so that you and Mr. Granger might be married. You have changed your mind about him, it seems."

Mary did not know how to respond to this. His hand grasped hers in such a way that she could hardly think. She wanted to think, wanted to be clearheaded and strong, wanted him to believe that she was engaged. But she did not want to tell him a lie. It might be useful to deceive Lady Baldridge and so avoid harangues and questions, but, in spite of what she had told Lady Melrose, it made her ill at ease to deceive Lord Mallory. She stared at the hand that held hers and searched for something to say.

Lady Baldridge saved her by announcing the arrival of the carriages. Hugo let go of Mary's hand, and as she hurried to the cloakroom with her ladyship, she realized that he had not answered her invitation. She donned her wrap and allowed Emily to lead her to the exit, wondering all the while if he would indeed come to her the next morning. Should he fancy he already knew what message she proposed to give him, he might consider the visit superfluous. He might depart for the country before she could fulfill her promise to Lady Melrose.

It was crucial now to send him packing, not only because she had struck a bargain with the flaming-haired widow, but

also because she wanted to settle things with Lord Mallory
once and for all. Matters between them hung in the air, like
the lanterns Lady Miselthorpe had strung from the chandeliers. It was critical to put an end to hope, let him know
without any trace of doubt that she would never accept his
proposals, no matter how many times he rescued her from
Limpsfield or held her hand over the strawberries.

She thought of sending him a note, stressing the urgency
of a visit, but she dismissed the idea. To seem to plead went
sorely against the grain with her, and she would not give
such a man the satisfaction of thinking that she wished to
see him. No, it would have to be done without a note. Her
intuition told her that he could be counted on; in spite of his
belief that she was engaged to Theo, he would come. He
must come.

CHAPTER NINE

"There is a person to see you, sir," Hawks said.

From the valet's frigid expression, Hugo deduced that his caller belonged to the dunning species. He made sure that Theo had not yet returned from the ball, then signaled Hawks to admit the visitor.

"Mr. Grisby," Hawks announced, ushering in a green-coated fellow whose face shone with perspiration.

Lord Mallory watched the man take out a handkerchief and dab his upper lip. The fellow's nervousness struck him as odd. He had never before encountered a nervous bill collector. Such fellows generally were too full of indignation to be nervous. "You may come right to the point, Mr. Grisby," he said. "And when you have presented your bill, I will tell you with perfect truth that I cannot pay it."

Grisby wiped his forehead and replied, "I have more than one bill, your lordship. I have bought up a number of your bills."

"My creditors were duly grateful, I warrant."

"So grateful that they were willing to take twenty percent of the value."

"Twenty percent is better than nothing, which is what they had from me."

"I anticipate that a great number of your creditors will share your view."

"Then you expect to buy up more of my bills, I collect, and no doubt you are about to tell me why. But first I must tell you, if you have a daughter for me to marry, you had better think again. My heart is, alas, already spoken for."

Grisby smiled dyspeptically and said, "I do not come with that sort of proposal, my lord. Nothing so arduous as that. Nothing in the least obvious or distasteful. No, all I ask is that you provide me with a bit of information."

"I knew my relations to be a very expensive set of fellows. What sort of information is worth the value of their bills?"

"Information of a military sort."

Hugo regarded him coldly, replying, "I am no longer attached to the military."

"Nevertheless, you have friends who are. They will certainly have access to information regarding troop movements on the continent."

Instead of replying this time, Hugo seized Grisby as though he meant to separate the man's head from his neck. He contented himself, however, with holding Grisby tightly by the collar and propelling him to the door. Grisby gasped in an attempt to breathe. When Hugo let go of him, he pulled himself up with soggy dignity and declared, "I have these bills, sir, and I will have more. Another gentleman in my place would see you in prison over them. You are fortunate that I give you the opportunity to buy them back."

At that, Hugo opened the door and, thrusting Grisby forward, he said, "Go to the devil." He slammed the door after him and then looked at his hands in distaste.

He took a moment to calm himself before summoning Hawks to say, "You are not, under pain of death, to admit that fellow again."

"Of course, sir. But suppose he proves as persistent as the others?"

"Never mind. We are going into the country tomorrow. I doubt he will find us."

"Thank heaven for the country, sir."

"I must wash my hands now, Hawks. That fellow has drizzled all over them."

When Theo came in, he found Lord Mallory preparing for his journey on the morrow. "Well, I have taken Lady Melrose home," the young man said. "But I can tell you, she is definitely put out with you."

"I am used to it. And so is she."

"Nevertheless, you ought not to have taken off like that without a word to anyone. We hunted for you a full half hour before the footman told us you had gone."

"I would not for the world have interrupted your conversation with the ladies. Once Miss Ashe and Miss Hanks had left, you had much to do to make new conquests."

Theo settled himself in a chair and stretched out his legs. "Do you really think I have made any conquests?" he asked. "You may be right, you know, for Lady Miselthorpe introduced me to Miss Miselthorpe, who thought my cravat was tied in the most unusual manner."

"Good God. Have you added Miss Miselthorpe to your list?"

"I cannot be sure. Something in her eye told me she was only laughing at me."

"That would not prevent her from succumbing to your manifold charms, my lad. Why, she might feel for you no more than she would feel for a pathetic orphan she had taken under her protection, and still she might persuade herself to marry you."

"Marry Miss Miselthorpe? I'm afraid I cannot entertain such an idea, your lordship. My affections, as you know, are placed elsewhere."

"Have you nothing left over for the poor girl? Heretofore, you have been most generous in dispensing your affections. Do you mean to leave her empty-handed simply because she teased you about your cravat? Or is it because her mother decks out her house like a Moroccan bazaar?"

"She is very pretty, to be sure," said Theo uncertainly, "and I do not like to contradict you when you have been so good to me and shared your rooms with me and shown me about, but I do not think I am the sort to play with one woman's affections while I am in love with another.''

Lord Mallory treated him to a cynical look and declared, ''In that case, Theo, you will have to find yourself other lodgings.''

Aghast, Theo stood up. ''Have I offended you, sir? If I have, you must tell me, and I will apologize at once. I confess, I am not knowledgeable in the ways of London as yet and may have blundered without knowing it. But I will make it up. You are the last man in the world I would wish to offend.''

''I am deeply sorry,'' replied his lordship, ''but I am sure you will find other rooms as much to your liking as these.''

''Is it because I won't make up to Miss Miselthorpe, as you advise? I take your advice at every opportunity, sir, but I thought in this instance you would not mind if I declined.''

''But I do mind, Theo. You have gone to all the trouble of ingratiating yourself with Miss Ashe, Miss Hanks, and Lady Melrose. Why do you stop there? Why not Miss Miselthorpe? Why not Lady Miselthorpe as well? If you made love to her, she would no doubt refurbish her house in the country style.''

''If she did, I'm sure I would be most flattered, but I do not like Lady Miselthorpe.''

''You stick at petty points, my lad. The object is not to like the ladies you woo but to amass as many conquests as will add to your reputation with the *ton*.''

''I have no skill in that line, I'm afraid.''

''You are too modest. One lady, at any rate, means to marry you, and at least one other would give an arm to take her place.''

''Did she tell you she means to marry me?''

''She gave me to understand as much.''

Clapping his hand, Theo beamed at the ceiling. ''Thank you for telling me. You have made me the happiest man in London.''

''Excellent. You may show your gratitude by quitting these premises as soon as possible. I leave for Sussex tomorrow. You may use the two weeks I am gone to seek another place to sleep.''

Theo fiddled with his cravat and sighed. ''You are really very angry with me.''

Lord Mallory rose, saying, ''Yes, my boy, I am, and, therefore, good night.''

Drawing the window curtain, the maid informed Mary that it promised to be a dreadful morning. The street was invisible beneath a heavy fog—''a pea souper,'' the girl called it, the kind that dampens the air and chills the bones to the very marrow.

This did not augur well. Mary sat up in her bed and put her feet over the edge, thinking back to the hopes with which last night's spring breeze had infused her. Now, in the gray light of day, she began to feel apprehensive.

At first, she selected an apricot morning dress, certain that the richness of the color would cheer her. Then she recalled Lord Mallory's expected visit and chose instead a high-necked gray frock with a starched collar ruff. Its primness suited her mood, not to mention the mood of the weather and the task she had in hand.

The situation in the breakfast parlor did little to allay her apprehension. Lady Baldridge's biscuit, topped with butter, sausage, and honey, sat untouched on her plate. Emily, whose plate was empty, put a handkerchief to her eyes and sniffed. Whatever they had been saying was interrupted by Mary's entrance.

Seating herself between them, Mary watched the footman fill her cup with coffee. She sipped quietly, looking from one woman to the other and back again. Emily spread her handkerchief over her face and sobbed. Lady Baldridge glowered at her breakfast and said, ''Miss Hanks wishes to return to Sussex.''

''I don't wish it,'' Emily cried. ''I have no choice.''

''If you know what the child is raving about, Miss Ashe, I wish you would tell me.''

''Emily thinks her heart is broken,'' Mary said, ''but she is mistaken.''

At this, Emily gave her friend a piteous look, while Lady Baldridge gave forth with an irritable sigh.

"It is always the way on the morning after a ball," said her ladyship. "I have never seen it to fail. One is bound to recall all the most foolish remarks one made, all the idiotic jokes and missteps on the floor. One never thinks of the partners one had; only those one longed to have and didn't. One never thinks of the refreshments, except insofar as they have soured the stomach. One can't recall a single pleasant dance or acquaintance, and one ends by vowing to stay away from the next ball, though it be given by the Prince himself. But one always forgets these gloomy rumblings in a day or two. One begins to remember a charming flirt, a well-placed witticism, a nicely executed turn on the floor, and one ends by accepting the next invitation with a hopeful heart. There is not a young lady born who has not experienced it. It is nothing to fly to Sussex over."

"It is not that," Emily said through tears. "It is Mr. Granger."

"I don't know why you should cry over him," said her ladyship. "He asked you to dance first. Miss Ashe ought to cry, if anyone ought to. But you don't see her sniffling away her appetite, do you? She's far too sensible a girl for that. Would you like a piece of fruit, Miss Ashe? You must put something on your plate."

Emily buried her face in her handkerchief once more and essayed a muffled apology.

Relenting a little at the sight of the weeping girl, Lady Baldridge patted her head. "Well, you just cry all you like," she said soothingly, "for I know exactly how you are feeling. I awoke this morning with blisters on my feet and a wish for nothing but bland porridge. But now I think on it, I shall have my biscuit and sausage, for cook will suspect that I am displeased with him if I do not. And I shall have just a spoonful of the cream in my coffee, and a bit more honey on the biscuit, though I much prefer raspberry jam and wish now that I had not finished it all as soon as it was made."

"You must eat something, too," Mary whispered to Emily. "And you must dry your tears, for I have news."

Emily put down her linen and looked at Mary with a questioning face.

Mary smiled, saying, "Oh, no, I shall tell you nothing until you have eaten."

Inhaling deeply, Emily strove to induce a few morsels down her throat. "Have I eaten enough? Will you tell me now?" she pleaded.

"It is all settled," Mary whispered. "He is not to marry Lady Melrose."

"He told you so?"

"Gracious, no. Theo knows nothing to the purpose. I have arranged it with Lady Melrose."

Emily grew despondent once more. "Then he still loves her," she said.

Before Mary could protest, the butler brought her Lord Mallory's card on a salver. Pressing her lips together firmly, she stood up. "I will tell you everything as soon as my visitor is gone."

Because Lady Baldridge could not see whose name the card bore, she remarked, "No doubt Mr. Granger has come to apologize. I wouldn't let him off too easily, Miss Ashe. He deserves to be punished before he is forgiven."

The mention of the name distressed Emily again, and as Mary left the parlor, the sound of Emily's sobs followed her.

She entered the library to see Lord Mallory studying a portrait by Mr. Reynolds. He gazed at the arrogant pretty face as though he would glady murder the lady. As he had not given his greatcoat to the footman, Mary deduced that he did not mean to stay long.

She was in the midst of thanking him for coming, when he cut her off abruptly. "I will give your father the news of your engagement," he said, "but you must write it out. The announcement must come from you."

Mary hesitated. She did not wish to put a lie to paper, if she could possibly help it. "That is not what I wish to speak with you about," she said.

He turned to face her and watched her walk to a chair.

Declining her invitation to sit, he paced and paused once more to inspect the Reynolds.

"Lord Mallory," she began in a formal tone, "we have agreed to be civilized in regard to the events that drove me to London. I am content with the arrangement, for I would not give grounds for idle talk by appearing resentful and cold in your presence. Nevertheless, I am afraid my behavior may have given you a false impression."

"In what way?"

"In this way: that you may cling to the hope that I will change my mind."

He peered closely at Mr. Reynolds's rendering of a sharp nose and replied, "You are right, Miss Ashe. I do hope you will change your mind, for I do not think you will be happy with Mr. Granger. Furthermore, I am bound to tell you this engagement of yours will not succeed."

Surprised, she did not reply.

He looked at her again and this time sat down. "You are thinking, I believe, that a marriage with Mr. Granger will patch things up between you and the squire, but it is not so. Your father will no longer accept Mr. Granger as his son-in-law. He is set on having me. I don't know why he insists on it, for he cares as much for titles as he does for Lady Babik's gossip. Still, that is how the matter stands."

"I surmised as much, and that is why I asked you to come today."

He waited for her to go on.

"I want you to tell my father that you do not mean to marry me, indeed, that you do not wish to marry me. I must say, your lordship, it would be perfectly reasonable if you said you wanted nothing further to do with a woman who has spurned you as I have done and who has run away from home in the determination not to marry you. My father would understand, I think, if you refused any further part in an alliance with his daughter."

Hugo looked at his hands and then at Mary. In a moment, he smiled. It was a tiny, bitter smile and caused the muscles in his jaw to tighten. "I regret that I have not earlier had the opportunity to correct a false impression of yours," he said.

"Let me do so at once by assuring you I have already told your father many times over that I will not marry you. I told him the day you left Dearcrop. If the truth be known, I told him at the outset that I would not endeavor to press you in the least if you did not wish to have me."

"That is impossible."

"You think because the squire is a mild, good-hearted sort of man that he would not behave so obstinately? I confess, I thought so myself at first. But the Ashes appear to have as many ways of being stubborn as the Mallorys have debts, and that is a great deal, I can tell you."

Here Mary's icy composure began to give way. She was going to be forced, she saw, to revise her tactics. "If you pursue this matter because of the money, let me assure your lordship that I am in a position to offer you a substantial sum by way of compensation. I am possessed of a fortune independent of my inheritance and am disposed to be generous in order to be rid of you."

Hugo smiled broadly. "It must be a wondrous thing to be so rich," he said. "We Mallorys, of course, know nothing about such things. Still we have not sunk so low as to sell what we have already given away."

Cautiously, she said, "You maintain you have told him—in no uncertain terms—that you have given up the suit. Why, then, do you continue to pay so many visits to Sussex?"

"I find the country affords a pleasant means of hiding from my creditors. You are aware that I am a patron of the hiding arts."

"And you are aware that it will not take your creditors long to find you out. No, there is another reason."

"True enough. My visits are on the squire's account, not yours. I like the old gentleman, and he is lonely since you've gone."

"Is that all?"

He rose and returned to the picture. The lady's red dress and sparkling jewels appeared to distress him. "No," he said. "There is no reason to hide it, I suppose. I have another motive for going."

"I thought as much."

"I want to persuade him to have you back."

"That is very kind of you, I'm sure."

"It isn't any such thing. It is infuriating to be caught between the two of you. In my life, I have never met such a proud, obstinate pair, and I want nothing so much as to be done with you both."

Mary swallowed hard. "In that case, you ought not to go today. You ought to send your regrets instead."

"Believe me, I would like nothing better. Only I will not rest peacefully until I've squared matters with you and extricated myself from your little war. I tell you, Miss Ashe, nothing I saw in India, not even when I was wounded in the arm, compares to this crossfire I'm caught in now."

"I regret you have been made uncomfortable, sir. I always regret the civilian casualties in wartime. But I, too, am discomfited. You ask me to believe your assurances, and, at the same time, my father remains angry with me. He will not even answer my letters. If you had spoken to him as you say you have, why are we still estranged?"

"I wish I knew. But if you doubt me, I invite you to apply to Mrs. Chattaburty for corroboration of everything I have said. She has heard me tell your father, plainly and directly, that I have no intention of asking you to marry me. She heard it the first time I said it. She heard it again when I was last in Sussex. She will hear it yet another time tomorrow. And just to make it as clear as I can, I assure you I will never propose marriage to you again."

This clear statement certainly satisfied the terms of Mary's agreement with Lady Melrose. It did not in the least satisfy Mary, however. His words worked on her like thumbscrews, forcing her to throw out every opinion she had held as certain and replace it with one she had considered impossible. He did not cherish hopes of marrying her, only of being rid of her. He did not continue to pay his attentions out of any regard for her, but out of a wish to make up what he had caused her to lose. He did not plan to ingratiate himself with her father in order to gain her hand, but in order to effect a reconciliation.

Mary did not want to believe him, but her heart told her he spoke the truth. Hugo had offered Mrs. Chattaburty by way of verification, and he had laughed at her bribe. He was genuinely fond of her father, genuinely troubled by the rift in that quarter, and genuinely anxious to put as much distance between himself and the Ashes as he could.

In a confusion of emotion, Mary stood up and looked about her. She saw ornaments and furnishings she had never noticed before, a Sèvres vase, a rosewood chest, a pink cushion. She began to feel as though she were in an alien land, and it struck her that she must get used to this room, and to all the rooms in this place, that she had put off becoming comfortable at Baldridge House in the conviction that she would soon be returning home. Now, it developed, she must acquaint herself with her London surroundings, for she might never again see Dearcrop in her father's lifetime.

She turned around and looked at Lord Mallory with an expression he had never before seen on her face—resignation. Her shoulders, nay, her entire bearing expressed a woman drained of energy and unable to feud any longer.

With quiet dignity, she said, "I am obliged to thank you, my lord. You have done exactly as I wanted. You have told my father you have given me up, and I was foolish enough to think that that would change everything. But I see it hasn't. Unfortunately, I do not seem to be able to absorb that fact, the fact that it makes no difference to him at all, the fact that he does not regard what you want any more than he regards what I want. He simply wants no part of me, and you may have the satisfaction of knowing you are not the only one who has given me up."

"I have not given you up."

"Forgive me, your lordship. I have heard so much to surprise me this morning that I am a little bewildered. Did you not say you had given up all hopes of my accepting you? Did you not say you wanted nothing more than to be done with me, my father, and our quarrel?"

"Yes. But it does not follow that I give you up."

As Mary looked at him through full eyes, her thoughts jumped unaccountably to Emily. She imagined the girl still crying her eyes out, and at that moment there was no one she envied more. If a genie had appeared to Mary now from out of one of Lady Miselthorpe's exotic brass vessels, inviting her to name her fondest wish, she would wish to be Emily, indulging in the relief of tears and anticipating the comfort of a return to home and family.

Her hands clenched, and she stared straight ahead without comprehending what she saw. Hugo came close and took her fists in his two hands.

"You will not have me as your husband," he said, "but I do not mean to disappear into the fog on that account. You will always have me as your friend, Miss Ashe. And if you mean to marry Mr. Granger, you will have need of all the friends you can muster."

At that he looked down at her fists and, one at a time, he opened them. Gently, he kissed one palm, then the other, and, in another moment, he walked from the room.

CHAPTER TEN

It was often said that as winter infected London with melancholia, so May infected it with determination. As soon as the season began to draw to a close, the *ton* pursued the pleasures of the town with feverish intensity. In this regard, none was so infected as Lady Baldridge. Heretofore, she had regarded herself purely in the light of a mother hen, sheltering her young ladies under ample wings. With the burgeoning of spring, however, she determined that her two gloomy charges should wring the utmost gaiety from the dwindling season. Accordingly, she herded Miss Ashe and Miss Hanks to the opera house and filled her box to overflowing with bowing admirers. At balls, she procured them so many partners that by the end of the evening their shoes were in tatters. At Epsom Downs, a balloon launch, a masquerade, and a picnic, she insisted they murmur encouragement to the horse they had bet on, climb into the basket with the balloonist, costume themselves as milkmaids, feast on pigeon pie near a duck pond, and for pity's sake, to do it all with a smile.

The approach of June produced no diminution of her determination. Indeed, it appeared to exacerbate it, for the rumor reached London that General Wellesley had crossed the Douro River and beaten back a very surprised Marshal Soult and his twenty-five thousand troops. The French retreat to Oporto inspired Lady Baldridge with as much triumphant glee as it might be thought to have inspired the victorious general himself, for her ladyship succeeded in wearing down Emily's resolve to return home and in somewhat dislodging Mary's fearsome scowl.

She kept Emily in town by crying. "Oh, you cannot leave, Miss Hanks, not when our Miss Ashe has pined her appetite entirely away. I wish I knew what to do for her. Perhaps the special license will set her up again. Now that she may be married to Mr. Granger, she will not have to cry for no reason at all."

"I do not think a special license will answer," Emily replied sorrowfully.

"That does not surprise me, given that young man's abominable behavior. Why, he has not been to visit her at all these past weeks. I expect he is much taken up with Charlotta Melrose and that is why he neglects her so, and though Miss Ashe pretends to be lighthearted, I am certain she feels the slight, for she would not even taste the haricot of lamb cook prepared Sunday last."

As Emily was sincerely troubled by her friend's dejection, she agreed to stay on in London.

Lady Baldridge wisely saw that a very different strategy was required in Mary's case. Whereas gentleness and an appeal to compassion were all that were necessary to win over Emily, nothing but a stern appeal to sense could influence Mary. Consequently, Lady Baldridge screwed her jowls into a censorious frown and said, "If you persist in feeling sorry for yourself, Miss Ashe, Mr. Granger will cry off altogether."

"Gracious," said Mary, caught up short, "am I feeling sorry for myself?"

Lady Baldridge remarked that perhaps her lowness of spirits was not quite so ungrateful and self-indulgent as it appeared.

"If I have been ungrateful and self-indulgent, then I beg your pardon. I don't mean to cosset myself and will stop it at once."

"You are a most determined young lady. I daresay Wellesley is nothing to you."

"Then I am determined to overcome this homesickness of mine. Still, I cannot help wondering how you will like being saddled with me for the rest of your life."

The prospect of being saddled with Miss Ashe did not dismay her ladyship in the least. She crowed with delight at the idea of having the young woman take up permanent residence in Green Street, but she feared it was not to be. Mr. Granger would in all likelihood weary of his red-haired amour and reappear to claim Mary for his own. And as the special license was now at hand, the two young people would marry and leave her a lonely old woman to rattle around a big house with no one but cook to console her.

"You have the special license?" Mary asked.

"Here it is. You must tuck it somewhere safe."

Mary went at once to do exactly that. She set it in the enamel box next to the Reverend Hardie's letter, reflecting as she did so that a more current reminder of her foolishness would perhaps stand her in better stead than the old one had.

Another potent reminder of her foolishness appeared the next morning in the person of Lady Melrose, who called to inquire if Miss Ashe knew the whereabouts of Lord Mallory.

"He left London some weeks ago," Mary told her.

"Ah, I wondered why I had not heard from him. I don't suppose you might tell me where he's gone?"

"Yes. He is with my father."

Mary's precise knowledge provoked considerable displeasure on Lady Melrose's pretty face.

Noting it, Mary said, "You are not jealous on that account, I hope. I have done exactly as you asked. I have sent him packing. Is it my fault he packs off to Burwash?"

"You have kept your end of the bargain then?"

"I did my best, but as it developed, it was unnecessary, for his lordship had long ago given up hope of our ever marrying, and so he assured me in the plainest language. He even offered me proof of his retreat, which was an unlooked-for piece of generosity, I must own."

Lady Melrose brightened. "Why did you not write and tell me this?"

Abruptly Mary stood up. "I do not know. I do not know anything of late, except that I am not to go home again. London is my home now."

"Do not be so downcast, Miss Ashe. You cannot have forgotten Mr. Granger. I am prepared to hand him over to you, and have been prepared since our last tête-à-tête."

"I am sick to death of Mr. Granger."

"A pity, for you are about to have him on your hands again. As you have kept your word, so shall I keep mine."

"You may do as you please."

Looking vastly pleased indeed, Lady Melrose prepared to depart. She paused at the door, however, to look at Miss Ashe, saying, "Have you by any chance received a visit from a Mr. Grisby?"

"No."

"He has been all over town inquiring after Hugo."

"A creditor, I suppose."

"Whatever he is, I do not like him, and I suspect he means Hugo great harm."

"I suspect he means to be paid what is owed him."

"He may get round to visiting you, Miss Ashe, and when he does, I beg you will not tell him what you have told me, or anything else either."

"You may have reason to protect his lordship, madam, but I do not. Indeed, by protecting him I may prolong his sojourn at Dearcrop. That is the last thing I wish to do."

"I desire to see Hugo leave Dearcrop every bit as much as you do; yet I cannot help feeling that he is safer there than in London. Will you promise me to say nothing of his whereabouts to Mr. Grisby?"

"I will not promise anything of the kind, your ladyship. I have made one bargain with you, and that is as much as I have stomach for."

Charlotta appraised her shrewdly. "My dear Miss Ashe," she said at last, "if you had succeeded in teaching yourself to care as little about Hugo as you like to think, then it would cost you nothing to promise."

Before Mary could think of a rejoinder to this, Lady
Melrose swept from the house.

Hugo gazed at the Mother's Room in the conviction that
he had never in his life been anywhere so congenial. During
the past weeks, he had vowed time and time again to quit
Dearcrop and attend to his obligations in London. Then time
and time again he had repaired with the squire to the
Mother's Room and asked himself why the devil he should
leave such a friendly spot merely in order to return to such a
tiresome one.

What did London hold for him, after all, but the promise
of Lady Melrose hanging on one arm and Theo Granger on
the other? The one creature to whom he had freely offered
both arms spurned them passionately. Indeed, she evinced
no eagerness where he was concerned except to buy him off.
She found him as distasteful as he found the oily Grisby,
whose blackmail had so enraged him that he had booted him
out the door and then neglected to do anything about the
fellow. But then he was no more able to do anything about
Grisby than he was about Mary. Wellesley was in Europe
celebrating his recent victory over the French and too distant
as well as too preoccupied to absorb a warning. Even if he
were in England, there was nothing Hugo could tell his
mentor about spies and traitors that he did not already know.
Meanwhile, Grisby was buying up his notes all over the city
to strengthen his bargaining power. As a result, London
represented not only Charlotta coquetry, Theo's perfidy, and
Mary's scorn, but also Grisby's grimy sweat all over his
hands.

In contrast, Dearcrop offered comfort and delight. Mrs.
Chattaburty, nay, all of Burwash, charmed him with gossip
and parties. The Babik ladies, both mother and daughter,
renewed their invitations to him to stay at Furringdale.
Squire Ashe doted on him and, in his turn, he had grown
amazingly fond of the old man.

It was a source of wonder to Hugo that someone as
implacable as the squire could evince such sweetness and
kindness. From these tender qualities Hugo derived the hope

that the old man was on the point of relenting toward his daughter. Hugo could see how desperately he missed her and believed it was just a matter of time before he was persuaded to have her back. Could he effect a reconciliation, he would be free to return to town with a clear conscience and renewed vigor for eluding the bill collectors.

Meanwhile, he sat with the squire in the Mother's Room, surrounded by Mary's childhood toys, and although the two men never spoke her name, they gave each other unspoken permission to think of her. In these shared moments, when each knew where the other's thoughts bent, they smiled at the tangled marionette and the headless doll and imagined they could hear the rustle of a dress at the door.

For some days after her visit with Lady Melrose, Mary anticipated a note from her concerning Theo, but none came. She had just begun to think she was fated never to receive letters in the post, when a visit from the young man himself rendered a note superfluous.

Mary extended him a warmer welcome than either of the other two ladies and invited him to sit down and tell them how he got on in the absence of Lord Mallory.

"I am in a fair way to losing every friend I've had in London," he said wretchedly.

Emily turned her head away. Lady Baldridge regarded him coldly and murmured something about it's being no more than he deserved. Mary, however, flashed him a smile, one that shone with the first genuine pleasure she had known in some time.

"Is it as bad as that, my brother?" she asked.

"I do not see how it could be any worse. First I managed to offend his lordship—I know not how—so that he insisted I leave his lodgings and find my own. I leased rooms in a house that turned out to be a thieves' den, and in the time it took to retrieve my stolen belongings, I neglected you and Miss Hanks and Lady Baldridge, whose looks tell me they are greatly put out with me, and justly so. And so if that were not enough, Lady Melrose has thrown me off entirely, saying I am a lout, a pest, and a booby."

"How awful for you," Mary said merrily.

"It is the way of fashionable ladies when they become bored, Mr. Granger," Lady Baldridge said, "and you must learn to be thankful that you are out of the clutches of such a one as Charlotta Melrose. Meanwhile, you shall stay to supper, and I shall tell cook to make a fricassee of sweetbread."

Lady Baldridge then hied herself from the room to consult with her chef, while Emily, deep in thought, moved to the bay window and looked out.

Mary took Theo's hands in hers. "You have not lost your friends in Green Street," she said. "I have been thrown off, too—by my father—and so there's a pair of us now."

Theo shook his head. "I know all about it. My father has written to say he fears the squire is lost to all reason on the subject. But then he is not surprised, after seeing what rancor your father has borne him all these years. Fortunately, Lord Mallory is there, pleading your case daily."

"Do not speak of him. Rather let us talk of Emily."

The reference inspired Theo to glance at the girl, whose slender back faced him like a reproach. "Will she forgive me, do you think? Will she forget how selfish my friendship with her has been up to now?"

"Yes, she will. But you must proceed cautiously, my brother."

"Advise me, Mary, for I have made such a muddle of things that I am unsure of my ground."

"Well, you must begin by talking of inconsequential things. On no account are you to speak of Lady Melrose, for if all you do is pour out your heart to Emily, she will feel you use her merely as a shoulder to cry on. You must consider her feelings, as much or even more than your own, and endeavor to cheer her and be cheered by her."

"But I do not feel cheerful, not in the least."

"I know, but you must do as I say. If you cannot, then I beg you will take yourself off and leave us alone altogether, for I do not think Emily's heart will withstand another disappointment."

His head, which had bowed low over Mary's words, now shot up. "Miss Hanks has had a disappointment in love?"

"She has."

"Who is this villain?"

"That I cannot tell you, and you must never ask her about it, for she is striving to overcome her despair. I can say, however, that the young man was only foolish, not malicious, and did not mean to break her heart."

"Miss Hanks and I have a good deal in common, it seems."

"You always had, only now you have more. Just be sure you do not dwell on past calamities. Attend to the present and all will be well again before you know it."

"I shall do as you say," Theo vowed, and Mary reflected that it was a fine thing indeed to be so eagerly heeded.

Although Emily always sat in his company as if a witch's spell had struck her dumb, Theo made sure not to notice. He accorded her the softest of attentions, asking permission to see her drawings or to sit with her in the window seat or to give her a bit of marzipan on her plate or to buy her an ice from a vendor in the park. Emily received these attentions as though she expected that they would be withdrawn as soon as they were given, and Theo at last grew so bold as to ask her if she was angry with him. In response, she blurted out that she could never be angry with him. She was only afraid.

So amazed was Theo at this reply that he related the particulars of the conversation to Mary. The two of them were following Lady Baldridge's carriage in a curricle, looking forward to lunching alfresco and watching the magicians and clowns at a fair. Marring their anticipation of delight was the fact that they had been unable to prevail upon Emily to accompany them.

"She says she is afraid of me," Theo lamented.

Mary found this so amusing that she laughed until her ribs hurt. Then, noticing Theo's indignation, she did her utmost to curb her merriment. "Forgive me, but you must have imagined it."

"I did no such thing. She said that she was not angry with me, only afraid."

"I am surprised. I thought she would trust you again."

"Why on earth should she distrust me?"

"By the same token, why should she trust you? When a girl's heart has once been rent to pieces, she builds a protective fortress around it. One does not win such a fortress with the snap of a finger. One must be patient."

"I shall be as patient as Joshua."

"It was Job who was patient, you dolt."

"Yes, but it was Joshua who crumbled the fortress walls."

"Do you plan to march on the poor girl?"

"Well, I have to do something, Mary. I'm in love with her and I'll be dashed if I will make a muddle of that."

"Well said! Oh, the style is a bit bald and wants polish, but the sentiment is perfect."

"You do not disapprove?"

"And what if I did, Theo? Would you give her up?"

"Not for anything."

"You are a very romantical fellow, my brother. Now all we have to do is convince Miss Hanks of it."

The fair inspired no stratagems for achieving that end. It did, however, supply Mary with a new idea. She was standing by herself observing a two-headed, four-legged prodigy and waiting for Theo and Lady Baldridge to return with some refreshment, when she heard herself addressed. She turned to face an elderly gentleman who proved to be Lady Baldridge's neighbor, Mr. Figget. Painstakingly, he asked after her ladyship and her cook and let slip the information that as his uncertain health made town living uncomfortable, he meant to remove from Green Street and let his house.

Mary asked Mr. Figget all manner of questions about his house. It was, she learned, not nearly as large as Lady Baldridge's but no less neat, modern, and commodious. Lady Baldridge's house, if he might be so bold to suggest it, was rather large and grandiose, whereas his was cozy and more suitable for a creature forced to live alone.

"May I come and see it?"

"By all means."

Mary said nothing to her companions about her meeting with Mr. Figget, but on the morrow, at the earliest opportunity, she crossed the cobblestones to his house. Approaching the tall black grille that enclosed a small rose gargen, she regarded the three narrow stories. It might well be a home, she thought. It might well serve as a center for her, now that she had lost her center, an anchor, now that the anchor she had depended on was out of reach.

Mr. Figget took her through the rooms, pointing out proudly how spacious they were for so small a house, how shiny and well-oiled the wainscoting had been maintained, how brightly the cream-colored walls complemented the marble fireplaces, and how convenient the street was to every conceivable location in London. Though it was not Dearcrop, not filled with mementoes of her mother and touches of her father, not the scene of her childhood adventures, still it was everything Mr. Figget represented, and Mary thought she would do well to let it.

Before making her decision, however, she went into Lady Baldridge's breakfast parlor and entreated her ladyship to come with her outside.

"But I have not yet breakfasted," Lady Baldridge said.

"It will wait," Mary urged, "but this may not. Someone may walk off with my prize while I am debating."

Regretfully, Lady Baldridge accompanied Mary into the street. Together they stood at curb, and as Mary pointed across the cobblestones, Lady Baldridge followed the direction of her finger.

"There it is," Mary declared.

"All I see is Mr. Figget's house, and while it is a very fine house, though awfully cramped and plain, it is not worth waiting breakfast over."

"Mr. Figget means to let the house, your ladyship, and I am thinking of letting it from him."

"You intend to squeeze poor Mr. Granger into that? Why it is barely wider than a chimney."

"I intend to let it for myself."

"It is hardly practical, Miss Ashe, for you will only have to give it up when you are married."

"I do not plan to be married."

"You shock me, I must say. It was my impression that

you had forgiven him and were on the best of terms, as though Charlotta Melrose had never existed."

"We are on the best of terms, your ladyship. I love Theo, but as a sister loves a brother."

"It is true that he has been unforgivably foolish, but I did not think he was so bad as to be jilted, and if you will not have him, I do not know who will. You heard him yourself— Lord Mallory has thrown him off; Charlotta Melrose banishes him from her door; and Miss Hanks will not so much as look him in the eye. I depended on you to be kind to him."

"I am being amazingly kind to him, I assure you. I mean to see him married to someone who loves him and who will make him the very best of men. That someone, however, is not myself."

"I daresay, I might have saved myself the trouble of scaring up a special license for you."

"I treasure it and assure you it is very useful to me."

"I do not understand one word of what you say. Why on earth would you let a house for yourself when you may return to your father now? Since you do not quarrel with him any longer over Mr. Granger, you ought to pack your trunks and go home where you belong, though I vow I shall miss you to tears."

Mary looked down. "I'm afraid I have not been completely truthful with you, my lady. I allowed you to think Theo was the cause of the rift between my father and me, when in fact it was Lord Mallory."

"Good Heavens! You have not fallen in love with Hugo! I wish I had a bite of toast to help me make sense of this."

"My father wished me to marry his lordship, and I refused."

"Your father wished you to marry him! My dear girl, I do not mean to alarm you, but have you considered the possibility that your father is mad? It may even run in the family, for I recall a look in your eye when you stood with Hugo at Lady Miselthorpe's ball. I thought at the time that it was the look of a madwoman. You need not be ashamed; these things run in many of the best families—in only the best families, I daresay; just look at the poor King and his son.

Oh, your father must surely be mad to try and marry you off to Hugo!''

"My father is not mad," Mary replied, a little nettled. "And Lord Mallory himself thought it would be an excellent match."

"Of course he did. The poor fellow is in such a sad case with his lands and his relations and his debts that he would marry a warthog so long as she had money enough. It was arrant madness for your father to punish you on Hugo's account. One would have to be mad to think the two of you would suit."

"Why does the match strike you as so unsuitable, my lady? Everyone, excepting myself of course, seemed to think it ideal."

"You were very wise and brave to run away as you did. You saw, and very wisely too, that marrying Hugo would be disastrous. He is a man of the world, while you have seen little outside of Sussex. He dallies with far too many women and regards his penniless state with far too much insouciance. You, on the other hand, are a serious, sensible young woman. The idea of matching the two of you is absurd."

"But Lord Mallory and I have a great deal in common, your ladyship. We share the same opinions regarding people. We are both interested in India. And he cares for my father nearly as much as I do myself."

"Faugh! I could more easily match porridge with ale or port with turbot."

Vexed, Mary said, "The point is, your ladyship, that I am not welcome at Dearcrop any more now than I was last winter when you took me in. I have therefore decided to set up my own establishment, and I can think of no better one than this, which will put me close to you."

"You can be even closer if you simply stay on with me. There is no need to go setting up your own house, you know. You are welcome to live with me as long as you like."

"You are very kind, but I must begin to make an independent life for myself."

"Independence is a very fine thing, my dear, but it is not an antidote to loneliness."

"You are right," Mary replied with a smile. "The antidote is to live across the cobblestones from you!"

On that, the two women returned to the house, where Lady Baldridge consumed enough smoked fish and toast to compensate her for the inevitable loss of her young companion.

Mary unveiled her news to Theo and Emily that afternoon as they played silently at silver loo. "I am relieved to hear you have taken a home," Emily said. "My return home is long overdue. I was unwilling to go while you still needed my company, but now I can leave London with an easy heart."

"You are not leaving!" Theo cried, rising and upsetting the game.

"I miss my family and am needed at home."

Theo threw a desperate look at Mary, then taking a breath, said, "You cannot leave, Miss Hanks, not before we have settled matters between us."

"I did not know we had matters that required settling."

"In point of fact, we have only one matter. I love you."

Emily stared at him, then at Mary, whose beaming smile and reassuring nod persuaded her she had heard aright.

Pleased at his own boldness, Theo demanded, "What do you say to that, Emily?"

The girl thought a moment, then ventured to reply, "It seems that every time I declare my intention to go home, I am fated to change my mind."

CHAPTER ELEVEN

For some days Mary observed the removal of Mr. Figget's belongings, a procedure that required all her patience to endure, for now that she had determined to set up her own establishment, she was anxious to get on with it. Impatience ought to have dwindled with the arrival of her appointments but, in fact, just the opposite proved true. She could not view the rough handling of her painted screen, bed, and pianoforte without crying out to the servants to take care. Heartily she wished the move already complete so that she might put an end to waiting.

Interrupting Mary's watch at Mr. Figget's door, Lady Baldridge inquired whether she could spare a moment from her occupation to tell her what in heaven's name had possessed Mr. Granger and Miss Hanks. "They look at each other so oddly. He is very pale and sickly, if you ask me, while she smiles and smiles and smiles. Do you suppose they are as daft as your poor father?"

"I suppose they are forming an engagement," Mary said.

"Do they mean to elope? Will you give them the special license?"

"I don't believe Theo has asked her to marry him as yet, but when he does, everything will be done in proper form. He assures me there will be no elopement. The banns will

159

be posted at the Oxdale church in Sussex, and they will return home for the wedding.''

"So he has thought it all out, has he?''

"Yes, and I can't help feeling rather proud of him.''

"I would be happy for them if it did not mean I was losing their companionship as well as yours.''

"You are not losing mine at all. I shall probably hang about your parlor as much as my own.''

"You say so now, but once you are in your own house, you will entertain only the most fashionable young people and forget my very name.''

"If I am so ungrateful as that, you have my permission to pound on my door until I come to my senses.''

Lady Baldridge sighed that young people always carried things their own way, and it was no use arguing with them. At that juncture, they returned to her ladyship's house, where the servant handed Mary a card. She had a caller, he informed her, and must go at once, as the visitor's mission appeared most urgent.

Surprised at the name on the card, Mary hurried to the parlor.

"Mrs. Chattaburty!'' she cried, opening the door.

That lady immediately stood up, her hard stone face looking haggard and drawn. "Miss Ashe,'' she said, "will you consent to return to Dearcrop?''

"Yes.''

"Thank heaven!'' the lady murmured and sank down again into her chair. "He said you would agree to come. I did not think you would be able to forgive so readily, for you have been used abominably, but I thank God I was wrong.''

Mary then had the servant bring some refreshment for her visitor. "You look very tired,'' Mary said. "You are not feeling ill from the journey, I hope?''

Shaking her head, Mrs. Chattaburty said, "It is your father who is ill. That is why I am come to fetch you.''

Mary felt as though a chill wind had penetrated her bones. Unable to speak, she waited for her visitor to continue.

"How many days will you need to prepare for your return, Miss Ashe?"

"As it happens, my things are already packed."

Mrs. Chattaburty was too preoccupied to inquire further and therefore accepted Mary's state of readiness without comment. "I have sent the coachman to refresh the horses. I did not wish to keep them standing, not knowing how long you would be out."

She drank a little of the wine brought by the servant and waved away the fruit and cakes he offered. "Like the horses, I shall rest the night and return for you at daybreak," she said.

A thousand questions raced in Mary's mind, but, struck by the weariness in Mrs. Chattaburty's voice and the sudden aging of her granite face, she refrained from interrogating her. There would be ample time, once they were on the road, to acquaint herself with the nature of her father's illness. Until then, she would cling to the hope that the squire's hypochondria lay at the bottom of this summons to come home, that he had used the excuse of an ailment to get her back to Dearcrop.

Rising with a sigh, Mrs. Chattaburty went from the house, leaving Mary to wrestle with her emotions.

The first of these was gladness. She had been entreated to come home at last. Rejoicing soon turned to agitation, however, as Mary began to fear that the reason for the entreaty might in reality be very grave. It had never entered her mind that her return to Dearcrop might be colored with sorrow. She had looked for affection—and only that—to mend the breach. Now a new element had to be reckoned with. Once it would have been enough just to be sent for. Now, she saw, it might betoken something dreadful.

The butler had no sooner ushered out Mrs. Chattaburty than he was obliged to announce another caller—Mr. Grisby by name, who begged a minute alone with Miss Ashe.

Smiling nervously, he apologized for intruding upon her privacy. He wiped his forehead with a dainty finger, saying, "I believe you are acquainted with Lord Hugo Mallory?"

Having sprayed this question, he drew a wisp of soiled linen from his pocket.

Mary could hardly tell what was more distasteful—Mr. Grisby's question, or the oily beads on his lip. Turning her head away, she nodded.

"Perhaps you might tell me where he has gone?"

"You have bills of his, I suppose."

"I do. But I am unable to locate him. No one knows where he's gone. Do you suppose he has left England? Has he, by any chance, gone to join Wellesley? Did he say where?"

As she surveyed the man, Mary recalled Lady Melrose's warning. If Lady Melrose desired her to keep mum, then surely she ought to tell. She felt sorely inclined to tell, for if Grisby reached Burwash right away, Lord Mallory would be forced to find a new hiding place, far from her father. Consequently, he would in all likelihood be gone from Dearcrop by the time she got there. She bestirred her imagination to summon up a picture of his lordship hounded by this repulsive fellow.

To her disappointment, it was not as sweet a picture as she had anticipated. She began to wonder why she should rely on such a man as Grisby to rid Dearcrop of its interloper when, in a matter of hours, she would be in a position to do it herself. It was far better to confront Lord Mallory face to face than to use some contemptible worm to do her work for her. Of course, she would not lie to Grisby for Lord Mallory's sake; at the same time, it did not suit her just now to tell the whole truth.

"I just hope that wherever his lordship is," she answered, "he is sufficently dismal as to have a foretaste of debtor's prison."

This piece of acrimony caused Grisby to pause in the act of mopping his nostril. "I suppose he has offended you, too, Miss. He was excessively rude to me on the occasion of my recent visit to his lodgings. These soldiers often turn out ruffians, I daresay, and hardly know how to treat a respectable female, much less an honest man of business."

Mary bridled at being classed with the likes of Mr.

Grisby, so much so, in fact, that she promised herself never to tell him the truth if she could possibly help it.

Taking the card from his pocket, Grisby handed it to her. "Should you hear news of his lordship," he said, "you may send for me at once. Day or night. Any hour at all. Remember."

Looking at the damp thumbprint on the card, Mary replied, "I think I can safely promise not to forget you, Mr. Grisby."

The moment he left, she tore the card to shreds.

In the morning, Mary hastily bade her friends good-bye. Lady Baldridge charged her to rest easy on the matter of the house; she would look after it as though it were her own daughter's. Emily and Theo hugged her, after which Mary stepped into her father's carriage. It pulled away with a lurch, and she neither drew the curtain aside nor looked back.

Mrs. Chattaburty napped for several hours, preventing Mary from learning more about her father's condition. The delay fueled her imagination with all manner of terrifying possibilities. Her reliance on her father's hypochondria grew shaky and at last gave way altogether. After an hour spent in speculation, she persuaded herself that she would reach Dearcrop too late to do more than execute her father's lavish funeral arrangements.

At last the coachman stopped at an inn, where the noise of barking dogs and flurried chickens woke her companion. Over a plate of cold meat and a bowl of berries, Mary questioned her.

"It began with a little cold, nothing uncommon or worrisome, or so we thought," said Mrs. Chattaburty. "But a week or two brought a sore throat. A cough developed next and it seemed he could not shake it. Meanwhile, his spirits, which have been depressed since your flight from Sussex, grew alarmingly low, and he began to have night fevers, during which he would cry out."

"It was good of you to be with him during this time."

"I did not observe these things firsthand, Miss Ashe. It was Lord Mallory who told me about them."

"I see."

"It was Lord Mallory who said you would come as soon as you were asked."

"It requires no great powers of discernment to know that I would come home as soon as my father sent for me."

Here Mrs. Chattaburty stopped chewing her beef and was forced to gulp it down. She paled, looked distressed, and inhaled deeply. "Your father did not send for you," she said. "Lord Mallory did."

Mary did not comprehend at first. "My father does not wish to see me after all?"

"He has no idea of your coming."

Closing her eyes, Mary quelled an impulse to bolt.

"His lordship and I begged him every day to send a note or a word to you, but he would only turn his face to one side and say he would not hear of it. Then, these past days, he got so bad that Lord Mallory took it upon himself to have you brought back."

"He took it upon himself!"

"Yes, and a very risky thing to do it was."

"I daresay, the shock to my father may worsen his condition."

"Lord Mallory is convinced your presence can only improve the squire's condition, and the doctor quite agrees with him. His lordship sent to London for Sir Geoffrey Malfrey and sets great store by his prescriptions. There's no gainsaying his lordship has taken a great deal upon himself."

"Is my father dying, Mrs. Chattaburty?"

"Doctors will always say a patient is dying, for if he does, then they appear to all the world as wonderfully sagacious, and if he recovers, then the miracle is owing to their excellent skill."

"You say his lordship risks a great deal. I do not understand that. What can be risked by my return if it is not the danger to my father's fragile condition?"

"I am speaking of the risk to his lordship."

"It seems to me his lordship is established on very firm ground."

"That will no longer be the case if you should tell your father who it was that sent for you."

"Yes, I see. My father will be angry with Lord Mallory if he learns the truth."

"Perhaps even more than that. It occurs to me, Miss Ashe, that you have it in your power to cause a breach between Lord Mallory and your father, for the squire was adamant that you were not to be summoned."

"But what choice do I have except to tell the truth?"

"You might choose to say you come of your own inclination, that you desire to beg your father's forgiveness, that your only thought is to be reconciled with him."

At the suggestion, Mary's chin tilted upward and her dark eyes flashed with disdain. "And why should I lie to protect Lord Mallory?" she inquired coldly.

"I cannot tell you that," Mrs. Chattaburty said. "You must see the reason yourself."

Mrs. Buxton, the housekeeper, embraced Mary, while the other servants wiped their eyes with their aprons and sighed in relief that the mistress had finally come home. As soon as Mrs. Chattaburty took her leave, Mrs. Buxton led Mary to the sickroom.

Hesitating at the door, Mary did not go inside. Instead, she asked the housekeeper to peek in and see how things stood. After a moment, Mrs. Buxton whispered that the two gentlemen were asleep. Once before they had napped like that in the late afternoon after the squire had had a bad night. The squire took hardly any food these days and thus his strength was gone by midday, and as for his lordship, well the poor gentlemen read to Squire Ashe and wrote letters for him long into the night, and so it was no wonder that he could barely keep his eyes open during the day.

Peering through the crack in the door, Mary saw her father. He slept restlessly and looked small and childlike in the great carved bed. His face was thin and white, and his fist, which lay over the counterpane, clutched and unclutched.

Lord Mallory slept in a Chesterfield, a book fallen open on his lap. He was unshaved and wore no coat. His shirt collar was unbuttoned, and Mary could see the even rise and fall of his chest.

"Do not disturb them," she told the housekeeper. Closing the door, they went to see about the unpacking. That done, Mary ordered up some dinner, the proportions of which would have warmed Lady Baldridge's generous heart.

She was joined at dinner by Lord Mallory, who thanked her for coming so quickly.

"Apparently Mrs. Chattaburty did not expect I would. But then I have always had the power to surprise the women of the neighborhood."

"I never doubted you would come."

His blue eyes were tired. Conversation appeared to cost him some effort. Despite this he looked remarkably handsome, and although they sat at opposite ends of the table with a candelabrum winking between them, still Mary could not be unaware of his large presence. More than ever, it was an attractive presence and its very attractiveness heightened her sense of being displaced in her own home. Ironically, she thought, she ought to feel grateful to the one who had displaced her, for he had brought her here.

"Mrs. Chattaburty informs me that my father has not been forewarned of my coming. I have therefore refrained from taking him by surprise."

"You did right. I had thought to be here to greet you and explain the preparations we would need to make, but unfortunately I fell asleep."

"What preparations do we need, my lord, before I may see my own father?"

Hugo studied his plate. "It is very hard that any preparation should be required at all. It ought not to be so. You ought to be able to go to him at once."

"But that, in your view, would not serve?"

"I will go to him after dinner and tell him you are here."

"If you do not mind, I would like to prepare him a broth first. I understand he eats little and as he is particularly fond of my broth, I may be able to induce him to take a few spoonfuls."

"What do you mean, 'if I do not mind'? You have no need to ask permission in your own house."

"It is clear that I must defer to your better knowledge and judgment in this case. It is clear, too, that you are master here now and I do not anticipate that you will disappear into the fog merely because I have returned."

Hugo pushed his plate away. "Sending for you as I did was doubtless high-handed of me, but I never deluded myself that I was master here. Tell me, Miss Ashe, did I do wrong to send for you? Would I have done better to wait until the squire asked for you himself?"

Bowing her head, Mary replied, "No."

After a moment he poured himself a glass of wine. "Thank you," he said and drank.

"But you know it would have been better had he asked for me himself."

Lord Mallory put down his glass and smiled a little. "He asks for you every day, only he does not say the words."

Rather than let free the sob that was locked in her throat, Mary did not reply.

"You do not believe me."

"I have learned to believe everything you say, my lord."

He looked at her, surprised.

"I did not go to my father directly because I felt you would need to prepare him and that you would know how to do it."

"It costs you a great deal to admit as much. I thank you for making the effort."

"Stop thanking me!" Mary cried. She rose abruptly from her chair, saying, "You know very well it is I who ought to be thanking you."

He regarded her with a smile. "That rankles, does it? I am the last person in the world you would be beholden to."

"How dare you answer for me."

"I do not answer for you, Miss Ashe. But I know you. I have committed you to memory, as completely as the squire has memorized *Arthur.* I read you every day, as I read

Arthur to him every day, and I have become so familiar with each page, each turn of phrase, each nuance that I can recite you by heart.''

Mary hardly knew how to reply to this. He had indeed read her well, and she did not like it, any more than she liked having his accurate readings thrown back at her. She was not an ungrateful person; yet it was true she did not like being beholden to anyone, and especially to him, to a man she had spurned as an opportunist, a man she had thought devoid of honor and principle, a man she had assumed incapable of cherishing any genuine regard for her father or herself.

"As soon as you have told my father I am come back," she said, "you will be free to leave Dearcrop."

"The country suits me wonderfully well this time of year."

"I am certain your relations will be glad to see you at Domville."

"Domville! That is the first place my creditors will look for me."

"Ah, that is why you stay on here. You are hiding."

"Certainly. It is what I do best."

Mary flushed at this but refused to be disarmed. "If it is hiding you require, I trust Lady Melrose will be only too happy to assist you."

"Charlotta never hid in her life. She is far too fond of show. Nevertheless, she would not scowl at me as you do, Miss Ashe, and as soon as I have spoken to the squire, I shall write her ladyship. Will that satisfy you?"

Mary found that, in fact, the prospect of having his lordship seek refuge with Lady Melrose was not in the least satisfactory. She did not say so, however. Instead she rose and excused herself, using the pretext of preparing a broth to escape from the room.

Lord Mallory was closeted in the sickroom for some time. As she stood in the hall, listening for a sound at the door, Mary grew apprehensive. Every additional moment signaled her father's continued resistance. If the squire had been glad of the news that she had come home, his lordship would have come out long before this. The fact that he remained inside meant he was still endeavoring to persuade the squire to see her.

When Hugo emerged, quietly closing the door behind him, she searched his face for a sign of hope. She could find none.

"Do not let yourself be discouraged," he said.

"I cannot go in if he will not say he wants me."

"Do not demand that. Let it be enough that you want him."

"I must know he wants me."

Hugo took her by the shoulders. "Then know it. Know it because I tell you it is so, even if he will not."

She looked into his drawn face. As before, she believed he spoke the truth. But she did not believe she had the courage to act on it.

Hugo dropped his hands to his side and walked down the hall. In a moment she heard his brisk step on the staircase.

Entering the sickroom, Mary saw her father quickly turn his eyes away from the door. She approached the bedside and knelt. Many minutes went by before she could think what to say, minutes during which the squire kept his eyes fixed on a point in space. It seemed at first that just being this close was enough, that she was satisfied, even grateful, to have the comfort of his nearness. At least he did not order her from the room. At least he did not reproach her. After a time, however, it was not enough, and she bestirred herself to speak.

"Papa, let me stay."

"Why did you come?"

"I've wanted to every minute."

"Do not pity me, Mary. I cannot endure it. Who told you I was ill?"

"I wanted to come, Papa. I ought to have come before this. Now I am here, let me stay."

"Of course, you may stay," he answered in a weak, childlike voice.

He had grown thin, so much so that the skin hung loose

and transparent on his cheek. Seeing how he had withered, she grieved. What did it matter, she asked herself, who was right and who was wrong, or who made the first move to heal the breach, or who was the first to give in? What did points of pride matter in the face of real suffering? She had only to look at him to know what was important and what was not.

"Can you not even look at me, Papa?"

"No."

"Are you still so angry?"

"I am not angry."

"But you turn your face away."

"How am I to look at you? I am ashamed."

"Then you don't hate me?"

"I hate what I have done and I do not know how to undo it."

"As of this minute, it is undone."

"For you perhaps, because you are young."

"If I were young, Papa, you would not have had to put yourself to all the trouble of finding me a husband. No, it is undone because I want it to be. I declare it undone."

"I could declare it undone, too, if it were not that I have come between you and Hugo. There I have done a great wrong. If I had let the two of you alone, all might have been well."

"If you had let us alone we never should have met at all."

"Exactly so. By interfering, I have made you both miserable."

"I am not miserable, Papa. Neither is Lord Mallory."

"You do not need to pretend, daughter. I know you speak as you do only to appease my conscience, but I tell you it will not be appeased. I cannot see why either of you should forgive me. If you were wise, you would go back to London and live a happy life there." He followed this with a spasm of coughing, during which Mary induced him to sit up against his pillow and drink a swallow of a soothing elixir.

Having quieted him, Mary sat next to him on the bed and told him, "I know exactly what is to be done, Papa, and it

can only be done here, not in London. I know how to make
everything right again."

"Do you?" he asked in amazement, turning his eyes to
look at her.

"Of course I do," she said brightly.

"You are so lovely, child," he said. "I remembered it
every day, but I had forgotten that your eyes were so black
and fine."

"I mean to remind you daily now."

"I don't know why you should want to stay. I have made
such a muddle of it all."

"You must allow, Papa, that I played a generous part in
the muddle-making."

"I cannot allow any such thing. You did only what you
were forced to do."

"We won't speak of it anymore. I have declared it to be
undone and undone it is. All that remains is for you to say
you will let me try to make it right again."

"I suppose Hugo will have to leave now."

"He has his own affairs to tend to, I expect."

"I don't know how I shall recover without him."

"I will look after you now."

"I daresay, I should recover twice as fast if you both
looked after me."

"Then I will ask him to stay awhile longer."

"But do you think he will, after what has passed between
you?"

"I anticipate no difficulty in persuading him to stay."

"Ah, I wish I could believe you. I cannot help thinking it
is all up with us."

"No such thing, Papa. I mean to take care of everything."

"What do you mean to do?"

"I have made you some broth. I mean to have Mrs.
Buxton bring it up."

He sighed. "I am glad it is no worse."

"What did you think I meant?"

"I do not know. I feared you might be overeager now to
please me at all costs and that you would declare your
readiness to marry Hugo."

"You feared it, Papa? Is that not what you wanted?"

"A long time ago I wanted it, but you know, lying here in this bed, wakeful at night because I do nothing all day but tend my fever, I have had much time to think. I have learned that I wanted Hugo for myself as much as for you. I came quickly to depend on him, you see. I was afraid that if he married someone else, he would be lost to me. I thought to secure him by making him my son-in-law, and in my foolishness,· I expected you would fall in with my selfish plan. If you had not been so strong, daughter, I am afraid I would have sacrificed you to my comfort."

"I always knew that Lord Mallory meant a great deal to you. To tell the truth, I was jealous of it, but I am learning not to be jealous any longer."

"You will not marry him, will you? You will endeavor to forget I ever demanded it?"

"Lord Mallory has taken an oath never to offer for me again, so you may rest easy, Papa."

"And I have taken an oath never to suggest it again. Ah, I have been wanting your broth a long time," he said with a sigh, and Mary thought there was in that breath something like contentment.

Mrs. Chattaburty came some days later to sit with the squire so that the young people could amuse themselves together. The moment she entered the hall, however, she learned that the young people were not at liberty to amuse themselves. Lord Mallory had a caller who bumped into Mrs. C. in the hall, causing her to shudder.

On the steps, she met Mary, who was just coming down.

"What a dreadful man!" Mrs. Chattaburty said. "I declare, he is a veritable drizzle. I do hope Lord Mallory does not end up with a soiled coat. I do so like that fawn coat of his and would cry to see it go limp."

"His lordship has a visitor?"

"I can say that much with truth, but I cannot say that the fellow is a friendly visitor for he wears a stormy look and promises to drench Lord Mallory. I vow, when he bumped into me, he dampened my chignon. Happily his lordship has friends at Dearcrop.''

''My father is genuinely fond of him.''

''I was speaking of you, Miss Ashe. You have kept mum, I see.''

''Have I?''

''Of course, you have. It's been some time now, and Lord Mallory is still here.''

''I would not distress my father. It might set him back, you know. And, besides, his lordship helps keep watch in the sickroom. I could not do it alone.''

''Naturally not.''

''I would do anything for the sake of my father's health.''

''You have made a wise decision.''

''My father cannot spare his lordship just now.''

''You need not justify your decision to me, Miss Ashe. I am in perfect agreement.''

''Are you, Mrs. Chattaburty? I daresay, I do not think my other neighbors will agree so readily. They will censure me, no doubt, for allowing Lord Mallory to continue at Dearcrop. Perhaps he ought to remove to the inn.''

''That would be impractical when his lordship is needed here.''

''You are disposed to be charitable, Mrs. Chattaburty.''

On this, Mrs. C. turned to Mary with her granite countenance cracked in an astonished smile. ''No one has ever accused me of that, Miss Ashe. No, it is you who are charitable. Had you been disposed to recall incidents of the past, you might not have welcomed me at all today, or let me visit my friend the squire.'' So saying, she gathered together her skirts and made her way to the sickroom.

Mary descended the staircase to see Mr. Grisby stalk down the hall. He stopped when he saw her, saying, ''Good day to you, Miss Ashe. How very sly you are!'' Whereupon, she watched him spray through the door, which the servant made sure to bang shut against him. She then turned to see Hugo leaning against the doorpost of the library, his arms folded and his smile deepening.

"I am delighted to find you are acquainted with Mr. Grisby. Perhaps I owe his kind visit to you. If so, you must allow me to thank you. He is a highly amusing fellow, and I take pleasure in refusing to pay him yet again."

Angrily, Mary said, "I told him nothing. I would not give such a man the news that the world was round."

"Of course you wouldn't. I ought to have known. You must forgive me, Miss Ashe. You must forgive Mr. Grisby's abruptness, too. It is my fault, I own. I have angered the poor fellow, and not for the first time, nor the last, I'm afraid."

Mary walked slowly toward him. "I am afraid, too," she said. "I am afraid your presence at Dearcrop makes it impossible for you to attend properly to your affairs."

"Are you hinting that I ought to leave?"

Reddening, Mary replied, "I do not hint any such thing. If I wished you to leave, I would say so straight out."

Hugo laughed. "Am I to understand, then, that you are glad to have me stay?"

"You are to understand that my father wishes you to stay and that it would distress him to see you dunned."

"Since it would distress him to see it, I shall make sure Grisby does not come here again."

"Moreover, he would be distressed at your financial difficulties."

"You may tell the squire that Mr. Grisby has not been successful in collecting a penny from me; nor do I anticipate he will ever be."

"Lord Mallory, perhaps my father might advance you something to relieve your present straits a little."

Hugo contemplated her face and said, "I told you once, Miss Ashe, you do not need to pay me to withdraw my addresses. I have withdrawn them as a present to you. I have nothing else to give, at least nothing that will please you half so much. Consequently, I wish you would be grateful for the gift and not try to bribe me again."

"You made it quite clear that you do not intend to offer for me again, sir! I do not require a repetition of the vow."

"What, then, do you require?"

She looked at his face, which wore a careless, skeptical smile, and her thoughts leaped at once to her enamel box. Therein lay all the reminders of her foolishness over the past years. But taken together they had not the power of making her feel half so foolish as Hugo Mallory did. It appeared she could not offer him sympathy or assistance without making a bumbling business of it. Perhaps, she thought helplessly, she would do well to give it all up, as her father liked to say. She was accustomed to teaching her heart how to behave sensibly, and she would do so now, but she could not help regretting that the only time his lordship was able to read her accurately was when she did not wish to be read at all.

Quietly she turned to go, but he stopped her. "I think I may have been mistaken just now. It occurs to me that your offer of assistance may have been merely generous."

Facing him again, she said, "It is not generosity, my lord; it is friendship."

His expression grew serious.

"You once told me you would not give me up because the time would come when I would need all the friends I could muster. You must permit me now, sir, to return the favor."

"Very well," he said.

"You will accept my offer of assistance, then?"

"Certainly not. I have no idea of paying Grisby, who merely buys up what bills he can find and in return gives honest tradesmen a fraction of their worth. I never contracted with the man and owe him nothing."

"Unfortunately, the law is not likely to see it quite as you do, my lord."

"I know. Nevertheless, I stick to my point, which is all the more reason why I shall probably need all the friends I can muster."

Meeting his blue eyes, Mary extended her hand to him.

CHAPTER
TWELVE

"I have never known you to be so closemouthed, Harriet," Lady Babik complained. She shifted uncomfortably in her chair, as though she no longer regarded her place of honor in Mrs. Chattaburty's sitting room with her former complaisance.

"Harriet has told us what we wanted to hear, that the squire improves daily," Mrs. Turnbull said. "I do not know what more she could say."

"That is nothing to the point," her ladyship snapped. "I vow, you are as innocent as Imogen."

Imogen Venable looked up from her teacup. "If that is not to the point," she said in a hurt voice, "I wish you would tell me what is."

"Why, it is that Miss Ashe and his lordship have lived together at Dearcrop nearly the whole summer now. It is a scandal, and I wonder why the parson has not said anything about it."

"I do not know what he could say," Mrs. Venable replied, rising to her husband's defense. "The squire sees no one, excepting Miss Ashe and his lordship and Harriet. And even if Mortimer did see him, I am sure he would not distress him by talk of scandal. Unless, of course, he thought it was his duty to do so. Do you think he ought to, Harriet?"

Hearing herself addressed, Mrs. Chattaburty looked at each of her visitors in turn. Her face grew hard but she kept mum.

"Well, it is a scandal, for all Harriet's ridiculous silence," Lady Babik declared. "Miss Ashe ran away from Lord Mallory to prevent a marriage and now she lives at such close quarters with him that she will have to marry the man to save her reputation."

"I do not think," Mrs. C. said, unable to restrain herself any longer, "that Miss Ashe's reputation suffers in the least. No one can be unaware of the care she has shown her father. Lord Mallory has deen devoted as well. Between the two of them, they have saved him. It's as simple as that."

"Well, I would be obliged to you if you would tell me how long this shocking arrangement will continue, now that the squire is reportedly on the mend. Does Miss Ashe expect society's indulgence forever?"

"You may ask her yourself," Mrs. Chattaburty said. "She proposes to stop by as soon as she has paid her compliments to Mrs. Hanks."

"She is to visit Mrs. Hanks? Oh, what I would not give to be a fly on the wall during that little tête-à-tête," Lady Babik said with a laugh. "How it must have astonished Miss Ashe to hear the banns posted for Theo Granger and Emily. Instead, I could almost feel sorry for her, losing her only hope of a husband to her best friend. I wonder she can continue the friendship. But these events must bring her folly home to her. She will certainly be a spinster now."

"Unless the parson forces her to have Lord Mallory," Mrs. Turnbull said. "Frankly, I do not think he will bring it off. If she would not marry Lord Mallory to please her father, she certainly will not do it to please the parson, with all due respect, Imogen."

"I do not understand," Mrs. Venable cried. "Did not Miss Ashe always intend to be a spinster? Did we not say so in this very room not six months ago?"

"Now I recall, you are right," Lady Babik replied.

"Harriet said—I remember it perfectly now—that she was eccentric for that very reason. Did you not say so, Harriet?"

Mrs. Chattaburty adjusted her imposing person in her chair. Her expession was glacial as she directed a reply at her ladyship. "Miss Ashe was and remains the most eccentric young woman of my acquaintance," she proclaimed. "To come to her father as she did, to insist that all be forgiven and forgot, to befriend the man who was the cause of her fleeing from her home, to welcome me as though I had played no part whatever in the scheme against her—this is eccentricity indeed!"

"I detest sarcasm," Lady Babik said.

"You would like sarcasm well enough if his lordship had offered for Miss Babik instead of Miss Ashe," Mrs. Chattaburty returned.

Before Lady Babik could cry out against this charge, Mary was ushered into the room. The four stricken faces that greeted her entrance announced at once that the ladies had been gossiping about her. There was something familiar and comfortable to Mary in that knowledge, so much so that she bestowed on them a warm, nostalgic smile. Shaking each woman's hand in turn, she said. "It is so good to see all my old friends again."

"I daresay, we had all thought to see you before this," Lady Babik remarked.

Mary apologized for neglecting them all since her return to Sussex. "I have not gone out these past weeks. Indeed, I was shocked to find, when I rode in the curricle to Hanks Cottage, that there is a breath of fall in the air. I had no idea August was going forward all this time."

"How does your father?" Mrs. Venable inquired solicitously.

"Better. A little better each day. He is able to walk about a little and his nights are more restful. He thanks you and the parson for the books you sent, for although they are not *Arthur*, they are, he says, not entirely without interest."

"The apple butter will serve him better than books, I expect," Mrs. Turnbull said. "Does he take it?"

"He took it for the first time last week, with a piece of

toast and a cup of tea. I did not have to tell him who sent it, Mrs. Turnbull. He knew as soon as he tasted it.''

"And how does Lord Mallory?'' Lady Babik asked.

"I have no idea,'' Mary replied. "I hardly see him, for when he is with my father, I must sleep, and when I go to the sickroom, he must sleep. Our only relief from his routine, I'm afraid, lies in Mrs. Chattaburty's kind visits.''

"I suppose you and his lordship are together much during those visits,'' Lady Babik suggested.

"Not very often. I must tend to the household while Lord Mallory attempts to conduct his business from Burwash.''

"I suppose he was conducting his business when I saw him outside the inn Monday last,'' Lady Babik said, "and from the look of it, it was a rather nasty business, too.''

Mrs. Chattaburty here induced Mary to sit down and taste a biscuit, but this did not distract Lady Babik from her tale.

"He was engaged in the most lively conversation with a very odd gentlement in a dreadful green coat. I can't think why the gentleman struck me as so disagreeable. Certainly his nose was well formed enough and his eyes were not overlarge. He had a wet way of speaking, though; I could see the spray from his lips and he talked very fast, saying that if his lordship did not pay up what he owed, the consequence would be prison. The fellow—I will not call him a gentleman—said it would give him profound pleasure to send his lordship to Newgate.''

"What did Lord Mallory say?'' Mary asked.

"He said he did not give a farthing what the fellow did, or words to that effect. I do not eavesdrop, you know.''

"This is mere tittle-tattle,'' Mrs. Chattaburty said. "I have too much respect for Lord Mallory to gossip about his difficulties, and I am sure Lady Babik feels as I do.''

"You are wrong, Harriet,'' her ladyship said. "If one of my relations is in difficulty, I am obliged to express my regret. Another person in my position might gloat, and not without just cause, for he has treated us shamefully, but I cannot see Lord Mallory hounded by creditors without feeling heartily sorry for him and without shuddering to

think what might have become of us all had a certain
marriage taken place as he led us to hope it would.''

To restrain herself, Mrs. Chattaburty popped a piece of
cake into her mouth.

Mary, however, set down her cup and plate and stood up.
''Thank you,'' she said solemnly. ''You have enabled me to
see that Lord Mallory's affairs continue to suffer severely as
a result of his lengthy stay at Dearcrop, and though it
distesses me to think we have kept him from tending to his
welfare, still I am obliged to you, Lady Babik, for your
information.'' With that, she bid them good-bye and took a
hasty leave.

''I don't know why Miss Ashe should feel obliged,'' said
Mrs. Venable in perplexity.

''I don't know either,'' Mrs. Chattaburty said. ''I am sure
I do not feel obliged.''

''I, on the other hand, feel very much obliged to Miss
Ashe,'' Mrs. Turnbull said. ''If she were one jot less eccentric than she is, what in heaven's name should we have to
talk about?''

When Mary returned home, her father was asleep, and
Lord Mallory was nowhere to be found. The servants did
not think he had gone out and therefore could not tell when
he was expected to return. A footboy told her he thought his
lordship might be in the library, but when Mary opened the
library door, the room lay empty. Mrs. Buxton suggested he
might have taken a walk in the garden as it was such a fine
day, and even if his lordship hadn't gone out to sniff the
roses, said the housekeeper, Mary ought to go herself and
get a little bloom on her cheeks.

Taking this advice, Mary stepped out on the lawn, walking briskly until she came to an expanse of hedge sculpted
in a maze. She paused at the entrance to contemplate her
situation, which struck her at this moment as something of a
maze in its own right.

From the moment they had met, her relations with Lord
Mallory had taken unexpected twists and turns; no sooner
had she found her way out of one cul-de-sac, it seemed,

than another loomed just around the next hedge. In the general course of her life, she did not permit obstacles to daunt her; if she could not get round them, she simply leaped over. But in his lordship's case, she felt as though she was always groping her way about.

Lady Babik's tale was an obstacle in point. It came back to Mary afresh now, and it seemed to reproach her. There was nothing new in it, she allowed. His lordship had aways been deep in debt. Indeed, one of the first things he had ever said to her was that he hoped he might one day be able to pay his tailor. What was new was the part she and her father had recently played—albeit unwittingly—in the deterioration of his affairs. He had allowed himself to be persuaded to stay at Dearcrop. Had he not been assisting her in the squire's care, he might by now have been able to extend his credit, or borrow the funds to pay off his creditors, or sell off another piece of Domville. He might even have found an heiress to marry and make all well again.

She shivered and opened the gate in the hedgerow. At the first bend, she admitted to herself that her anxiety on his lordship's account was another new twist. Not long ago, she had viewed his debts merely as proof that he was a fortune hunter. Now she viewed them wholly otherwise. They appeared to place him in the greatest jeopardy, personified by Mr. Grisby and his dewy brow. Typically, Lord Mallory treated the matter with indifference, almost as though he did not care what happened to him. For an instant, Mary envisioned him languishing in debtor's prison. She imagined him laughing it off with great style and wit, and she imagined him cold and pestered by rats.

She turned into another hedgerow, determined that she would never let it come to that. Before Mr. Grisby should level one more threat, her father would prevail on his lordship to accept a gift, a very large gift, as a token of friendship. The squire would act as soon as she told him about Lord Mallory's straits, and if her father did not feel well enough to bestir himself, then she herself would do it. One way or another, Lord Mallory would be free. She would have nothing with which to reproach herself. On the contrary, she would be able to say that she had repaid his friendship in equal measure.

Finding that the turn she had taken led into a cul-de-sac, Mary turned around. At this moment, she could not summon the patience to find her way out, so she sat down on a marble bench to think. Soon she was absorbed in contemplating the image of Lord Mallory, not in prison this time but free of debt. She imagined him spending most of his time at Domville, initiating improvement on the estate. This would, of necessity, prevent his attendance at Dearcrop. Any time he might spare from Domville would be taken up in London, where he would live the life expected of a marquis. Chief among his obligations there, she supposed, would be to cast about him for the means of producing a little marquis.

The maze, it seemed, had now worked its way around with so many twists and turns that it quite took Mary's breath away. She saw now that saving Lord Mallory meant losing him altogether. He would no longer tiptoe into the sickroom to shake her gently awake, whispering that as he had come to resume the watch, she must go to her bedchamber and rest. No longer would he light her to her chamber door, frowning because she looked pale and peaked and denying that he looked just as bad. No longer would she find him the next morning, asleep in the Chesterfield, his coat on the floor, his cravat hanging loose on his chest, his dark head profiled against the high back of the chair. The money he was soon to receive would free him to leave the routine they had established. She regretted it with all her heart; yet she could not but wish to see him get on with the business of his own life.

"Miss Ashe," Lord Mallory said. "What are you doing here?"

She looked up to see him standing at the entrance to the cul-de-sac. He wore a hat to shade him from the autumn sun and he carried a number of papers.

"I lost my way," she said.

He folded up the papers and nodded. "I am glad I found you, for I have something to tell you."

Moving over on the bench, she permitted him to sit beside her.

"I have good news," he said.

"I should welcome some."

"After the squire and I took our turn about the room today, he did not go right back to his bed. I wonder if you can guess what he did.

"He came downstairs to take tea."

"Why, so he did. How did you know?"

"He told me he meant to surprise you."

"That is nothing, however, to what happened next."

She looked at him and saw him smiling.

"He sang me two hymns and asked which I thought would best please the mourners at his funeral."

Mary's black eyes grew brilliant. "In all this time, he has not spoken of his funeral."

"Until today."

She began to laugh, and Hugo laughed with her, saying, "There is more. He asks me to read through Cicero and Tacitus in search of an epitaph."

"He does not mean to choose one from *Arthur*?"

"No. I suggested it, of course, but he would not hear of it. It would be too conceited of him, he said."

"He really is on the mend, I see. Thank you for telling me, Lord Mallory."

In response, he looked down at his arm, on which, in her emotion, she had put her hand. When he looked at her again, he was no longer laughing.

She drew her hand away, feeling awkward and foolish, and studied the surrounding walls of hedge.

"Which brings me to a second piece of good news," he said. His tone, more subdued now, had lost its playfulness. "I will be leaving Dearcrop."

"I expected as much."

"I daresay you think my departure long overdue, but I could not in good conscience leave until the squire could spare me."

"Are you sure he can spare you now?"

"Fairly sure. I will await Sir Geoffrey's final word on it

when he comes tomorrow, however. I expect him to say I may leave at once.''

"So soon? Well, I suppose there are many matters requiring your attention, and we have kept you from them far too long.''

"As a matter of fact, I have some letters here that tell me I had best return to London as soon as possible.''

As the letters looked to Mary like bills, she said, "Lord Mallory, my father and I cannot allow you to leave without taking with you some expression of our gratitude for your kindness. I beg you to accept something that will assist you in your present difficulties.''

"Are you offering me money again, Miss Ashe?''

"I am sorry if I have done it in a way that offends you. I hope you will overlook it. All I ask is that you accept a gift.''

"I am not offended. It is impossible to offend a Mallory in regard to money. We have none to be offended about; nor do we pretend to any pride on that head either. In matters of friendship, however, it is quite another story. Not for nothing did my scribbling ancestor sing its praises.''

"You are refusing then?''

"Your father has continually offered me money, and I have continually refused.''

"Is it so wrong to let a friend help you?''

"I will not have it said that I gained in any material way by my friendship with your family. Besides, I doubt I will have need of any gifts. One of these letters comes from General Wellesley, who summmons me to the capital. There is talk, it seems, of his being made a viscount. If it comes to pass, as he deserves, then there will be much for me to do. Some of it will, I make no doubt, provide me with a subsistence.''

"But what if it should not come to pass?''

"Then I rely on my second correspondent, Lady Melrose, who claims to have a scheme that will make my fortune. As a rule, I discount her ladyship's schemes for they always promise to land me further in debt, but she takes her oath that this one will not cost me a groat.''

Mary stood up and put a hand to her cheek. "Heavens, I had forgotten all about Lady Melrose!"

"She has not forgotten about you, though. She begs to be remembered in the warmest terms. Moreover, she asks me to remind you of the delightful conversations that passed between you in London and of the many interests you have in common. I had no idea the two of you had become so well acquainted."

Stricken, Mary could not reply.

"I am also to tell you that you must send me packing back to London at once. It seems she will not be able to make my fortune for me unless I present myself on the spot."

"In that case, I will certainly not be so selfish as to try to keep you here."

"You need not be so selfless, Miss Ashe. You might at least try."

Mary walked to the hedge and fingered a leaf. "If my father's condition threatened to decline as a result of your departure, I would try to keep you here. But as he is nearly well again, that expedient is almost certainly unnecessary. You are at liberty to choose, my lord, as you should be. Lady Melrose flatters me by thinking I could send you packing or in any way influence your decision."

"I am not at liberty to choose, unfortunately. I have no choice but to return to London and to the tangle that I laughingly call my affairs."

Rising, he offered her his arm so that they might make their way back to the house. In silence, they walked through the maze of hedge, and after losing their way two or three times, they accidentally came upon the gate.

Hard by an oak tree, Lord Mallory bowed to take his leave. Mary stopped him, speaking aloud the concern that had occupied her thoughts during their walk. "Will you promise me, Lord Mallory, that if General Wellesley should have nothing for you, and if Lady Melrose's scheme is not to your liking, you will allow my father to advance you a loan?"

"It seems to me you take a very gloomy view of my prospects."

She regarded him seriously. "I would not like you to do anything against your wishes simply because you were constrained by the want of money."

"You have come to know me very well now, Miss Ashe, well enough to know that while I may not always be able to do precisely as I wish, still I never do what I do not wish."

"In that case, I will not be gloomy any longer. I shall bid you a cheerful good-bye and wish you God's speed." She held out a hand to him, which he took firmly in his, and she produced a brilliant smile.

"You don't look the least bit cheerful," he observed.

"I shall practice, my lord. By the time you leave, I shall dazzle you with my good cheer."

"On the contrary, you will grow more and more cheerless as the wedding approaches."

"Wedding? What wedding?"

"Mr. Granger's. You need not pretend to be offhand, you know. Mr. Granger's latest act of perfidy has rung the church bells for some weeks now. I had come to know the young man as a thoroughgoing coxcomb, but, I confess, it never occurred to me that he would jilt you for Miss Hanks."

Her cheeks pink, Mary said in a low voice, "He never jilted me. Engaging himself to Emily is the most sensible thing Theo has ever done. It is the kindest thing he could have done for me."

"I agree. He was completely ill-suited to be your husband. Still, he ought to have behaved better. He was engaged to you."

She circled halfway around the oak. "That was a deception," she said. "We were never engaged."

He circled the tree in the other direction coming face to face with her.

"You are not in love with him?"

"I would hardly throw him at Emily if I were."

He laughed. "And I gave him the character of a lothario. Why, at this rate, Lord Byron will take orders." He smiled at her and asked, "Why did you let the world think you were engaged?"

Mustering all her courage, Mary replied, "I thought it would prevent you from renewing your addresses to me. I flattered myself that you meant to do so. I did not know you had resolved never to offer for me again."

His smile vanished and the lines of his jaw grew taut. "I knew my offer was repugnant to you, but I did not know it was as much as that. So, I did not merely inspire you to run from your home in the night; I did not merely cause you to break with your father, I also managed to induce you to live in fear of my addresses, so much so, in fact, that you deceived the world in order to avoid them. I daresay, the most diabolical villain in the blackest gothic tale might take a page from my book."

"I never thought you a villain!" Mary cried. "I have come to know you as the most honorable man of my acquaintance. I made sure you were a fortune hunter; then you scorned to take my money. I believed you stood between my father and me, then learned it was wholly his pride and my stubbornness that stood in the way. I presumed you curried favor with him out of mercenary motives, then discovered I have you to thank for his very life. When it seemed that you had taken my place in his heart and home, you became the means of reuniting us. When I let you believe I was engaged to Mr. Granger, you took my hand and said you would never give me up. No, you are not a villain, my lord. But you are a sorcerer. You are Merlin— turning my every conviction to doubt, transforming whatever I think I know into its opposite, until I do not trust my own mind anymore."

Hugo studied her gravely, as though he feared she was about to faint dead away at his feet. Seeing that she continued to stand, however, he replied, "I am sorry to have distressed you so, Miss Ashe. It would have been better if my character had been as bad as you thought. Then your mind might have been completely easy. Perhaps it is just as well that I return to London."

Mary leaned her back against the oak and did not reply.

He walked a few steps closer. "At the risk of confusing you further, Miss Ashe, I must tell you I am greatly complimented to be thought a Merlin. Heretofore, I have been a firebreathing dragon. Merlin is a step up, I think. It gives me hope that I may one day attain to Launcelot."

Unable to meet his look, Mary turned her head, thinking that he outshone all the clanking habitués of Camelot taken together. Then, recalling something that gave her a pang, she replied, "That, I am afraid, depends on Lady Melrose."

Sir Geoffrey Malfrey bent over the sickbed so that his wig threatened to fly into the coverlet. For some time he hummed and ahhed over his patient. Mary and Hugo looked from his face to the squire's, awaiting the verdict. After knitting his brows, shaking his head, and poking the squire here and there on his person, the great physician announced he thought his lordship might go to London without causing the squire to die of a relapse. This news did not appear to please Mary or his lordship as much as Squire Ashe expected, and as soon as Lord Mallory left to escort Sir Geoffrey to his carriage, he expressed his surprise.

"He ought to be glad to go," the old man said to his daughter. "What's he to do here with an old fellow like me? He should be riding and dancing and looking for a way out of his debts."

"He is very attached to you, Papa."

"Yes, he is," the squire said with satisfaction.

"And you are very attached to him as well. In all candor, I wonder you are able to let him go with such a light heart."

"Ah, my dear, I no longer interfere in the goings and comings of young people. Give them their head, I say, and smile at it. In the end, all that matters is that you have their affection, and it is not necessary to have the power over them of saying 'yea' or 'nay.' It is a lesson I have learned from you, my love, and I trust I have learned it not only painfully but well."

"It is thanks to me then that you take no pains to keep his lordship here?"

"That is it precisely. But I thought you would be glad to

bid him good-bye. I can see you have become perfectly comfortable with him now and do not hate him as you used to, but it cannot be easy to spend every day in the house with the gentleman who sent you fleeing from his proposals as far as London."

"I do not dislike London as much as you do, Papa."

"Nevertheless, you may be happy at last, for you have had everything your own way, and it's no more than you deserve. Theo Granger is to marry Miss Hanks, who says she will sing the psalm at my graveside, and therefore you need fear nothing further from that foolish young man. Hugo promises to send me an epitaph from London and to be out of your hair by first light tomorrow morning, and as he and I have both sworn never again to press you on the subject of matrimony, you may be a spinster to your heart's content. We shall have our house to ourselves once more and may amuse ourselves with visits from Lady Babik and Miss Babik and all the others we have not seen for so long. Then, in no time at all, there will be a wedding, which I mean to be well enough to attend, for I know how pleased you will be to see it is someone besides yourself tripped out in white veil and trains. I am glad things have turned out so well for you, my dear, for I have really only wanted your happiness."

"Yes, Papa, everything has turned out exactly as I wanted," Mary said. "I am the most fortunate woman in the world."

At dawn, Lord Mallory permitted his valet to iron his cravat and tie it on neatly before setting forth in the cart with the valises. That done, Hugo walked down the hall to the squire's chamber. Opening the door a crack, he looked at the sleeping old man, whose steady breathing and contented snore bore witness to another restful night. Satisfied, Hugo pulled the door closed and made for the staircase. He paused before Mary's chamber door, listening for a sound, but hearing nothing, he headed straightaway down the steps and out the door.

The morning was chill, and a fine blue haze covered the ground. The smell of fall invigorated him and he thanked

the boy who led forward his mount. He was on the point of
taking the reins when out of the corner of his eye he caught
a flash of movement. Turning, he saw Mary emerge from
the haze and come forward.

He dropped the reins and went to meet her. "This is very
kind of you, Miss Ashe," he said.

"It is you who have been kind, and you must allow me to
thank you before you go."

"Certainly I will allow you," he said and, touching his
fingers to her cheeks, he kissed her.

The stableboy, astonished at the sight of his mistress in
Lord Mallory's arms, nearly let the frisky chestnut get away.
He caught the reins just in time to hand them to his
lordship, who walked deliberately to his mount, swung
himself astride and galloped off into the morning fog. The
boy watched Mary slowly ascend the steps, take one look at
the departing rider, and enter the manor house. He then
dashed to the kitchen to regale the servants with the news
they had for so many weeks longed to hear.

CHAPTER THIRTEEN

When Lord Mallory was ushered into Arthur Wellesley's study, he was surprised to see his old friend look up at him from his desk with a tired smile. In the old days, the general's finely hewn features had been animated with purpose. Today, however, they looked thin and pinched. As the two men shook hands, Mallory felt tension in his grip, and he watched him take a breath of effort as they sat down.

"I've not been patient, awaiting your visit," Wellesley said. "I'm glad you've come at last."

"I guessed your letter implied more than it said. I take it there is not just your new title at stake here."

"My new title!" the general said in disgust.

"Kindly do not disparage titles. I have one or two myself, remember."

"Yes, I do remember, but this idea of elevating me has created such a ridiculous stir that it may never come to pass at all."

"It must come to pass. England will show her gratitude, you will see."

"England, as usual, cannot quite make up her mind, my friend. There are those who say I've led too many retreats from hard-won ground."

"They are fools."

"I am not so certain of that. It is true I have hung back; you see, I prefer caution to casualties. But I shall be tenacious in future, not for any titles I may garner, but for the hope of bringing this war to an end."

"You were more than tenacious at Oporto."

"It was surprise that won the day, not tenacity."

"Do you mean to meet Bonaparte head-on at last?"

"I should like that. We have much in common, Boney and I. We are both of poor families, both ambitious, both unreasoning patriots."

"You have nothing in common," Hugo contradicted. "He is short, you are tall. He calls himself by his first name; you cannot do so because Arthur has already been spoken for. He is greedy for empire; you lead armies into battle because you are called."

"I would like to think you are right. And, after all, he has the easier job of it, if I may say so, for he is the political as well as the military head of his nation, whereas I am at the mercy of a monarch and a parliament."

"But you have the advantage over him, if I may say so, for you were educated at Eton, then in France, a combination he cannot hope to conquer. If he had attended English public school, perhaps he might have a chance. As it is, however, you will always know what he is thinking, while he will always struggle to out-think you."

"In that case, I look forward to meeting Bonaparte on the field of battle one fine day. In the meanwhile, I will content myself with a viscountcy."

"You have earned your title well."

"Perhaps you would like to earn yours, too, Hugo."

"I'd like to earn something. That is why I am here. I am hoping you will provide me with the means of paying my bills."

"I can put you in the way of an opportunity, I think, but from what I hear, your family's debts are beyond the little I can offer. Why have you not done something before this? It is not like you to let things go so far."

"I have done what I could, but there is nothing left to pawn, nothing left to sell. I must either become a highwayman or husband to an heiress. Which do you think the more honorable vocation?''

"Neither. England calls, and she has first claim on you. Your creditors cannot dun you if you are out of the country.''

"Am I going traveling then?''

"You are, if risking your neck and dealing with scoundrels appeals to you as it used to.''

"There is always the hope I will get myself shot through the brain and need never think about bills again.''

"You may not get yourself shot, Hugo. England is not finished with you yet.''

"May I know where I am going?''

"You may, but it is not to be made generally known. If anyone asks, you must say you are going into the country or some such ruse as that.''

"Rest easy on that head. No one will ask.''

"I doubt that. Your tent was always bustling with the comings and goings of pretty females. I can't imagine our difficult circumstances have dampened their ardor. But you must let them think you go to the country; tell them you must hide from the bill collectors.''

"Hiding is great sport indeed, but will I hide alone?''

"Absolutely alone, except for a coffer of gold.''

"Excellent company. And where are the two of us off to?''

"Lisbon.''

"That is very amusing, Arthur. I suppose the French will welcome me with champagne before they separate my neck from my shoulders.''

"Your orders are expressly to avoid the French. You are to meet only with the Portuguese regulars. They are readying to join with us against Bonaparte.''

"You trust these fellows?''

"I trust they know the British do not mean to occupy their country or set up a puppet monarchy. Other than that, I trust them to let the British lead their important fighting for them.''

"And are we to pay for the privilege?''

"In a fashion. The coffer is to allow them to replenish their armies and armaments. Both are exhausted, but I do not mean to hand over the gold without getting written assurances in return. That is why I am sending you."

"Do you realize what will be said if it is ever discovered who it was you sent to Europe with so much gold? You will be ruined, I think. Even I am shocked at your willingness to place so much treasure in the hands of England's foremost debtor."

"I cannot agree with you, Hugo. In the first place, if the discovery is made, what is the worst they can do? Make me a duke, I daresay. In the second place, you are not England's foremost debtor. That distinction is reserved for the Prince. And in the last place, I have faith that those in power will eventually back me, that England will one day prevail in this war, and that Hugo Mallory will always reward my trust in him."

"When do I go?"

"That is still uncertain. The gold must be secured and the papers drawn up. You would do best to be prepared to leave at a moment's notice. Meanwhile, if you must say good-bye to anyone, you must do it so as not to arouse suspicion. I would not have you put anyone else in danger."

"What sort of danger?"

"There is a fellow named Grisby who is in the employ of our enemies. By enemies I hope I mean the French and not my critics here at home."

"As it happens, I am acquainted with the man. He buys up all my bills and threatens me with prison unless I spy on you."

"Ah, we might turn that to our advantage."

"It's too late. I've booted him out by his breeches too often. If I did a turnabout now, he would be sure to guess the reason."

"Then you must continue to put him off. He is not dangerous in himself, but his friends might be, and therefore you must set it about that you plan a sojourn in the country, with a charming female companion, if possible."

"I see. I am to hint that a lady has consented to ruralize with me?"

"Surely there are ladies of your acquaintance who still want to know where they might visit your tent in private of an evening. You cannot have changed that much since I last saw you.''

Hugo laughed. ''I have lately lost the knack of entertaining ladies in private, I'm afraid.''

''Where did you spend the summer, my friend. In a monastery?''

''No, at the bedside of a very sick old man.''

''A likely story. Next you will be telling me you have fallen desperately in love and have sworn fealty to your lady for all eternity.''

''That's exactly what I will be telling you.''

''Fancy you thinking you served Arthur of Camelot instead of Arthur of Dublin.''

''I believe I can distinguish one Arthur from another. I can distinguish them well enough to know that you are asking me to get my heart shot to pieces when I no longer own it.''

''Ah, Hugo. This is very bad news. I had depended on you to have your wits about you and not leave half of them behind when you went abroad. There is nothing romantical in the business we have in hand. It will be tedious, dirty, wet, and dangerous, and I depend on you to get out of it alive.''

''You can depend on it; I have every reason to live.''

''You must not tell this lady about our plan, no matter how tempting it may be. Rumors about your mission will ensure our failure. Besides, she may be in danger from Grisby when he can no longer get his hands on you.''

''It is Grisby who had better look out. If I do not reduce him to a mizzling handkerchief, she will.''

''I like her very much already. But I am serious, Hugo. All our hopes for Iberia rest on our success in Portugal, and our hopes for Portugal rest on your success in Lisbon.''

The engaged couple returned to Burwash escorted by Lady Baldridge, who followed in her own capacious carriage. There to greet them at Hanks Cottage were their parents, an assortment of siblings, and Squire and Mary Ashe. Embracing, squealing, and weeping went all around until Lady Baldridge tired of the noise and inquired whether there was not a bite of something to eat. On that note they went inside to a collation spread out on the table. After she had eaten her fill, her ladyship permitted Squire Ashe to be introduced to her. She eyed him with skepticism, and, noting that he looked almost robust, inquired as to whether he had really been sick all this time or merely pretending. He answered that, in truth, he had nearly died. When Lady Baldridge exclaimed at this, he soothed her by saying it was not so bad after all, for as he had completed most of his funeral arrangements, no one would have been put to much inconvenience if he hadn't recovered. Lady Baldridge concluded from this reply that the squire was every bit as mad as she had always suspected, and she resolved henceforth to humor him in whatever he said and then dismiss it altogether.

Delighted to meet his daughter's erstwhile hostess, the squire regaled her ladyship with the details of his illness, then turned to see Emily and Mary huddled together and smiling. He saw Theo approach them and saw them draw him into their intimate midst. They kept the young man engrossed, until Mary quietly withdrew to leave the lovers alone. The squire then saw his daughter smile wistfully at the two young people, who were as fond as any two unmarried people generally are, and he saw Mary dab the corner of her eye with a handkerchief. For a time, she looked into space as though her thoughts were elsewhere, then frowned as though her thoughts had taken an alarming turn. Seeing all this, the squire began to wonder if his daughter was really as happy as she ought to be.

A question about the wedding, just a few weeks away now, roused Mary from her preoccupation. With considerable relief, the squire saw her enter into the planning with genuine enthusiasm. She joked, offered suggestions, and teased Theo. After a while, however, her mind seemed to wander again, her gaze drifted off, and the wistful expression returned. That she was not happy was apparent to her father. He had only to discover the cause.

He thought Lady Baldridge might be of assistance to him in that endeavor, and so, some days later, he paid her a visit at Hanks Cottage. But when he arrived, he found the household in turmoil over the smallness of the rooms. Lady Baldridge's person filled them to overflowing, so that there was much conjecturing over how to take out furniture and walls so as to add to their guest's comfort without totally disrupting the lives of everybody else. Amidst the discussion, Squire Ashe could not so much as get a peep in, and when the Grangers arrived clamorously and solved the dilemma of the small rooms by offering Lady Baldridge their cottage—the one that was to serve Theo and Emily as home—the squire gave over all hope of claiming any of her ladyship's attention.

He returned to Dearcrop to find Mary in the Mother's Room with an enamel box on her lap. She shut it when he came in and appeared grateful when he forebore to question her about it. Excusing herself, she disappeared, pleading a great many letters to write, then reappeared a moment later with an anxious look and a letter in hand. The post, she announced, had arrived from London.

The letter, addressed to the squire, had come from Lord Mallory. It said that he had met with Wellesley and had attended the ceremonies making him Viscount Wellington of Talavera. He ended by hoping the squire was well and that he would remember him to Miss Ashe. The squire handed Mary the letter and watched her study it. After some time, she said gravely that Lord Mallory had a fine strong hand.

These proceedings had the effect of increasing the squire's concern. Not only was his daughter unhappy, but he also began to suspect that Hugo was the cause. He knew Mary did not hate the gentleman any longer. It had been manifestly clear during the summer months that the two got on extremely well, as well or even better than when they had first met. Thrown together as they had been for weeks, it was possible that Mary had been reminded of what she had originally admired in his lordship, before the marriage arrangements had exploded and spoiled everything. Not only was it possible; it was also probable, thought the squire, for to be in Hugo's company for any time at all was to learn to love him.

Over the next few hours, Mary asked to see the letter

again and again, until finally her father gave it to her to keep. When he asked her what she meant to do with it, she replied offhandedly that she had a place where she kept such things. It interested him to know that she meant to keep the letter. Putting this clue together with some others, he reasoned that Mary was certainly in love with Lord Mallory and that her present low spirits were the result of her separation from him.

As he ruminated on this turn of events, he thought he really ought not to be surprised. He had seen the love between men and women turn to hatred often enough. Why could not the opposite be true as well? But if it was indeed true, what was he going to do about it?

It was this thought that led him to Mrs. Chattaburty's house. He answered her welcome with trepidation, recalling another visit to her and the events that it had set in motion. More than anything, he wanted to avoid another muddle, and he began by saying that he had come because, more than ever, he relied on her sagacity in matters of love and marriage.

Mrs. Chattaburty's eyebrows rose at this, transforming her stony face into a statue of surprise. What could the squire mean? she asked. As far as the Ashe family was concerned, all matters of love and marriage had been settled. She would not hesitate to tell him what she had so often told him before he took ill, to wit—it was wrong to press a woman to marry and drive her from hearth and home. It was fortunate for them all that things had turned out as well as they had.

The squire, knowing full well he was about to embark on another disastrous course, smiled wanly and hung his head.

Furthermore, his hostess continued, the squire had come through his illness as fit and as rosy as they could have hoped. He was able to visit, to ride, and to plan his rites of entombment. Once more he enjoyed a wholly blissful family life. What did he want to go dredging up love and marriage for?

"Mary is in love with Lord Mallory," the squire answered.

Mrs. Chattaburty inhaled deeply. "If she is, I do not wish to know about it."

"You must help me, dear lady," the wretched father said. "Mary is so unhappy."

"There is no point in your moving your lips, squire, for I cannot hear you."

"If you do not advise me, I do not know what I will do."

"Mr. C.'s sow has proved barren and there's nothing for it but to eat it. On the other hand, I expect to see my newest grandchild at Michaelmas."

"Take pity!" the squire cried. "For if you do not, I shall be reduced to asking Lady Babik for advice."

On this threat, Mrs. C. relented. "Very well," she said, "I will advise you. But you must promise to do exactly as I say. I do not give advice just to have it ignored."

"I think too well of your advice to ignore it. If I had listened to you months ago, Mary would not have run away."

"Well, since you promise, then my advice is this: Do nothing."

"Nothing? I cannot stand by and see her so unhappy. Should I not write to Lord Mallory and ask him to come back? I might say I have had a relapse and require his care. Or I might tell him the truth."

"Do nothing."

"In any other instance, I might agree. But now, when Mary's future happiness is at stake, I cannot do nothing."

"You must allow your daughter to decide her own future. And you must keep mum."

Nettled, the squire rose from his chair. "I do not like your advice, Mrs. Chattaburty."

"I find, sir, that advice is excellent in proportion as it is unpleasant. I only wish I had given this piece of advice months ago."

Striding to the door, the squire shook his head. "I am disappointed."

"I am afraid you do not have much faith in your daughter."

"Certainly, I do. She is an intelligent, handsome woman. That is why I want to make everything right for her."

"She must make it right for herself. Have faith in her, sir, and let her do it. If you interfere again, you may rob her of her chance."

Hesitating, the squire thought about these words. Then, taking leave of his stern advisor, he left the house. He paused to look up at the gray cloud that bulged in the west and wondered aloud what in the name of all that was holy he was going to do now.

As Hugo had returned to London in the same month that most of the *ton* returned from the summer respite, he was absorbed into the life of the town without remark. To inquiries as to how he had entertained himself during the past weeks, he responded as he had to Arthur Wellesley— namely, he had tended the bedside of a sickly friend—and this answer was universally received with arch looks and knowing smiles. A rumor went round that Lord Mallory had spent the hiatus in rural seclusion with a mistress whose identity he was too discreet to disclose. He was, therefore, scrutinized minutely on every occasion to see which lady attracted his particular notice, and each of his dance and card partners shone briefly in the gossip of the day.

He spent most days closeted with Viscount Wellington and some nights as well, for it proved that Mr. Grisby had a constable in tow who lay in wait at his lordship's door. Various changes of lodging deterred Grisby for a time, but he always managed to dog his lordship's footsteps to each new direction.

"You had better get me to Lisbon in a hurry," Hugo told Wellington. "Capture by the French would be preferable to being stalked by this drizzly phantom."

The viscount replied with a small loan out of his own pocket, a loan that permitted Hugo another change of lodging.

Paying a visit in Green Street, Lord Mallory was disappointed to learn that Lady Baldridge had removed to Sussex. He walked from her house, his tall figure bent against the breeze, and envied her ladyship's proximity to Dearcrop. London struck him as strangely thin and tedious. Card parties, balls, afternoons at White's, the conversation of beauties and dandies—they all set him to yawning. His thoughts dwelled on walks in the hedge maze and leavetakings in the dawn.

Thus, when a note from Lady Melrose arrived, he read it with something like gratitude. The note had been written a week before but had been prevented from reaching him by his frequent change of lodging. Charlotta had scrawled a fiery scolding—why had he neglected to visit her since his return to town? He knew very well that she required his attendance at once and that she had his future in view. Why did he put off coming?

He read the scolding with a smile and, glad for some distraction, set forth to pay his respects.

Charlotta did not take him to task in person as she had in writing. On the contrary, she tossed her flaming curls in the most enchanting manner and said that she was overjoyed to see him. Patting a sofa cushion next to her, she invited him to look out the window and admire the trees in their autumnal slendor.

"Do you recall, Hugo, the time we passed together in India?"

"What is there in the changing of the leaves that brings India to mind?" he asked.

"Nothing. I think of India often. I wonder if you do."

"I recall that I was shot twice through the arm and in consequence cut a fairly ridiculous figure at a ball."

"Is that all you remember?"

"I think you want to tell me what you remember, and I am not unwilling to hear it if it is pleasant."

She lowered her lashes and began, "Do you remember a night when I came to your tent?"

"It is difficult to say. There was more than one such night."

"On this particular night, I was quite distraught."

"That is hardly a clue, Charlotta. You were always distraught."

"I came to tell you my father had engaged me to Binky."

"Ah, yes. I believe you said you wished to throw yourself on a pyre and burn to death, Indian fashion."

"Death by fire seemed preferable to giving up a man I loved to marry one I despised."

"You were very young, Charlotta. Now, I am certain, you are glad you did not burn yourself to death, for you are a lovely widow with a comfortable income. You have everything you could want."

"Yes, I am glad. I would be gladder still if you would allow me to place my comfortable income at your disposal."

"You are offering me money, my dear? That is a turnabout."

"A lovely widow with a comfortable income is in a position to offer it instead of demanding it. But I am not merely offering you money, Hugo. I am offering you myself."

He regarded her seriously. "Would you elope with me to the country?"

"Of course. I have always loved you, Hugo, in my odd way."

Troubled, he looked away, but she turned his face back to hers with a white silken hand. Then she kissed him on the mouth. At first, Hugo did not move. Then he put his arms about her waist and pressed her close, seeking in her lips the taste of country morning fog. He was still seeking when Charlotta pushed him away and stood up.

"How dare you!"

Hugo laughed. "You are as changeable as the leaves on the trees. Well, what now?"

"I have not changed at all. My kisses are as they always were. Yours have grown tepid."

"I must be sorely out of practice."

"There is only one way you will do better and that is to kiss Miss Mary Ashe!"

The smile faded from Hugo's face. "What do you know about Miss Ashe?"

"I know that last spring you could not keep your eyes off her. I know that she followed you to Sussex, where you evidently spent a blissfully pastoral summer. I know that you came back to London and forgot to visit me."

"You imagine you know a great deal."

"Do not pretend with me, Hugo. You love her as much as she loves you."

"You may go on with these lofty sentiments if you wish, Charlotta. I would by no means deprive an old friend of an indulgence that gives her so much pleasure. But you ought to know, since you claim to know so much, that I have sworn never to offer for Miss Ashe and that she would have made me swear it if I hadn't already done so."

"Well, I hope you keep to your bargains better than she does. She promised to send you packing, and this is how she sends you!"

"She made a bargain with you?"

"I told her I would give up Mr. Granger if she would give you up. I certainly kept up my end, for as you must know, Mr. Granger is to marry Miss Hanks. It would not be boasting to say that the engagement would never have happened if I had decided to hold onto that young man."

"Did Miss Ashe agree to give me up?"

"She pretended to be totally unaware of the power she had over you, saying that she could not influence your actions one way or another. She pretended she would like nothing better than to send you packing, but I saw through that easily enough."

"How do you contrive to be so perspicacious?"

"Love is my métier, my dear. I have studied it from girlhood. I know as much as there is to know, perhaps more. The only thing I do not know is how to find a proper husband."

Hugo laughed again. "I take it you are withdrawing your generous offer?"

"It would not matter to me that you did not love me. I would have made you love me in time; I swear I would. What does matter, however, is that you love Mary Ashe, and your vow only proves that you would spend your life with me mooning about her. I think far too well of myself to marry you under those circumstances."

"It appears I have lost a companion in the country on account of a kiss. I must endeavor to do better in future."

"Would you have accepted my offer, Hugo?"

He rose, walked to where she stood, and replied, "No."

"I thought as much."

Then, as though she had had a change of heart, she looked at him intently. "Are you absolutely certain?"

Gently, he nodded.

"But what will you do? It is no secret that your affairs are in complete disarray and that you are on the point of being installed at Newgate."

"I have something in mind, Charlotta, but it requires your help, and for the life of me, I cannot think why you should help me."

"What more can I do? I have offered you everything, and you have refused."

"And you would be wholly justified in refusing me in your turn."

"You will kindly permit me to do my own refusing. Now tell me what it is."

"I would have it put about that you are going with me into the country. An elopement would be implied, naturally, I will ride with you to the outskirts of the city. After that, a gentleman wearing my coat and hat will escort you to your destination."

"I see what your scheme is, Hugo! You mean to make Miss Ashe jealous. You hope that will force her to accept you. Meanwhile, I am to have my name besmirched throughout the world."

"I was sure you would refuse. It would be madness not to."

"I complain, Hugo, but I do not refuse. I deem it one of the great pleasures of life to complain of you. But I will not deny myself the greater pleasure of making Miss Ashe jealous, if only for a short while. Nor will I deny myself the pleasure of riding with you."

Smiling, he took her hand in his. "This is very good of you, Charlotta."

"The world will not agree with you, my dear. But fie on the world! Between then and now, and between here and there, I may yet induce you to change your mind."

CHAPTER FOURTEEN

Squire Ashe sat in his chair by an unlit grate and observed to himself that he had now come full circle. Nearly a year ago, he had sat in that very spot, wondering how to insure his daughter's future happiness. Since that moment, the only accomplishments he could point to with certainty were his own about-faces. He had begun as a man who did not care one way or another whether his daughter remained a spinster, and had ended as one obsessed with the idea of marrying her off. He had begun with no thought of what would happen to his daughter once he had departed this vale of tears, and had ended by going to extreme lengths to see that she would be loved and cared for. He had begun as a man who had never entertained the possibility of dying; he had ended as one to whom planning for that inevitability was one of the chief joys of life.

These changes might have ended disastrously for him had he not been fortunate enough to spend some time loitering in Death's anteroom. Death had proved a good friend to him—assisted by Lord Mallory and his forgiving Mary—but he could not always rely on that noble trio to rescue him. If the interference he presently contemplated should make a muddle, he might not get off so easily this time.

In the past few days, he had followed Mrs. Chattaburty's

advice to do nothing, not because he believed she was right but because he was rendered immobile by indecision. He had watched his daughter's increasing preoccupation with the intention of broaching the subject of Lord Mallory, but whenever an opening did present itself, he backed off, not knowing what to say or how to say it.

This restraint cost him much. The color in his cheeks, which had been so hard won, now faded. He picked at his food and sighed indifferently at the card table. When the stonecutter set before him samples of marble used in the finest grave markers, he could hardly muster enthusiasm. In the evenings when Mary read to him, he drummed his fingers. In the mornings when neighbors came to call, he tapped his foot. He peered at the tea leaves in his cup for long periods of time, as though he hoped to read in them a message.

Mary, meanwhile, also had a great deal to occupy her thoughts. She went to Littleton Vale to assist with wedding preparations, then retired to her bedchamber to open the enamel box. One by one she sorted through the mementoes, wondering what they might teach her now. Afterward, she would put them by and go out into the world once more to beam upon the bride and groom.

Busy though she was with her private thoughts and public façade, Mary could not help but notice the decline in her father's spirits. His pallor and listlessness were not lost on her; nor was the sigh he produced whenever he looked at her over his newspaper. Thus, when she came into the room and found him seated in his great chair, looking for all the world as though he were a mourner at his own funeral, she said, "I think I shall send for Sir Geoffrey."

The squire peered up at her through sorrowful eyes and declared, "It is not I who am ailing. You are the one, my dear, and you need not pretend otherwise."

Mary colored a little at this. "I imagined I was doing a very fine job of being cheerful. Evidently I fool no one."

"You fool everyone but me. If I am unhappy, it is because you are."

Mary drew up a chair next to him. "Papa," she said

earnestly, "I ought to have listened to you and married Lord
Mallory when I had the chance."

"No, I ought to have stayed out of it. You two might
have been married by this time had I not interfered."

"If you had not interfered, I should never have loved him
in the first place."

"Ah, it is all such a hopeless muddle. Our mistakes arm
themselves against us and beseige us unmercifully."

"I do not intend to surrender, Papa, at least not yet."

"I am afraid, my dear," the squire said, shaking his head
in despair, "it is all up with us."

"Perhaps I can still do something."

"I'll be stapped if I know what to do."

"Papa, I must see Lord Mallory. And I must do it before
he sees too much of Lady Melrose."

The squire nodded, then looked puzzled as he suddenly
bethought himself that he had never heard of Lady Melrose.

Seeing that puzzled look, Mary explained who the widow
was and what designs she had on his lordship.

"But he does not return her feelings, Mary. He loves you,
I am certain of it."

"Nevertheless, his affairs are in such a desperate state
that I fear he may be induced to make a Smithfield bargain."

"Ah, you feared it was Emily who would do so. Now it is
Hugo who is on the brink."

"She will do everything in her power to marry him, for in
her way she loves him as much as we do. But if I am there
to persuade him otherwise, then you shall have a son-in-law
at long last, and I shall have a reason to throw my little box
into the fen."

"What do you mean to do?"

"I shall go to London."

The squire paled and said nothing for some while. At last
he ventured to say, "London will be difficult for you, my
dear. Lady Baldridge will not be able to accommodate you
as she did before. Nor will your good friends Emily and
Theo be there to keep you company."

Mary shrugged this off lightly. "I have a house, Papa. I
took it just before returning to Dearcrop. I will send a

servant to ready it for my coming. Once there, I shall be too busy with Lord Mallory to be lonely.''

"Nevertheless, my dear, I think I ought to accompany you.''

Mary looked at her father in astonishment. Then she burst out laughing.

"I know why you are laughing at me,'' the squire said with dignity. "Indeed, it is no more than I deserve. But I would make any sacrifice to keep Hugo from the clutches of a dragon.''

"She is not a dragon, Papa. She is very beautiful.''

"Even so, I would go a good deal further than London to see Hugo again.''

"Ah, you are anxious to get those epitaphs.''

"To tell the truth, I am surprised I have not received them. He did promise, you know.''

"I make a promise, too, Papa: You shall have a good deal more than epitaphs to look forward to. What say you to a grandchild named Hornbeak Arthur Mallory?''

"I say you would do far better to have a daughter named Mary.''

Mrs. Buxton, who had scorned the suggestion that anyone but herself would know how to make the squire comfortable in London, had everything in readiness by the time the master and the young mistress arrived. Mary marveled that her father had come through the journey in such fine spirits. He hummed to himself and looked about the hall of his daughter's house with fervent curiosity. Although he appeared somewhat tired when they sat down to a light supper, he was soon refreshed with a bowl of hot broth and a peach.

Afterward, Mary brought him her very own writing desk, a fresh sheet of paper, a quill, and a pot of ink. She stood behind him while he pursed his lips and penned a single sentence announcing his arrival in London with Mary and their desire to see Lord Mallory as soon as possible. The moment he appended the final period, Mary seized the paper, blotted it, folded it, and instructed the footman to deliver it at once to his lordship.

Too tired with traveling to await the reply, Squire Ashe retired for the night, saying that he would still keep country hours even in town. Mary was thus left to pace in the library alone. Within the hour, the footman returned to report that as Lord Mallory had removed from his lodgings, he had been unable to deliver the letter. This piece of news bewildered Mary for some time, until it occurred to her to send to Lady Baldridge's house for young Jeremy.

A short while later, the butler ushered in a taller, plumper, rosier Jeremy than she remembered.

"How do you get on, Jeremy?" she asked.

He grinned by way of an answer.

"Do you get enough to eat?"

"Yes, but I must eat like a proper person now. Mrs. says I must not steal any more."

"And do you mind Mrs.?"

Here Jeremy shifted on his feet a little. "I does what I can," he said with a pained look. "Mrs. says she will make me a pork pie if I do."

"Inducement indeed. Do you like tarts with your pie?"

Jeremy's eyes opened wide and he swallowed hard.

"I thought you would. Tell me, do you remember Lord Mallory?"

"Aye. He is a right one."

"I think so, too, and I would gladly tell him so, but I cannot find out his direction."

"Was you thinking of apple tarts or lemon?"

"Jeremy, you are a very resourceful young lad. Suppose I sent you to deliver a note to Lord Mallory and when you arrived at his lodgings, you learned that he had removed from there. What would you do? What would you do if I promised you a plate of apple tarts?"

Brightly, he responded, "Why, that's easy, Miss. I should talk to the landlady. Mayhap she'd know where his trunks had been sent."

"Good!" Mary said. "I see I have chosen my man well. Now, off you go."

Summoning the butler, she gave orders that the coachman
was to escort Jeremy to his destination and to keep the
horses standing until the boy should return. When they were
gone, she rang the bell. Mrs. Buxton arrived moments later
to receive her mistress's request for apple tarts.

Their arrival on a plate was soon followed by the return
of Jeremy, who wore a triumphant grin and carried a slip of
paper.

"Here is the direction, Miss. Shall I go there now?"

Taking the paper from him, she hugged it to herself and
answered, "The morning will do as well. Now you must eat
your tarts."

But, in fact, the morning brought the news, borne by a
discouraged Jeremy, that his lordship was no longer to be
found at the direction they had been given the previous
night. According to one of the tenants, Lord Mallory had
not even spent a week on the premises before removing
himself and all his belongings to another house. Where he
had gone, the tenant could not say; nor could the landlady
be located to be pumped for information, though the child
had haunted her stairwell throughout the morning.

When Mary relayed this news to her father, he looked up
from the *Times* with a glum expression. "This is the worst
possible news," he said.

"Not when you recall Mr. Grisby," Mary replied. "Hugo
may not have gone off with Lady Melrose at all. He may
only be hiding from Grisby."

"That fellow who dunned him in Burwash?"

"The very same."

"I never liked him."

"I don't recall that you ever met him."

"I never did, but Lady Babik told me all about him."

"There is perhaps cause for rejoicing if Hugo's creditors
have kept him too busy to become engaged to Lady Melrose.
Did the *Times* carry any announcement of an engagement,
Papa?"

"No, there was nothing. Poor Hugo. I do not like to think
of his being unhappy."

"I doubt he is unhappy. He enjoys sparring with the soggy Mr. Grisby."

"It did not occur to me that Hugo amused himself in such a manner. If it is as you say, then I ought not to do what I had resolved to do."

"You have a plan, Papa?"

"I had the notion of going to see my solicitor and asking him to buy up Hugo's notes from Grisby. But I would not like to deprive Hugo of his entertainment."

"In this case, I think you might take the liberty."

"You do not think I would be awfully high-handed in doing so?"

"I think his lordship is a great believer in being high-handed when circumstances demand it. I wish you would do it, Papa. I, meanwhile, will send for Jeremy and another plate of tarts."

That afternoon, the squire ventured forth into the city. At the same time, Mary sent Jeremy out once more. To fortify him, she gave him a sack full of apples and cheese.

The squire returned well before Jeremy did, and he related a conversation with the solicitor that presented the bleakest possible picture of Lord Mallory's situation. It was known all over London by now that his lordship's debts had mounted astronomically since the beginning of the summer, that the interest alone might deplete several small fortunes, and that the prospect of his ending up in prison became more likely every day.

No word came from Jeremy that day nor the next. Mary's imagination began to plague her, and her father's frequent declarations that catastrophe was imminent fueled her fears even more. She feared that Hugo had already been hauled off to Newgate, and this notion haunted her to such a degree that she sent a servant there to inquire after him. When she heard that no Lord Mallory was to be found at the prison, she sighed with relief and immediately envisaged Hugo hiding out from the Bow Street runners in a foul-smelling, vermin-infested Whitechapel slum. Worse than that, she imagined him already married to Lady Melrose.

To complete her misery, she imagined Jeremy caught in

the act of stealing food. She regretted that she had only given him a small sack of stores and prayed that the landlady had not had the boy seized and sold to a white slaver. It soon developed, however, that no such fate had befallen Jeremy, for he came to Green Street the next day and reported that he had done exactly as Miss required. He had not ended his quest at the house where he had begun it. No, indeed. He had found the dratted landlady, who closeted herself with a bottle of gin instead of tending to the rooms above a bookseller's in Fleet Street. Jeremy had followed him there, and from thence to the Inns of Court, where Lord Mallory had resided for some days before removing to the house of the Viscount Wellington, whose servant had been prevailed upon to say in Jeremy's ear that Lord Mallory, having borrowed a tuppence or two from the general, had now taken lodgings near St. James. When Jeremy inquired as to whether his lordship was still to be found there, the servant had replied indignantly that of course he was; he had seen the gentleman with his own eyes that very morning when he personally delivered to him a private note from his master.

Having finished his story, Jeremy took a breath and regarded Mary with some pride.

"I could kiss you, Jeremy," Mary said. "But I warrant you would prefer apple tarts."

"That I would," Jeremy said with relief.

The tarts duly handed over, Mary and her father set out for St. James. The coachman set them down in front of a neat modern house, before which stood a coach and four.

"I fear Lord Mallory may have another visitor," the squire whispered, "and that we may be too late. They may be carrying him off even now."

They climbed the stairs to Lord Mallory's rooms and knocked on the door. Hawks, the valet, could not contain his joy at seeing them. He repeated "Squire!" and "Miss" in reverential tone until Mary inquired if they might see his lordship. Because his composure had utterly forsaken him, the valet led them straightaway into a charming sitting room, which they entered in time to hear Lady Melrose say, "Tomorrow then," and Lord Mallory respond, "Yes."

Paling at the implication of these words, Mary met Hugo's eyes. Then she walked forward resolutely with her hand outstretched. His welcome was a mixture of surprise, gladness, and displeasure. She could understand his surprise; she had counted on his gladness; but she hardly knew what to make of the displeasure, unless it signified that her coming had interrupted him in the act of making arrangements with her ladyship.

In contrast, Lady Melrose's greeting was simple to read. The lady was clearly irritated and that did much to reassure Mary.

Hugo performed the introductions and laughed to see Charlotta toss her auburn curls and direct a coy glance at the old man.

"I hear you have been dreadfully ill," Charlotta said in a soothing voice. "It is so disagreeable to be ill, I think. You were fortunate, however, to have Hugo at your side. He is such a tonic! I declare, he always knows the right thing to do and say to bring a body round again."

Squire Ashe, mesmerized by the manner in which this flaming beauty cooed at him, nodded his head vigorously, saying, "Ah, you have been ill as well as I, and Hugo sat at your bedside too."

At this, Charlotta directed a sly look at Hugo, a look that was not lost on Mary. Her ladyship then responded to the squire, "Let us say simply that he has completely cured me of what has ailed me for some years."

The squire drew nearer to her and caught the fragrance of her scent as she fluffed a white handkerchief at her white bosom. At last he managed to stammer that he was certainly glad she had been cured. "You will visit us in Green Street, I hope," he invited.

Charlotta simpered a little before answering, "I should be delighted. Unfortunately, I leave London tomorrow."

"Could you not leave the next day?"

"You make it very tempting, squire."

Over the course of some minutes, the squire endeavored to persuade her to succumb to the temptation.

Meanwhile, Mary scanned Hugo's face to see what she might read there. She was conscious of his eyes upon her, but she saw that they frowned as often as they smiled. He had responded to her greeting by taking her hand firmly in his. Now he dropped it and walked to the window.

"I cannot persuade Lady Melrose to put off her journey," the squire complained. "Mary, you shall have to do it."

Mary turned to her ladyship and said earnestly, "Lady Melrose, let me add my persuasions to my father's. So much has happened since we last met. It would give me great pleasure to explain it to you."

"I'm sure it would," Charlotta replied in a gay tone, "but it would give me no pleasure to hear it. I bid you farewell, therefore, and take with me this valuable lesson: It is useless to make bargains with innocent country girls."

On that she made an impressive exit, leaving the squire open-mouthed in admiration. Recalling him to the present, Hugo congratulated him on looking so well, and asked if he had come to collect his epitaphs.

The squire shook his head. "Do you know, I've given it much thought, and it occurs to me that I ought not to choose my own. When I am gone, you and Mary may put your two heads together and choose one for me."

For a moment it seemed as though Hugo would like nothing better than to put his head together with Mary's. Then, recollecting something, he smiled gravely and did not reply.

Squire Ashe, looking from Hugo's face to Mary's, grew alarmed. "Are you well, Hugo? You look as though you have grown thin. You have not eaten properly since leaving Dearcrop. I see it in your cheeks. You must dine with us in Green Street. Say you will dine with us tonight, and I will have Mrs. Buxton prepare you a hearty ragout."

Hugo put his hand in the breast pocket of his coat and felt for a paper. As he fingered it, he looked troubled. Then he said as mildly as he could, "What time shall I come?"

* * *

Dressed in a burgundy silk gown, Mary presided over the candle-lit table. With each sound of a fork on a plate, with each sip from her glass, with each nod to the attendant to spoon out another bit of sauce, her heart enlarged and warmed. She reveled in the mingled voices of Hugo and her father, in the shadows flickering on their animated faces, in the sweetness of their smiles as they glanced in her direction. So engrossed in these sensations was she that she hardly attended to the conversation. Thus, she was roused to the present with a jolt when she heard Hugo say that he was on the point of leaving London.

The squire protested, saying he would not permit it.

"I am afraid I am committed," Hugo said.

"Surely, you can put it off."

"It is impossible."

"But we have only just found you. Believe me, it took quite a bit of doing, too. We tracked you all over town for more than a week."

"When do you go?" Mary asked.

"Tomorrow."

Mary set down her fork. Rising from the table, she said in an unsteady voice, "I shall leave you to your cigars, gentlemen." She went to the door, turning to say, "Perhaps, when you join me in the drawing room, Lord Mallory, I may be able to persuade you to change your mind."

When she was gone, Hugo turned to the squire. "I would stay if I could, but there's no going back now."

"Do not be too sure, my son. The Ashes are a stubborn lot. We will go to any lengths to have our way."

Hugo smiled. "You would not have to go to any lengths if I had a choice in the matter. I would give much to be able to stay."

"Then you must do as I do—leave everything to Mary. Meanwhile, you must tell me about Lady Melrose. She is the most dashing creature I've ever laid eyes on. Indeed, she makes coming to London well worth the trouble."

After half an hour of conversation about Charlotta, during which the squire gleaned nothing definitive of his lordship's intentions in that quarter, the squire produced two exaggerated yawns and protested that he was unaccountably tired. "I suppose it's all that chasing after you, Hugo," he said as he excused himself for the night. "You must go to Mary in the drawing room, and the two of you must get along as best you can without me."

Bidding him good-night, Hugo entered the drawing room to find it empty. He sat down on a sofa and watched the door, expecting that his eyes would bore a hole in it. He could not tell what he wished for more—that Mary would come at once or that she would not come at all. There had been something in her eyes that told him why she had come to London. But the light in those black orbs must not be allowed to distract him.

He felt in his pocket for his instruction from Wellington and recalled the pleasure with which he had received the note. After a month of delays, changes of lodging, dodging Grisby, and cooling his heels, he had known at last that he would be useful. Folding the note, he had put it in his pocket and poured himself out a glass of French champagne to toast the fall of Bonaparte.

Hours later, Mary had walked into his rooms, filling them with the blue of her walking suit, the richness of her ebony hair, and the radiance of her expression. In a trice, pleasure had flown, taking with it all thoughts of Wellington, Bonaparte, and usefulness. He devoutly wished the European continent might go to the devil, that Wellington had not chosen him for his diplomatic mission, and that he had never agreed to go.

Rousing him now from these thoughts, Mary entered the room and closed the door quietly behind her. She wore the sari he had given her, and though it completely covered her neck and shoulders which had shone so charmingly during dinner, he found he could not look at her long without losing the resolution he needed to carry out his orders.

Seeing him direct a frown at the fire, Mary approached him.

"I wish you would not leave London," she said.

He fixed his eyes more firmly on the fire.

"You need not leave on your creditors' account. Nor is it

necessary to seek refuge with Lady Melrose. There are less extreme measures available to you.''

He looked up at her as she stood before him. "You are not going to offer me money again, I trust.''

"I certainly am, but you must take me along with it.'' On that, she sat down close beside him.

"Are you asking me to marry you?''

"I have no choice. You have sworn never to ask me again.''

He seemed as if he would kiss her then, but he held back. Undaunted, Mary placed her hands on his chest and kissed him. Whatever had made him hesitate before now melted. His arms went around her, pressing her close to him, and he swept his lips along her cheeks, her eyes, and her mouth.

When she was able to take a breath, she whispered, "Does that mean you accept my offer?''

"It means I love you.''

"And I love you, Hugo, though it is mortifying to admit it after all the fuss I've made.''

"Why did you wear this?'' he ran his hands over the soft fabric.

"Why do you think?''

"You mean to remind me of its origins, of a place that tempts one to forget everything else.''

"I mean to remind you that you cannot possibly tear yourself away from me, that you love me with such an overwhelming passion that you will put off whatever appointment you have set for tomorrow.''

He closed his eyes, tasting the lobe of her ear.

"You do love me with an overwhelming passion, don't you?''

She received an answer which, though spoken without words, was as eloquent as she could have wished.

CHAPTER FIFTEEN

Mary did not awaken when the girl came in to draw the curtains. Nor did she stir when a pot of chocolate was brought in on a tray. It was only when the girl shook her and whispered in a loud voice that the squire had sent her to find whether she was dead that Mary opened her eyes and smiled. Pulling herself up on her pillow, she asked what sort of day it was, and upon being told it was mizzling enough to chill the bones, she declared she knew it would be a charming day.

"Please tell my father I will be down very soon," she said. "I will join him at breakfast."

"The squire breakfasted hours ago, Miss."

"Well, he shall do it again—only this time he shall breakfast on good news."

When the girl had gone, Mary climbed out of her bed and sought out her enamel box in a drawer. Setting it on a table, she reviewed its contents one by one. It was not long before she came upon the special license, and, fanning herself with it in a coy manner, she danced about the room until the girl returned to help her dress.

"Do you know what time it is?" her father asked as he greeted her.

"I can't say I do, but I trust you are about to tell me."

"It is past noon."

"Then I hope Mrs. Buxton will not delay in bringing me something to eat. I am famished."

"Did it not occur to you that I have been perishing for some news, my dear? I came down at six o'clock and have been waiting ever since."

"I apologize. I was up late last night."

After pondering this, the squire said, "That is a good sign, I expect."

"I expect you are right."

"If you have a heart, you will not tease me and keep me in suspense."

"I do not have a heart, Papa. I have given it to Hugo Mallory."

The squire took a breath of relief. "And so, when will you be married, my dear?"

"We did not discuss a date, but we may marry this very day if we like for, as it happens, I have a special license."

"Gracious, I never would have thought of getting a special license. What foresight you have, child!"

"I am afraid I cannot take the credit for it. Lady Baldridge obtained it for me."

"Do you mean she knew you loved Hugo?"

"Let us say she knew I would need a special license one day and was kind enough to go to the trouble of getting one."

The squire shook his head in admiration. "I cannot help but marvel at the manner in which women always seem to know the right way to proceed in this business of matrimony. But tell me, daughter, what did Hugo say about Lady Melrose? Did he indicate that she would stay on in London now that he planned to cry off? Do you suppose I might visit her? Do you think my being your father might make a visit awkward?"

Laughing, Mary said that she and Hugo had not discussed Lady Melrose.

"That seems a little hard," the squire said. "I don't suppose her heart will be very broken, but even a little broken is difficult."

"You are wonderfully tenderhearted, Papa. I cannot say, however, what Hugo's plans for her ladyship are."

"Well, he did say that he had changed his mind about running off with her?"

"Not in so many words."

"Well, what on earth did he say?"

"He said he loved me. He didn't say much after that."

"Then you are not certain he has changed his mind?"

"Of course, I am. He loves me and I love him."

In some anxiety, the squire protested. "What is that to the purpose, child? It's not the love we are after here; we've always had that. It's the change of mind we want, his promise not to elope with Lady Melrose."

"You may take Hugo's love for granted, but, as for me, it was the only question. Now that he has answered it, all the rest will follow."

At this juncture, the footman entered to set a breakfast of beef, egg, and muffin before Mary. She ate it with relish, pausing just long enough to say, "Please, Papa, do not work yourself up into a frazzle over Melrose."

The squire made an effort to calm himself. "Of course, everything will be well. Now tell me how Hugo asked you."

"I asked him," Mary said between bites.

Clapping his hands, the squire crowed, "Splendid! And what did he say?"

Looking up from her plate, she replied, "I can't recall that he said anything."

Her father's anxious frown returned. "Nothing at all?"

"His lips were occupied, Papa."

The meaning of this allusion did not immediately penetrate the squire's anxiety, but when it finally did, he smiled broadly and relaxed in his chair. "Quite right," he observed.

"That's better," Mary said, breaking a muffin in half. "If you had persisted in your fidgets, I should have made Hugo speak to you."

"Will he be here then?"

"I expect him today—any moment, in fact."

"What time did he say?"

"He did not say."

"Ah, yes. His lips were occupied. I understand perfectly well. You see, I am not the least bit fidgety."

At three o'clock, Mary changed her dress. She ordered Mrs. Buxton to prepare a lavish tea, and she poked the fire so that the room would warm quickly. The squire waited with her for some time at the tea table. When Hugo did not materialize, they were forced to proceed without him. Then, an hour and a half later, they grew sufficiently peevish to move to the drawing room.

Peeking through a window curtain, Mary saw that it was growing dark. She glanced at her father, who sat in his chair as though turned to stone. He had assumed this pose as soon as the twilight dimmed the sun. He now kept it as though he were not at liberty to breathe again until Hugo should present himself.

But Hugo did not present himself. At nine o'clock, Mrs. Buxton insisted that they might more efficiently do their waiting if they fortified themselves with something to eat. The squire refused, claiming no appetite. Mary ate a pear and tried to reassure her father, but he was beyond being reassured by words. At last, she sent for young Jeremy.

"Take this note to his lordship," she instructed the boy, who set forth on his mission with a vision of tarts in his head. In little more than half an hour, he returned with news of Lord Mallory: His lordship had given up his rooms. The landlady had been told not to expect him back. Jeremy had been unable to discover his new direction.

Squire Ashe started violently at this information. Mary went to him and laid a soothing hand on his arm. Her father clutched her hand and cried, "He is gone. It is all up with us now."

Pale but calm, Mary looked at Jeremy. "You may go to the kitchen and have something to warm you. You have done well. I thank you."

As the boy tiptoed from the room, the squire began to shake his head pathetically. "He is lost. We are lost."

"He will be back. He will come tomorrow. Or the next day. You will see."

"He will not come," the squire wailed.

Much to his sorrow, he proved correct. Days passed without a word, let alone a visit from Hugo. Mary spent each day at home, expecting to hear from him momentarily. The squire waited with her, thinking that for his daughter's sake, he must not allow his heart to crack. Mary would realize the truth soon enough and when she did, she would surely die. "Ah, that I should outlive my own child," he mourned. "My only solace is that I have learned how to make arrangements."

Mary's solace lay in sending notes to all her acquaintances in London to ask after Lord Mallory. The first to respond was Lady Miselthorpe, who wrote that his lordship had almost certainly gone off with Lady Melrose. Other letters arrived in the same vein, some expressing the opinion that Lord Mallory would never go so far as to marry the widow; others maintaining that he had done the prudent thing in light of his desperate straits. Mary replied to every one of these notes that the authors must surely be mistaken and that she would write them another time in hopes of hearing more accurate news.

She went to Lady Melrose's house and learned that her ladyship had indeed set forth for the country on the appointed day. Lord Mallory had been seen handing her into her carriage. Then he had mounted his chestnut to ride alongside.

Mary visited her father's solicitor and learned that Grisby had refused the generous offer to purchase Lord Mallory's notes. Attempts to renew the offer had come to nought, for the lawyer could not locate Mr. Grisby anywhere.

Mary wrote again to Lady Miselthorpe requesting Lady Melrose's direction in the country. In reply, she received a severe scold. "Your pursuit of Lord Mallory is stirring up talk," her ladyship wrote. "The gentleman is married and that is that!"

Some days later, she received a similar missive from Lady Baldridge. "My dear Miss Ashe," the good woman began,

Word has reached Burwash of Hugo Mallory's elopement. I beg you will not add to his lunacy by behaving like a lunatic yourself, which is what Lady Miselthorpe informs me you are doing. You have always been too sensible to regard him as an object. You wisely agreed with me, I recall, when I pointed out how disastrous any match between you must prove. That is why I am able to write Lady Miselthorpe and tell her that this rumor of your attachment to Hugo is mere flapping in the wind. A far more effective antidote to this gossip, however, is for you to stop chasing Hugo all over town. I advise you and your father to return home as quickly as possible before your father's unsoundness of mind afflicts you further.

Yours, etc., etc.

Mary had no sooner finished reading this than her father handed her a letter from Mrs. Chattaburty.

My dear Squire,

Lady Babik informs me that Lord Mallory has eloped with Lady Melrose. She says it is the talk of London and that Miss Ashe goes about town in search of his lordship's direction. I know Miss Ashe and Lady Babik too well to believe any of it. Still, I am obliged in friendship to suggest that you think of traveling abroad for a time. Now that you have braved the journey to London, surely you might plan a sojourn in Greece, where the weather is accounted quite seasonable this time of year. Much as I long to see my old friends in Sussex again, I fear that Lady Babik has made the climate uncongenial at present. As you have in the past flattered me by soliciting my advice, I trust you will not be offended at my presumption in offering it once more.

Sincerely and etc.

"Oh, what are we to do?" the squire cried.

"Well, we are certainly not going to Greece."

"Fie on Greece! What are we to do about you?"

"Why should we do anything? I am sure I shall find Hugo's direction shortly. It is only a matter of time."

"This is madness, girl. The man has gone off with another woman. You must stop pursuing him and learn to make the best of a bad business before it tears my heart to pieces."

Mary put her arm about his shoulder. "I don't believe he has run off with Lady Melrose, Papa. I can't believe it, not after what passed between us that last night."

"I want to go home, Mary," he said forlornly. "I implore you, give up this search. Do not make it impossible for me to go back to my own house."

"Very well, Papa. I will do as you ask. Just as soon as I have made one more visit."

Mary was fortunate in finding Lord Wellington at home, and, as soon as she was ushered into his study, she came right to the point. "Do you know where Lord Mallory has gone?"

He regarded her sternly and replied, "He was quietly eloping to the country until you kicked up a storm."

She shook her head. "That hardly seems likely, sir. He has been offered an opportunity to discharge his debts in full, an opportunity I have good reason to think he finds in every way satisfactory. It does not make sense that he would elope now and so suddenly, with no word to anyone."

The viscount straightened some papers on a table and stood up. "He was obliged to keep a rendezvous."

"There is no reason why he should keep a rendezvous with anyone but myself."

The viscount's eyebrows rose at this. "My dear young lady, have you any idea how much trouble I have gone to over this rumor of Hugo's elopement? It was no small matter to set it about, I assure you. And when I finally managed to deceive the world, you came upon the town, raising questions and doubts and demanding to know where he'd run off to. Well, you must stop it at once.''

"If he has eloped, I mean to hear it from him.''

"Miss Ashe, are you acquainted with a Mr. Grisby?''

"Regrettably, I am. I suppose *he* knows where Hugo has gone. He manages to hound him everywhere. But I cannot ask Grisby if he knows, for he has apparently left London.''

"He has left England.''

"Left England?''

"Exactly so. I believe he is en route to Lisbon. Now you will do me the honor of giving that some thought, and when I return with a glass of ratafia for you, you will tell me what conclusion you have reached.''

In the quiet of the general's study, Mary's thoughts leaped to Reverend Richard Hardie, then to the man who had hidden with her in the dogwoods at Dearcrop. She thought of the staggering sums he owed and of all she owed him. She thought of flaming red hair and of filmy blue-violet. From there, her mind traveled across the water to Europe, and she shuddered. There could be only one reason why Hugo had gone so suddenly, and although she had never for a moment believed that he loved Lady Melrose, still it was reassuring to know for certain that he had not gone off with her. Her hopefulness immediately dissipated, however, at the thought that Grisby had been more successful in finding Hugo than she had been.

"I wish he had told me,'' Mary said when the viscount returned.

"We had no way of knowing you would refuse to believe our splendid rumor. Everyone else seemed willing enough to believe. Besides, I enjoined him not tell anyone. The knowledge might have endangered you, too.''

She reached for the wineglass and endeavored to steady her hand. "Is Hugo in very great danger?''

"I can tell you this much—he is in very great danger of giving up his bachelor's state to marry a young lady from Sussex.''

She paused in the act of sipping the wine. "He spoke of me?''

"Aye, that he did, but he did not tell me nearly enough. I had no idea you might persist so stubbornly in seeking him out."

"It is true, my father and I have spent most of our time in London trying to locate him, but we had no idea it might cause harm. We only wanted to help Hugo."

"Perhaps if you will return home and say no more about it, no great harm will come of it."

"On the other hand, great harm may have already been done. Oh, why could I not have been an obedient, tractable woman? Why could I not have meekly assumed he had jilted me, like any sensible woman would have done? Now it may be too late!"

His lordship knit his forehead and tapped his fingertips together. "I pray it is not. Hugo's life is precious to me. There are momentous affairs at stake here as well."

Mary set down her glass and stood up. "I have made this muddle, and it is up to me to unmake it. If I have raised any suspicion that endangers Hugo or anyone else, I shall set it to rest at once."

"And how do you propose to do that?"

"I have not decided that yet, my lord, but I will see to it, I promise you. I will deliver all the assurances necessary."

"If you could divert suspicion, Miss Ashe, it might keep Grisby's friends in doubt. They may not be in a hurry to get shot up in Europe if they have good reason to content themselves here."

"I will do everything I can, my Lord. In your turn, you will please be so good as to deliver Hugo back to me in one piece."

He walked to her and, bowing smartly over her hand, replied, "Nothing would give me greater pleasure."

When the Ashes returned to Dearcrop, Mary was drawn into the thick of Emily's wedding preparations. The bride and groom sought Mary's company when they could not have each other's. They prevailed on her to assist in spiriting Lady Baldridge out of their house so that they might smuggle in china, plate, linens, and other articles essential to the sanctification of their marriage. They demanded her approval of the menu for the wedding breakfast, the position of the veil on Emily's fair head, and the purchase of a dozen chickens for their little coop.

The squire, who had little to occupy his mind besides his disappointment in Lord Mallory, grew irritable. The clamorous wedding plans inspired him to fidget. His daughter's behavior did little to calm him, especially when he overheard her whisper—to Miss Babik, of all people—that she had hoped to be married herself by this time, but, alas, she had been jilted. When the astounded Miss Babik picked up Pug, whom she had dropped upon hearing this tidbit, she inquired as to the identity of the gentleman. Hearing his daughter pronounce the name Lord Hugo Mallory, the squire sent for his carriage, returned to his home, took to his bed, and composed his deathbed speech.

When Mary found him thus, he cried, "Oh, how I wish you had not confided our disappointment to Miss Babik. It will be all over the county now."

"I suppose it was impulsive of me, Papa. Still, it is hard for me to contain my very natural resentment amidst all this marrying and carrying on."

"Do try to be more cautious, child," he begged. "I would not for the world have you the subject of hideous gossip."

"I have always been the subject of gossip. And, besides, it is all over London that Hugo is a jilt. The news would reach Sussex by some route or other if I did not broadcast it."

"Of all the muddles, this is the worst, I fear. Imagine, blabbing to Miss Babik of all people!"

"If we cannot confide in our good neighbors, Papa, in whom can we confide?"

"No one, my love. It is impossible to confide in anyone ever again."

"Nonsense. You must learn to trust people, as I have done. Oh, Papa, I cannot tell you what a fine thing it is to be able to say that one has faith in someone, despite all the evidence. It is worth everything to have that."

"I do not mind your having faith, my dear. I just wish you had not reposed it in Miss Babik."

After soothing her father as best she could, Mary went to her bedchamber for a final look at the enamel box. There was no point in hanging onto reminders of foolishness now, she thought. In loving Hugo, she had done exactly as she ought, and the hours they had spent together in Green Street confirmed that. He had held her with an ardor that had quite taken her breath away. He had touched her and looked at her as though he would burn the sensations on his memory. She understood that his love for her was solid and steady, and she knew as well as she knew her own name that she would always be able to count on it.

Mary's love for Hugo was much simpler to understand—it was every bit as stubborn and passionate as she was. Stubbornly and passionately she clung to the belief that he would be all right, that she had not harmed him, that she would be able to repair any harm she might have caused, that it would not be too late, that love could not be cruelly taken from her, now that she had found it.

She fingered the papers one last time before feeding them to the flame of a candle. One of them—the special license— she replaced in the box, not as a reminder of her foolishness, but as tangible proof that Hugo would come back to her.

Miss Babik obligingly spread word of the scandal. So successful were the efforts of that energetic young lady that several townspeople congratulated the squire on having escaped the clutches of a fortune-hunting son-in-law. Too full of emotion to reply to these neighborly greetings, he confined himself to the precincts of Dearcrop and did not go out again.

Lady Babik's powers of deduction led her to conclude that Miss Ashe had never really been engaged to Lord Mallory at all. The story of the jilt, she inferred, was no more than a fabrication. She took the opportunity of a sunny fall afternoon to stop her neighbors on the main street of Burwash and inquire why it was known in every corner of the world that Lord Mallory had left Miss Ashe in the lurch. Why was it noised about London that Lord Mallory had eloped with an heiress in order to elude his creditors? How could one possibly explain all this talk, she would be pleased to know. If it were all true, wouldn't every effort be made to hush it up?

As no answer came readily to mind on this occasion, the townspeople were forced to accept Lady Babik's explanation, to wit—that Miss Ashe had set about the rumor out of jealousy, that once his lordship had made it clear his affections were not placed at Dearcrop, she had flown into a snit and made sure to ruin the man's character. Of course, Lord Mallory's character was weak; her ladyship was forced to allow it. It was universally known that handsome men were weak where headstrong women were concerned. She could have predicted he would cry off; indeed, she was certain she had predicted it on numerous occasions. But Lady Babik could not help feeling sorry for the poor gentleman, who was not even there to defend his reputation. Naturally, she also felt sorry for Miss Ashe, who was too old now ever to interest another suitor and whose unhappiness was now assured for life. It was a pity that Miss Ashe had always been such an eccentric young lady, for had she been more conventional she might now be Lady Mallory. Nevertheless, she would not hear her relative's name dragged through the mud just to soothe Miss Ashe's wounded pride.

At this point in her exhortation, Lady Babik paused to take a breath and, inviting passersby to listen to her harangue, began it again from the very beginning. She was warming to her subject when Mrs. Chattaburty happened by. Taking in the spectacle of a group of townsfolk gathered round her ladyship's open carriage, Mrs. C. could not forbear interrupting. Her stone face locked in a scowl, she stated that Miss Ashe was completely blameless, that if his lordship had jilted her he was a toad, that if the townspeople believed it, they were toads, and that if she heard any of them repeat the scandal in her vicinity, she would call them all toads to their faces.

"Oh, you need not call me a toad," Mrs. Venable

exclaimed. "I have the greatest compassion for Miss Ashe and wish she may not die of mortification."

"Don't get on your high ropes, Harriet," Mrs. Turnbull said. "It is most likely Miss Ashe who has jilted his lordship, for she always does exactly as she pleases."

Mrs. Chattaburty carefully avoided looking at Lady Babik. Her loyalty to the inmates of Dearcrop did not exceed the bounds of prudence. In the heat of argument, she still remembered not to offend her superior in rank. She contented herself with staring down her neighbors until they looked heartily ashamed of themselves and began slowly to disperse. Then she turned a smiling face to her ladyship and inquired after the orchards at Furringdale, the health of Lord Babik, and the progress of little Pug in learning the trick of playing dead.

Before Lady Babik could reply, Lady Baldridge drove up in her curricle to demand everyone's attention. She ordered her tiger and coachman to pull her to a standing position, from which she declaimed mightily against scandalmongers and called back the dispersing listeners to hear her tale. She declared that no one dast say a word against Mary Ashe in her presence. She had known that young lady many months, had seen her in company with Lord Mallory many times, and had remarked how coldly they glared at each other. She had no opinion of Charlotta Melrose, who had more vanity than Yorkshire had sheep. It made perfect sense for Hugo to offer for Miss Ashe, given his appalling debts, but it made no sense at all for her to accept him. She was too sensible a woman to accept such a husband. Logically, therefore, no jilting could possibly have occurred; but if there had been a jilting, Miss Ashe would learn to bless the day.

The townsfolk absorbed this as they had absorbed all the previous information, with avid eyes and ears. When Lady Baldridge had gone, it was Lady Babik's turn again. Mrs. Chattaburty followed next, fixing her listeners with her granite face and liberally bestowing the epithet "toad" everywhere but on their ladyships. It took nightfall and the sweep of a dusty wind to scatter the talkers and hearers at last.

News of the ladies' historic meeting sent waves of excitement as far as London, and as the news was charged with the liveliest scandal, only the infants in their cradles failed to repeat the story of the infamous jilt. When the tale reached Emily and Theo, they worried that an oppression of spirits might soon jeopardize their friend's health. It never occurred to them, however, that Mary might actually have lost her reason until the morning on which they joined her in the sunny sitting room at Dearcrop and observed her play her mother's harp. She wore an expression of anticipation. Her dark eyes flashed as she sang a Scottish air with an uplifted voice and heart.

"I wish you would stop a minute," Theo snapped. "I can't talk to you above all that din."

Laughing, Mary lowered her hands to her lap. "There," she said. "You have no tact and less taste, but as you are dotty with love for my deserving friend, I forgive you."

"It is you who are dotty," Theo countered. "We're all worried about you, Mary. You are acting very oddly, you know."

"When have you known me to act in any other way? Did I not spend all that time refusing to marry you? Did I not then go ahead and make it impossible for you not to marry Emily?"

"There was nothing odd in all that. I am grateful, as you well know."

"Yes, but at the time you thought it very odd, if not perverse."

"That is true, but this is a different case. It is madness to sing at the top of your lungs as though you were glad of being jilted."

"I never sing at the top of my lungs. It is vulgar."

Here Emily stepped in to say in a more gentle manner, "Mary, my dearest friend, let us help you. You have done so much for us. Now it is our turn."

Mary pushed the harp upright and rose from the stool. With a warm smile she went to each of her friends and squeezed their hands. "If you will assure me that he is well, you will do more than I ever did for you."

When the young pair exchanged a glance, Mary went on, "Have you heard that Lady Babik defends him? She believes in him absolutely. It is quite wonderful, I think."

Emily and Theo's surprise turned to distress.

"This is not like you," Emily said in a low voice.

"It is true, I have not always appreciated Lady Babik's sagacity as I ought. Perhaps I have been too cynical, too untrusting in the past."

"You do not need to pretend your heart is not breaking," Emily said.

"There is no use fussing about my heart," Mary replied. "It will do just as it pleases. Once I could school it to listen to my head, but that time is gone. It doesn't seem to care whether Hugo has jilted me or not, as long as he is safe."

Again Theo and Emily exchanged glances. It did not seem as though their efforts benefited Mary in the least. Indeed, they suspected that Mary was succumbing to the tragic fate of many a jilted young lady and taking refuge in madness. Theo said that never having listened to reason before, Mary could not now drum any of it up for practical use. As for Emily, she held firm to the belief that the love of devoted friends and the kindest father in the world must at last bring her dear Mary to her senses.

The day of the nuptials dawned bright and unseasonably warm for October. After escorting the wedding party to the door of the church, Squire and Mary Ashe left them outside and entered the great oaken doors. As they walked down the aisle toward the front pew, a murmur arose among the assemblage that crowded both sides of the aisle. Aware that she was the subject of the murmurings, Mary put her hand on her father's arm and whispered to him to be of good cheer; he answered with a funereal moan. They took their places in their pew and watched Parson Venable search the altar for his spectacles and his text. Finding them at last, the clergyman moved to the top of the lectern steps and signaled the beadle to let the wedding begin. The great door opened with a creak as the beadle went out. When it opened again a moment later, letting a shaft of sunlight inside, an expectant breath went up from the assemblage.

Mary was surprised to see Parson Venable start and stare forward. She was surprised again to hear the door bang closed and instead of the patter of wedding shoes, to hear the sound of a single pair of riding boots echoing hard against the stone floor. The familiar step caused her to whirl around. There, with his arm in a sling and a riding hat pulled halfway over a white bandage, stood Hugo Mallory. In an instant, she ran up the aisle to him, oblivious to the curious stares of the onlookers.

With his good arm, Hugo pulled her to him and kissed her. The wedding guests turned to one another in astonishment, all thought of the bride and groom gone from their heads.

"I never did believe in the jilt," Mrs. C. whispered.

"I always knew he was not as bad as they said," Lady Babik declared, "though I am sure he was very bad."

"The disease has overtaken her completely," Lady Baldridge lamented. "She is incurable now."

Parson Venable called to Squire Ashe in a nervous tone. "Do they not know there is to be a wedding here? What do they imagine they are doing?"

"I suppose they imagine they are kissing," the squire said with a grin.

"I can see that! But what about the wedding?"

"That poses no difficulty," the squire assured him. "My daughter keeps a special license."

The parson stood tall and raised his hands, hoping to quiet the uproar in the church. But as it had grown beyond his power to calm, he shrugged and leaned over to Squire Ashe once more. "Lord Mallory appears to be wounded. How do you suppose he hurt his arm?"

"I don't know. I suppose Lady Melrose shot him."

The parson sent a hasty prayer heavenward, while the squire reveled in the spectacle of his daughter in Hugo's arms.

"Thank God you are safe," Mary said to Hugo. Then,

touching her fingers to his bandage, she added, "If this is Grisby's work, he will have much to answer for."

Hugo laughed. "Grisby is dispatched, thank you. If you wish to avenge my wounds further, you will have to take on the French army. And I pity them if you do."

"I have a half a mind to make them deserve your pity. But you are alive, I can breathe easy again, and we have other business to attend to."

"Business? All my business has been successfully concluded. Lord Wellington presents me to you with his compliments. Henceforth, this will be my only business." So saying, he nuzzled his face in her hair.

"Look around you, my love. Do you see all these eyes staring at us?"

At this, he gazed about him. "Who are these people?" he asked.

"They are here for a wedding."

"Well, let us not disappoint them."

"Theo and Emily's wedding.

"Ah, yes. I saw the two of them loitering outside the door. I expect they'd like to get on with it."

"I expect Theo will call you out for stealing his thunder in church."

"He will be out of luck then, for if there is any piece of me the French have not got to first, it is yours."

"And I shall take very good care of it, I promise you. But we must let those poor young people have their wedding now."

"And when they have done with the parson and the veil, we shall have our turn. I don't suppose anyone will mind. What is one more wedding when the folks are already gathered and the vestments already pressed?"

Slipping her hand through his arm, Mary walked with him to the front pew and a thankful, capering squire.